DIFFUSION

STAN C. SMITH

ISBN-13: 978-1515180456

ISBN-10: 151518045X

The indigenous Papuans in Diffusion speak one of approximately 800 languages known to exist on the western Pacific island of New Guinea, one of the most linguistically diverse areas of the world. At the end of this book there is a guide to the dialogue of the villagers. You may enjoy referring to it occasionally as you read the book.

In the text of the novel, each word or phrase is referenced by number, and the numbers correspond to the phrases in the language guide at the end of the book.

And following the Papuan tribe dialogue guide is a preview excerpt from **INFUSION: Diffusion Book 2**

DIFFUSION

Definition:

the transmission of elements or features of one culture to another

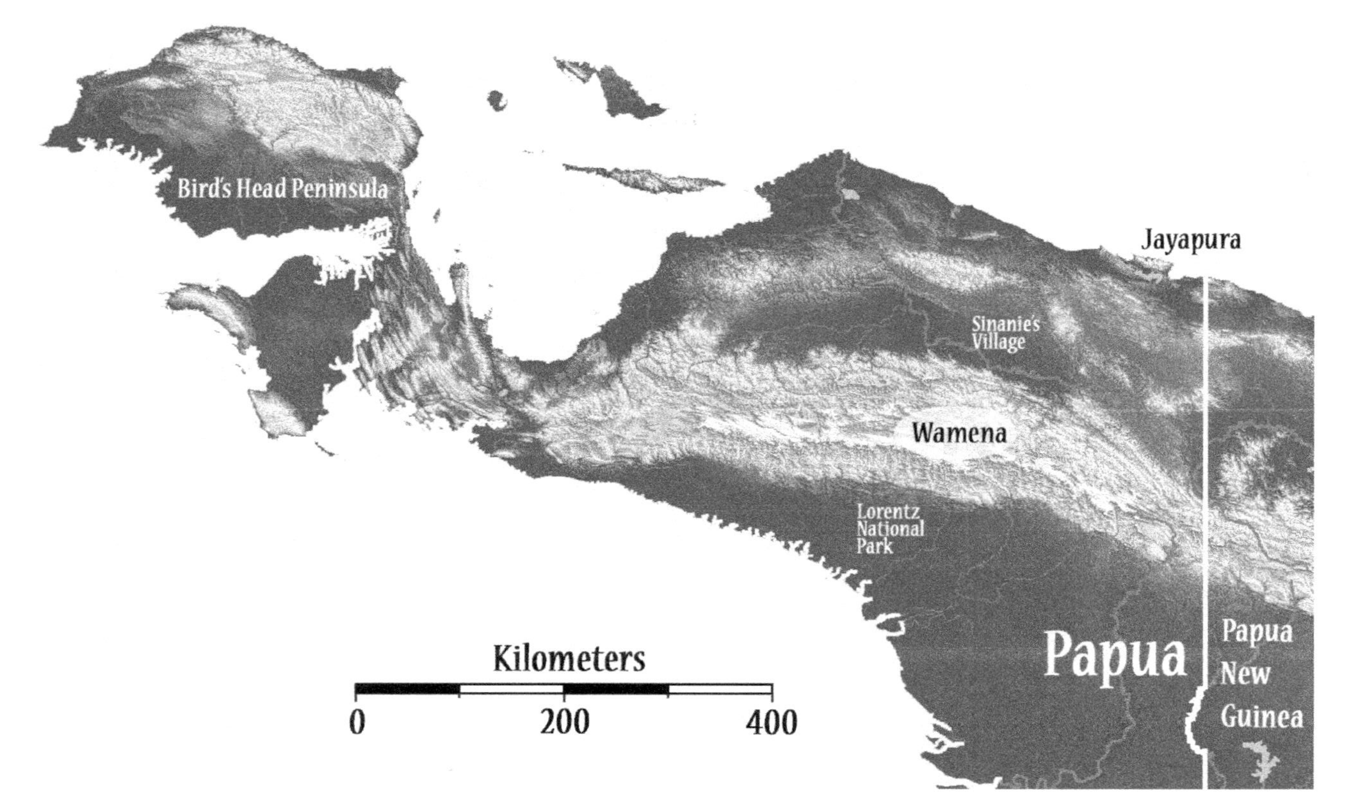

Bird's Head Peninsula
Jayapura
Sinanie's Village
Wamena
Lorentz National Park
Papua
Papua New Guinea
Kilometers
0
200
400

CHAPTER ONE

PETER WOOLEY WAS no longer willing to die. Closing his eyes against thorns and stinging sweat, he stumbled through forest understory so dense that running was impossible. He had slipped out of the village undetected, but there was little chance of losing the tribe's best hunters once they discovered his absence. If he could make it to the river and then cross without drowning, perhaps they would give up and let him go. And if he could somehow trek sixty miles to the coast without survival gear, he might then formulate a plan to prepare the world for what he had seen. Cruelly, he had been given a reason, but almost no chance, to survive.

Peter stumbled and fell. He rolled onto his back, sucking in the viscous air hanging over the forest floor. Sunlight pierced the canopy here and there, but otherwise he stared at a solid ceiling of vegetation that was unrelenting, stretching for miles in every direction and broken only by the occasional river. Peter's breathing gradually slowed. The constant trilling of insects soothed him and pulled his thoughts from despair to hope. Perhaps he might live to see his dear Rose. He had something to offer her now, a gift like no other. For years he had given his wife little more than heartache and concern over his disregard for his own life. She deserved more than that. Peter was a reckless wanderer with a habit of planning ever-more-perilous ventures before even completing the previous one. As Rose would say, he was willing to die for the sake of a thrill. And this time he had gone too far—a solo walkabout into the remotest forest, itself potentially fatal, but then derailed by an astonishing encounter.

There was movement above. A cat-sized creature launched itself from one tree to another, its long tail held rigid as ballast. It was a tree kangaroo, common in the forests of Irian Jaya, but Peter was sure this variety was unknown to science. The local villagers had domesticated it, and its presence above him indicated that they were likely in pursuit. Peter struggled to his feet. He had to keep moving.

He plunged headlong into a dense patch of plum pines, the trees tearing his skin and clothing. Something tugged at his throat, and the cord around his neck snapped. He turned in time to see a figurine slide from the ensnared cord and fall to the ground. It was a stone carving of a tree kangaroo—the same creature he had just seen in the flesh. For a moment he considered going back for it, then he looked to the trees above and spotted the real tree kangaroo. It stared back at him briefly and then headed back the way it had come, leaping agilely between tree limbs.

Peter cursed to himself. It was going to lead the tribesmen straight to him. Leaving the figurine, he emerged from the plum pines and broke into a run, only to be forced to skirt around another patch of them.

"Peter!"

Peter stopped cold. Samuel stood before him in his skin shorts and oddly gleaming vest. Peter felt a flame of hope. After all, Samuel had convinced the villagers to spare Peter's life in the first place.

"Samuel, I had to leave! I wanted to say goodbye, but I couldn't risk it. The others—do they know I've left?"

Samuel stepped closer, his expression grim. "They are aware. You must know you cannot leave this place. You cannot bring others here; it is not yet time."

Peter scanned the forest but saw no sign of the tribe's hunters. "They'll kill me, won't they? You can stop them. Please, Samuel! I can't stay here."

The man shook his head. "If I am to endeavor to save your life, you must agree to remain. Stay here with me, Peter. There is much for us to do."

Peter considered the offer. No doubt, there was much work to do. In fact, this was an absurd understatement. The substance the villagers possessed and protected was beyond Peter's comprehension. He was no more equipped to make progress with it than Samuel was—or the tribesmen, for that matter. No, it was too big. They needed help. He had to get back to civilization. He backed away from Samuel.

"All I ask is that you give me a chance. Try to hold them off."

Samuel's face showed genuine alarm. "Do not, Peter. I beg you."

Peter's heart sank as he realized Samuel wasn't going to help. He shook his head in regret and turned to run. Suddenly he realized a man was blocking his path. Peter glimpsed a familiar array of green lorikeet feathers in the man's hair, but by the time his brain registered recognition, it was too late to stop. Sinanie's spear pierced his gut. Peter grasped the shaft, but the man rushed forward, forcing him back and driving the spear deeper.

Peter tripped and fell onto his back. Sinanie pinned him down, forcing the spear in until the ground beneath him stopped it. The pain exploded and escaped as a garbled yelp. Peter could not move, and it became difficult to breathe. Strangely, what came to his mind was the meal he had shared with Sinanie only the day before. He wanted to speak, to explain to Sinanie that, for the first time in his life, he was afraid to die. But words wouldn't form, and they wouldn't be understood anyway. Sinanie stood above him, gazing coolly into his eyes. Slowly, the tribesman smiled. It wasn't a taunting smile. It was more like a small kindness.

Sinanie wasn't alone now. There were two others—maybe three. They intended to kill him, and they would do more than that. There were different measures of death. Peter knew this now; he had seen it with his own eyes. They would make sure his body wouldn't heal and would never leave this place. Rose would never know that he had almost become an important man.

One of the men dropped his spear and picked up a club-sized tree limb. He hefted the limb a few times, assessing its balance, and then swung it at Peter. The blow glanced off Peter's forehead. Stunned, but still conscious, Peter stared at the unrelenting canopy above. In the few seconds before more blows would come, he tried to imagine that he was relieved it was finally over, that he had done all he could. But he knew he hadn't.

From its perch in a coral bean tree, the tree kangaroo peered over its twitching snout at the scene below. Clubs pounded flesh until the flesh was no longer a man. And still the clubbing went on. Swirling dust and flying drops of fluid sparkled in shafts of sunlight in the small clearing. Visible light and energy of other wavelengths reflected and transmitted a brutal, but meticulous, task. Tremors from violent blows coursed through soil and up the dense wood of the bean tree to clutching paws. Vocalizations and pheromones made their way to the creature's ears and nostrils, adding to the scene an emotional layer of determination diluted by regret.

The creature filtered the incoming data, discarding certain parts and wrapping the rest into a coherent package of understanding. Cognitive feelers probed the package, twisting and shuffling layers, teasing out subtleties of meaning and ultimate consequences. The arrival of the man, Peter, had been significant. He had been almost equipped for what was needed. Now the man no longer existed, but perhaps he could still be important.

The tree kangaroo turned away from the laboring tribesmen. It leapt from tree to tree until it arrived at the churning brown river the villagers called *Méanmaél*.[1] By reverse-hopping, claws digging into tree bark, it descended to the water's edge and began gathering raw materials: decaying vegetation, chewed leaves, soil scraped from the forest floor, and water.

The creature worked without urgency because time was inconsequential. Others would find their way here. It was only a matter of waiting.

CHAPTER TWO

PAPUA (FORMERLY IRIAN JAYA)

42 Years Later

STANDING dead center in the Last Unknown, Quentin Darnell closed his eyes and inhaled the scent of ancient secrets. This experience was not possible back home, where every living or extinct organism had long been scrutinized and classified. Here, in the Central Highlands of Papua—sometimes called the Last Unknown —every breath yielded odors given off by microbes, worms, insects, and plants not yet identified. Which was exactly why they had come.

The others were approaching, so Quentin retreated deeper into the forest. As he moved through a stand of pandanus, a buzzing call, like a cicada, captured his attention. He spotted a most remarkable bird eyeing him from a low branch. It was a bird-of-paradise, but Quentin could not recall the specific type. Its black head, against a yellow chest and wings, was striking enough, but what gave the creature its impossible appearance were the half-meter-long blue feathers protruding from each side of its head. The feathers resembled curved, serrated swords folded over the bird's back and trailing behind. It was only a few meters away, and Quentin stood motionless to avoid spooking it. The characteristic noise of the group he'd been traveling with usually prevented such encounters, especially with animals as rare as this one.

Suddenly, the bird ducked its head, forcing the two swords to lift from its back. It dipped lower, and the swords swept forward before slowly arching backward again. It repeated the motion, and with each dip the feathers stabbed forward even more, until they finally pointed straight toward Quentin.

Voices broke the silence, disrupting the bird's mesmerizing face-off with Quentin. It fluttered away, its display feathers trailing behind, iridescent in the sunlight. Quentin sighed. The encounter had lasted less than a minute, but it would likely be the most serene experience he would have all day.

The boisterous chatter drew nearer. Any human voices would have been intrusive here, but these bore the tenor of American teenagers. One voice—it was Russ Wade—rose above the others.

"Mr. Darnell, are you taking a dump?"

Abruptly the entire group was upon him. Seven students, ranging from fourteen to seventeen, from eighth to eleventh grade, and Lindsey, Quentin's wife and colleague.

Lindsey emerged from the brush into Quentin's clearing first, leading the others. Her wavy, caramel-blond hair was still fresh from the air-conditioned ride in the minibus, and she wore a teasing smirk on her face, apparently pleased at having crashed Quentin's party.

Russ flashed his amiable grin and cartoonish eyes, making it impossible for Quentin to be mad at him. "You should've gone at the *losmen*," he said, still at high volume.

Ashley said, "Wow, you're funny Russ. Maybe consider shutting the hell up?"

Miranda, Ashley's best friend, frowned at her harshness. She said to Russ, "We just don't want you to scare off the animals."

Russ wasn't fazed. "Oh, you girls want to see animals? I thought you just came to see the *horims*." The other boys chuckled at the reference to the penis gourds worn by Papuan men, sometimes their only article of clothing. The teenagers discussed the gourds endlessly.

Ashley shaded her eyes and scanned the surrounding forest in a mock gesture. "Miranda, did you just hear a talking penis?"

Quentin glanced at Lindsey. She had a knack for intervening when the students' banter crossed the line, and he had a habit of letting her deal with it.

"Hey!" Lindsey shouted over the ensuing laughter. "This is our last field day, and we're wasting time."

Lindsey was right; they'd stretched their legs after the long ride, and it was time to get started. As they walked back to the minibus to collect the gear, Quentin mustered his enthusiasm to motivate the students once more. The kids were natives to a society of online computer games, where patience was as rare as a bird-of-paradise. Quentin also made a silent wish for this final day to go without incident. For three previous summers, he and Lindsey had brought students to the Central Highlands with no mishaps. Papua was an ambitious destination for a Missouri public school district, and more than one administrator had tried to stop the field trips. But Quentin's passionate requests to the School Board, emphasizing his deep connection to this place, had so far worked. Nevertheless, one fractured ankle or one case of chikungunya or malaria would bring it all to an end. It could even bring an end to his job.

At the minibus, Quentin said, "This is it, folks. We've talked up Lorentz Park for weeks. Today, you'll have your last chance to see things nobody has ever seen."

The eighth graders, Bobby, Carlos, and Quentin's own son, Addison, were attentive. The older kids were at least quiet. "Roberto and Russ, you guys are on insects today. Ashley and

Miranda, you're on plants. Addison, Bobby, and Carlos, you guys are on vertebrates."

Bobby beamed. He punched Addison's shoulder. "Vertebrates! What'd I tell you?"

Addison was slight-framed, pale, and rarely physical. He frowned and rubbed the spot on his shoulder. But then he held up his smartphone tablet, showing the mammal guide home screen. Quentin smiled at this. It was usually a struggle to get his son to use that damn thing for anything except *Kembalimo*, the language game that had become so popular the last few years.[2] Addison and Bobby were developing a friendship, and Addison could definitely use a friend, especially one like Bobby.

Bobby was among Quentin's favorite students. The boy was perpetually enthusiastic, in spite of his struggles with schoolwork and his parents' recent thorny divorce. Bobby was the only student who had actually earned his place on this trip. Two years ago, he'd shown up in Quentin's classroom after school, having heard about the previous summer's trip. He had asked an astounding number of questions and then had declared he would earn the money to pay his own way for the trip by the end of his eighth grade year. It had taken Bobby two years to do it, but here he was. The other students were here because their parents had paid for it, including Quentin and Lindsey's son, Addison.

Markus, their hired driver, slid from the minibus and straightened to his full height, six inches shorter than Quentin. Black skin and strong features indicated he was native Papuan, rather than Indonesian. Markus kept a tireless running commentary in mixed pidgin and English. Having driven taxis in Jayapura, the capital city of Papua province, he was amused by the odd activities of this group.

"I will help you today," he said. "We will find many *kumul*."

Quentin glanced at Lindsey. On their first day, they had taken Markus up on his offers to help, only to discover that he seemed to hate the forest and everything in it. When the kids had searched for reptiles, including snakes, he'd started referring to them as *longlongman* or *longlongmeri*, which meant crazy man or woman.

"No thanks, Markus," Lindsey said. "We'll be fine."

Lindsey took the older kids into the forest, and Quentin took the eighth-grade boys in another direction. They had agreed to stay within shouting distance of each other and the minibus, so before they had gone too far, Quentin stopped at a clearing and waited. The boys sat on the ground, succumbing to this familiar ritual.

At first it seemed quiet. There was no breeze, and the only sounds were from living, moving things. Feeding lorikeets shrieked in the distance. There was faint scratching, claws against wood, possibly a rat or possum. Nearer, they heard motion in the leaf litter —first to one side, then everywhere. Spiders seeking prey, snails gliding, millipedes and pillbugs rummaging through an endless food supply of decaying leaves, and insects of all conceivable forms, performing all conceivable functions. With each passing heartbeat, countless legs scuffled, antennae tapped and tasted, and mandibles and fangs crushed and killed.

"Did you hear that?" Quentin scanned the canopy with exaggerated movements. "That could be the *Mbaiso!*"

Bobby's eyes widened. "What's an *Um-bay-zo?*"

Quentin lowered his voice. "*Mbaiso* is Moni for 'forbidden animal.' The Moni say they are ancestors, returned in a different form." He paused. "If you find one, supposedly it can look into your past."

"Really?" Bobby whispered. Addison said, "Yeah, right."

They sat quietly. The chuckling of a honeyeater filtered through the trees.

"Have you seen one?" Carlos asked.

Quentin shook his head. "Only young people can see them, and they only appear if you have a deep love of the forest. The *Mbaiso* can tell these things about people."

The boys rolled their eyes, but they quickly rose to their feet, eager to start searching.

———

THE NEXT THREE hours passed quickly. The boys saw only two mammals: a rat that quickly scampered away, and a cuscus—a type of possum—high in the canopy.

The highlight of the day was a tree python, bright green with buttercup yellow spots. Addison had found it as he relieved himself in the brush. He'd yelled so loud that Lindsey, her students, and Markus came running. The python then became the most photographed snake in the Baliem Valley. At this point, the teachers decided it was time to head back.

Streaks of afternoon sunlight painted the forest as the group made their way to the minibus. The day's activities had reduced the exhausted students' chatter to occasional comments as they walked. Miranda and Ashley led the way, but Quentin stayed close behind. The two girls were best friends, but their differences had become apparent to Quentin during the trip. Both girls were popular at school, but Quentin now suspected this was due to their combined personalities. Miranda's syrupy sensitivity acted as a buffer to Ashley's rough edges and temper. Together, they were balanced, even remarkable. Apart, their peers would probably marginalize them.

Miranda stepped over a fallen tree and then brushed debris from her pant leg. "I so need a shower. Things are crawling under my clothes."

Russ was five meters behind, but he still heard her. "You need help getting them out?"

"Whatever, Russ."

"What does it mean, *whatever?*" Markus said. But then he stopped walking. His eyes were fixed on the forest ahead.

Miranda saw them first. "Look, there are people."

Four men emerged from the shadows. Markus spoke a greeting in Dani, but the men approached without answering. In Wamena, the town the Americans used for their home base, many Papuans could be seen wearing a combination of traditional dress and items influenced by the 21st century: a pair of shorts, a wristwatch, even a PVC pipe worn as a *horim*. But the men approaching them now had no ornaments or implements of modern origin.

Instead of the longer decorative *horims* seen in Wamena, these men wore short gourds cinched against their abdomens—the functional apparel of active hunters. Brown feathers from the wings of cassowaries fanned out from their headbands. Their noses held ornaments that appeared to be heads of black beetles, the oversized mandibles piercing the septum. Each man held a bow and several long arrows. Disfigured, flaking skin covered most of one man's legs. Quentin recognized this as *Grile*, caused by ringworm and easily treated where medical supplies were available. Their bodies were greased from the waist up, something Quentin had only seen in mock battles enacted for tourists.

The men ignored Markus and focused on the Americans. They began talking to each other. Markus looked at Quentin and shrugged.

Quentin tried Indonesian. *"Selamat. Siapa namanya? Dimana?"*

The men showed no understanding.

Markus spoke again, this time apparently digging into his knowledge of Papuan languages, and he exchanged some words with them.

"These men are going to Wamena," Markus said. "They talk about killing."

Quentin's gut tightened. Papua was an Indonesian province with a history of political injustices and violent resistance by the indigenous Papuans. Bringing students here a few decades ago would have been unthinkable. But tourism was common now, and typically the Papuans were friendly to visitors. "Tell them we don't want any trouble."

One of the tribesmen extended a sinewy hand and grasped Ashley's dark, curly hair. She tensed. The man rubbed the hair between his fingers, as if judging its coarseness.

"Ashley, relax," Miranda said. She smiled and placed her hand on her chest. "My name is Miranda."

The man released Ashley's hair and grasped one of Miranda's breasts through her shirt. Miranda's smile transformed into a stricken expression.

"Miranda *meri*, don't be afraid," Markus said, his voice unusually high. "They will go away soon; you will see."

The Papuan turned back to Ashley and reached for her breast, too.

Ashley blocked with her elbow. "Don't touch me, asshole!"

She then wheeled and slapped the man's face. The Papuan's head wrenched, and his feathered headdress flipped to the ground.

The forest clearing became deathly still.

Ashley stood defiant, her face red and fists clenched. The man recovered from his shock and lunged at her, ranting and pointing his finger. Lindsey was closer than Quentin and threw herself between them.

The man's companions suddenly filled the air with feral shrieks. But they were not angry, they were laughing. They hooted wildly, doubling over, dropping their bows and arrows to the ground and pointing at their dishonored companion.

The man stopped his verbal assault. Slowly, he picked up his headdress. He looked over Lindsey's shoulder at Ashley and spoke in an even tone, like he was stating a simple fact, perhaps *I dropped this hat on purpose*. He placed it on his head, restoring some measure of dignity.

Ashley was now trembling and tears streaked her face.

When the laughter subsided, Markus exchanged words with the men, and he seemed to relax. "These men will not hurt us," he said. "Now they understand."

"They understand what?" Lindsey said.

"That you are not from the government. And your students are *yangpela*, young people. *Pikinini*. I told them to come to the minibus. We'll give them food."

Still chuckling, the men gathered their weapons and walked away with Markus.

"Good God, Ashley!" Russ said.

"Drown in your own vomit, Russ!"

Russ raised both hands to show he meant no harm.

Lindsey touched her shoulder. "Are you okay, Ash?"

"No, I'm not!" She stepped away and stood with her back to them.

In the awkward silence that followed, Quentin struggled for the right words. Finally, he cleared his throat. "Well, I'd say we've learned some valuable things about—"

Addison interrupted him, "We learned that Ashley's bitchy temper could get us killed! She's such an idiot!"

Addison had typically been a silent, although brooding, observer when the entire group was together, and this outburst seemed to shock everyone. Ashley swung around with rage in her eyes, and Bobby even stepped away from Addison as if seeking a safer distance. The older boys, Roberto and Russ, glanced at each other and then started toward Addison.

Addison was seemingly unaware he had crossed a line. He continued, "Only a total idiot would hit someone who has a—"

Lindsey rushed in and clapped a hand over his mouth. "That's enough, son." Still covering his mouth, she guided him away from the group toward the minibus.

Quentin looked around at the remaining students. So much for Addison's progress with making friends.

Bobby was watching Quentin and seemed to detect his concern. He smiled, his adolescent blue eyes shining, and Quentin sensed that the boy was trying to reassure him. Bobby had a way of doing such things, which was another reason Quentin liked him. Bobby then turned to Carlos and gave him a shove. "Let's go, before Markus gives away all our food."

———

THE PECULIAR ASSEMBLY of travelers sat on the ground near the minibus and shared the food Markus had packed. Markus talked with the Papuans some, but he seemed unwilling to divulge further details about their destination and purpose.

As the afternoon sun dropped, the kids opened up to the Papuan tribesmen, trying to ask questions about their customs and gesturing wildly to explain their own equally puzzling lives. Russ and Roberto tried in vain to explain that they played in a garage band. The younger boys pantomimed a question about the *Mbaiso*, the mythical animal of Quentin's story. The Papuans simply shook their heads. Two of the men suddenly howled with laughter. Miranda had taken their photo and shown them the image on her smartphone's screen. Only Ashley sat quietly, keeping an eye on the Papuan she had struck. His name, they'd learned, was Pupun.

Resting on his elbows, Quentin watched. This encounter could have gone a different way. Perhaps those who had criticized this field trip were right; Papua was still occasionally volatile and was too dangerous. But bad things could happen anywhere. And Quentin was compulsively drawn to Papua, by a force he could comprehend but not suppress. If anything, Quentin was self-aware; Lindsey and occasional therapists had made sure of that. He understood his drive to overcome this place, to be a stronger man than his father. Bringing students here without incident was his way to conquer the Last Unknown. But perhaps it was going too far.

Lindsey jabbed his leg with her foot. "Where are you, hon?"

Quentin half-smiled. "Right here."

AFTER FINISHING THE FOOD, the Papuans disappeared into the forest. Everyone piled into the minibus, and they began the three-hour drive to Wamena. Soon the students began dozing off.

Lindsey said, "What do you suppose Pupun and his friends are up to?"

Quentin pulled out his smartphone to look at photos. "Maybe they're the last of a tribe. A disease wiped them out. Those four were immune, and now they're on a quest to find women—rebuild the tribe."

"And they thought they'd recruit Ashley," Lindsey laughed. "No such luck. They've wandered the forest for years, getting slapped by women."

Quentin snorted. "Or maybe they're guardians of a treasure. Their quest for mates continues because they haven't found any women worthy of it."

"More likely they've forgotten where they put it. They need help finding it."

Quentin ignored this. "Probably gold. The legend of the mountain of gold is true, and they're guarding it."

"Gold is boring. The treasure is a rare flower. When you smell it, you fall in love, then you search until you find your soul mate. That's Pupun's quest."

"You may be right," Quentin said. "Pupun had me smell this dried flower he had. Then everything was clear—I had to start my search."

Lindsey raised her brows.

"It took me about three seconds," he said.

She slapped his shoulder.

Russ spoke without opening his eyes. "You guys are teachers, for God's sake. You're making me sick."

———

As THEY DESCENDED into the Baliem Valley along the dark waters of the Uwe River, the ice-capped peak of Gunung Trikora hung in the mist to the south. The rugged peaks of the Maoke mountain range extended from the eastern half of the island, the independent country of Papua New Guinea, west to the Bird's Head peninsula in the Indonesian province of Papua. The Bird's Head peninsula was where Quentin's parents had introduced him to the tropics when he was six. They had wanted him to meet the Papuans they thought they knew so well. Quentin dismissed this thought. No point in ruining his mood by dwelling on the past.

As they entered Wamena, Markus braked sharply, startling Quentin and waking the others. The road was blocked by a group of Papuans.

"*Lauk,*" one of them said in greeting. His t-shirt displayed the Morning Star flag.

"*Lauk,*" Markus said.

Speaking pidgin, the Papuan requested donations for the Free Papua Movement. Markus spoke to Quentin, "You should give these men money, *tisaman.* They will be happy then."

Lindsey was already digging in her pack. "Here, Markus. Is a hundred thousand *rupiah* enough?"

"Plenty good, *misis.*" He took the money and handed it over.

The man glanced at the bill and smiled. "*Papua Merdeka!*" he said, and waved them on.

Lindsey said, "Markus, has the OPM been active?"

"You don't worry about this, okay *misis*? There is talk of protests, but tourists are very safe."

"What's the OPM?" Roberto asked.

Quentin explained, "It stands for *Organisesi Papua Merdeka*, the Free Papua Movement. Many Papuans want Papua to become an independent country. The OPM are freedom fighters. The flag on that man's shirt was the Morning Star. It kind of symbolizes their fight for independence. Occasionally in the past there's been serious trouble in Wamena."

Lindsey said, "Is something happening we should know about?"

"It's okay, *misis*. You'll see."

Markus drove to their losmen as the sun slid behind the mountain peaks.

CHAPTER THREE

The pig whimpered as the Papuan man gripped its hind legs. Another man grabbed the forelegs and pulled, lifting the pig from the ground. A third man then drew back his bow. The squealing pig looked directly at Bobby as the arrow pierced its side. Wide eyes pleaded for help, but Bobby couldn't move. Suddenly he realized the pig's cries were in *Bahasa*, the Indonesian language.

Bobby gasped and opened his eyes. The squawking continued, but it was only the morning chatter of Tika, the cockatoo in the losmen's lobby.

Last night's pig feast, arranged by Markus, had actually been fun. Butchering the pig had been done in the traditional way, and it had taken three arrows to kill it, but Bobby had been too hungry to let that bother him. While the food cooked, the Papuans had staged a fake battle. That was the best part. They'd painted their bodies with pig grease and soot from the fire, reminding Bobby of the Papuans they'd met in the forest.

Bobby kicked his sheet off. This was the last day, and Mr. Darnell had promised they could explore on their own. Carlos and Addison were asleep, so he shook their beds.

Addison sat up, his coiled hair smashed flat on one side. He stumbled to the bathroom.

Carlos mumbled, "I'm awake already." He heaved off the bed and started picking through dirty shirts and socks that covered the floor. "You know what I'm buying? One of those necklaces with lizard feet."

Bobby considered this. Carlos could probably get away with wearing one of those. It was because of his brother. Everyone liked Roberto. If Carlos wore a lizard-foot necklace, people would say, "Well, he *did* go to New Guinea with his brother Roberto." If Bobby wore one, they'd say, "That's disgusting."

Bobby didn't have much money for souvenirs anyway.

Addison came out of the bathroom. He had frizzed his hair up with his brush, and now it was like a caramel-colored mop hanging over his freckled face. "If you guys want Indonesian lizard-AIDS, go ahead and buy that crap."

Bobby looked at Carlos and rolled his eyes. Addison hadn't apologized to Ashley for blowing up at her yesterday and was still acting like it had never happened. He was clueless about things like that. Bobby got along with him okay, but Addison hadn't even wanted to come on this trip. The Darnells had made him, because Addison 'needed more interaction with his peers.' Addison was the only kid Bobby knew who played Kembalimo more than he did. This had given them something to talk about, and they some-times communicated through Kembalimo. But Addison could be a pain.

They got dressed and went to the lobby, where the group met each morning. They were the first ones there, so they passed the time talking to Tika.

The older kids, Russ and Roberto, and then the two girls, came dragging in with wild hair and pillow-creased cheeks. Bobby didn't have any siblings, and during this trip he had learned that older kids would sleep all day if they could.

Ashley's long frizzy hair was even wilder than the others'. She said, "Does that bird ever shut up?"

Bobby considered responding to this by telling them about his dream, but the older kids made him a little nervous. Especially Ashley.

Roberto yawned and eyed the pack on Carlos's back. "Where you guys going?"

"Wherever," Carlos said. "It's the only time we got on our own. Wanna come?"

"Maybe. Russ, you want to run with the twerps?"

Russ sat in a chair with his head in his arms. "After breakfast, I'm back in bed. You guys got too much energy. It ain't natural."

Bobby paced around, eager for the teachers to show up so they could start the day. He plopped into a chair and pulled out his smartphone to pass the time. Without a local SIM card he had no cellular access, so he used the lobby's Wi-Fi. He opened Kembalimo and browsed through his list of friends. Most of them were kids his age who spoke other languages, living in places like Brazil, Madagascar, and Bahrain. Kembalimo allowed him to talk to them as naturally as he could if they spoke the same language. Addison's name was near the top of his friend list. He stared at it for a moment and then tapped it. His screen went blank and then was populated with the 128 symbols of Kembalimo. Using his finger, he moved the symbols into groups. Each group contained specific information, because the symbols had gradually been assigned their own meanings as Bobby had played the game repeatedly over the last two years. The message he composed could be roughly translated as: *You need to apologize to someone.* Bobby tapped *Send*.

A few meters away, Addison's smartphone chirped. He pulled it out and stared at the screen, frowning. He then began shoving things around on his own screen.

A string of symbols appeared on Bobby's screen. Addison had

composed his message using the same 128 symbols, but Addison's symbols had different meanings than they did for Bobby. The game translated them into Bobby's own Kembalimo language, called a *lingo*. The message said: *Someone needs to apologize for almost getting us killed.*

Bobby made eye contact with Addison and tried giving him a disapproving look.

"You guys are real Kembalimo nerds." Russ had started pacing and he now stared over Bobby's shoulder at the smartphone, although there was no way he could understand the message in Bobby's lingo. "Addison's right there. You can't just talk to him?"

Bobby felt his face flush as all eyes turned to him. Even Ashley was looking at him.

"It's just a way to practice," he said. He shoved his phone back into his pocket. "I usually talk to people in different countries who don't speak English. We talk about all kinds of stuff."

Russ blew out a one-syllable laugh. "You just described the most boring game ever. Answer me this: Can you kill anything in that game, like Nazis or zombies?"

Bobby's face grew even warmer. "Actually, it's not a game. And there's no—"

Suddenly the teachers appeared and everyone's attention shifted away from Bobby.

"Good morning, scientists!" Mr. Darnell always said that, and like always everyone just groaned and herded to the long breakfast table.

At the table there were boiled eggs and bread slices with a bit of peanut butter on them. As they ate, Mr. Darnell reviewed the day's schedule. The flight to Sentani was at 3:30, and everyone had to be at the losmen by noon. Until then they could explore on their own.

Mrs. Darnell was against this and everyone knew it. Apparently Mr. Darnell had convinced her they wouldn't be kidnapped or killed if they had a few hours on their own.

When Mr. Darnell finished, she shouted for them to stay seated. "This is not our country; it's theirs," she said. "Ashley, what will you do if someone touches you?"

"I'll say *Permisi*, uh...*selamat jalan*."

"And just walk away," Mrs. Darnel finished it for her.

A few chuckles rippled around the table. The others wouldn't let Ashley forget her fight with Pupun. She must have been really scared to hit someone like that. Bobby had been that scared only a few times before. There wasn't much to be afraid of in Newton, Missouri. One time a growling dog had cornered him in an alley. He'd grabbed a rock and thrown it. He'd missed, but the dog had backed off. He hadn't thought about throwing the rock, it had just happened. Danger had a way of changing people.

———

Bobby, Carlos, and Addison burst through the door onto the street. The air smelled of strange food and pigs. Barefoot walkers and bicycle riders were everywhere, some with bundles balanced on their heads or hanging behind them from straps across their foreheads. Two Papuan men wearing only *horims* walked by, holding hands and talking to each other in Dani. Across the street a Papuan woman sat on the ground. Two naked children rolled an empty can around in the dirt next to her. An Indonesian boy, waiting with combed hair and white clothes for his mother to finish talking to someone, watched them play but didn't try to join them.

The three students decided to head for the Pasar Nayak market. As they walked, they passed Papuans squatting in the dirt with small piles of sugar cane, ginger root, or yellow tomatoes spread out on cloth before them. Bobby couldn't imagine they could make much money selling these, and he was tempted to give away the last of his own money. He thought about the Papuans they had met at Lorentz Park. Pupun and his friends had few possessions and maybe no money at all. But unlike the Papuans here, Bobby hadn't thought of those men as poor.

At the Pasar Nayak market, which was open on the sides but covered by a metal roof, they wandered for over an hour through endless rows of goods. Carlos couldn't find a necklace he liked, so finally he bought a machete in a sheath decorated with animals and the words, *Wamena, Indonesia.*

When they left the market, a Papuan man carrying a pile of t-shirts stopped them. He held up a shirt emblazoned with the Morning Star flag. The man had a warm smile and friendly eyes, and the boys liked what the teachers had told them about the freedom fighters, so they each bought one. This depleted Bobby's remaining money.

Addison shed his pack and pulled his new shirt on. He said, "How's it look?"

"Like a dumb-ass tourist," Carlos said, stuffing his into his pack. Bobby stowed his away, too.

They turned north on Sudarso, a street busy with activity, but as they made their way north, things seemed to change. People were shouting and running. Soon Bobby saw a mass of people in the street several blocks ahead. He stopped walking.

"Guys. I don't think we should go this way."

Addison kept walking. "Come on, I want to see what's going on!"

Suddenly two Indonesian policemen, wearing stiff tan uniforms and black berets, stepped in front of them, blocking their way.

"*Mau ke mana?*" said one of the policemen. The men were not smiling, and their brown faces sparkled with sweat. A pistol hung from each of their belts, balanced on the other side by a black club.

Carlos said, "Sorry, we speak English."

Suddenly, smoke billowed from the middle of the crowd ahead, followed by angry shouting. The two policemen turned and ran toward the crowd, leaving the boys staring in fascination. As Bobby instinctively began backing away, the crowd erupted into chaos and violence. Police billy clubs thrashed in the air above the heads, and people tumbled over each other trying to escape.

"Addison! Thank God!"

Bobby turned, startled. It was Mrs. Darnell.

"Where the hell have you boys been?" She grabbed the neck of Addison's t-shirt and started hustling them away from the violent crowd. She pulled out her walkie-talkie as she walked. "Quentin?"

Brief static and then a voice, "Yeah, Linds. Any luck?"

"I found them. We'll be at the airport in less than ten." She lowered the walkie-talkie. "Change of plans. We're leaving for Sentani now."

"Why are we leaving early?" Bobby asked as he tried to keep up.

She shot him a glance. "Do you really need to ask that? There are conflicts at the north end this morning. Remember talking about the OPM, and the flag?"

"Yeah. We bought t-shirts. Addison's wearing his."

Mrs. Darnell looked at Addison's shirt for the first time. She stopped walking. "I told your dad this was a bad idea." She shook her head and started walking again. *"It'll be okay, Lindsey. They'll stay out of trouble! Oh, and let's not buy local SIM cards for their phones, Lindsey. Why would they ever need them?"*

Bobby had never seen her this upset.

"What about the OPM?" Addison said.

"Some Papuans demonstrated by raising the flag. Things are getting out of hand. Now they're trying to get tourists out of Wamena." She nodded at the shirt. "Take that off. Now."

Addison started to pull it off, but when she looked away he shoved it back down.

As they approached the green domed roof of the air terminal, it became clear that something was very wrong. Tourists were everywhere, slinging luggage around, fumbling for money and paperwork.

Mrs. Darnell plunged straight through the crowd and into the building. Angry shouting and the odor of sweat filled the crowded space. She guided them through the confusion and out the other side. There they saw Mr. Darnell and the other kids sitting next to the airstrip. The luggage was piled on the grass beside them.

"Nice of you guys to join us," Russ said. "We've missed our plane like four times."

Mr. Darnell rose to his feet. "We should be able to board one of the Twin Otters," he said. "The larger planes are filled."

BOBBY'S EXCITEMENT grew as the plane bounced and rolled to the grassy edge of the airstrip, coming to a stop just in front of him. They had flown from Sentani to Wamena on a big Fokker F-twenty-something, and he'd had a lousy seat far from the window. But this was a proper jungle plane—rugged-looking and dirty white with blue letters that said *Merpati*. A door near the Twin Otter's nose popped open, and an Indonesian pilot climbed to the ground. He glanced at the Americans without smiling and then opened a baggage door at the rear of the plane and one on the side of the nose cone. He attacked the pile of luggage, throwing it in like he was angry at every bag. He was not having a good day.

Inside the plane, Bobby counted eighteen seats, jammed into a cabin not much larger than the minibus. Each row had two seats on the right and one on the left.

"Move your butt, Roberto. Miranda, don't touch me there!"

"Bite it, Russ!"

The older boys took the first row, then Ashley and Miranda, and then the Darnells. Addison and Carlos took the two seats behind the teachers, leaving Bobby by himself. He chose the single seat across from them, happy to have his own space by the windows.

The cabin was hot and smelled like fuel. Tattered fabric covered the seats. In fact, everything seemed worn out, like his dad's old car. Dents and gashes stippled the cabin wall. Suspicious substances caked the floor, gumming up the seams and screws. Bobby felt the same rush as when he boarded a roller coaster—helplessness mixed with anticipation. He looked out the window, his own private window, at the mountains encircling Wamena and the Baliem Valley.

It had been an exciting day, so far.

CHAPTER FOUR

THE HOTTER THE GODDAMN PLANE, *the longer you have to sit and wait*, thought Quentin. By the time Lindsey had found the boys, the larger planes had departed, leaving only a handful of Twin Otters. The airline's resources must have been stretched thin, for it appeared there would be only one pilot on this flight. Through the window, Quentin watched the pilot quarrelling with an airline official. Apparently the pilot's goal was to argue with every person at the airport before taking off.

Quentin moaned and shifted position. He twirled a small object in his fingers, a habit developed in his first year of teaching that helped calm his nerves. It was a raccoon *baculum*, or penis bone, that a student had bought while on a family trip to the Ozarks. The student had joyfully explained that Ozark boys once gave the four-inch bones to their girlfriends as tokens of love. Quentin had jokingly offered it to Lindsey when they'd first met, and she'd surprised him by revealing that she'd already collected *bacula* from a dozen different mammals to show her students. Every day since then he had carried it with him in the pocket of his trousers.

Lindsay smiled at his nervous habit. "Things could be worse."

"How?"

"We could be stuck here. The Papuans are uprising, and we'd be caught in the middle of it, an international incident. 'American Teenagers Involved in Civil War.'" She framed the headlines with her hands. "The kids would join the separatists. We'd have to go back and tell the parents they're now freedom fighters."

Quentin felt his stress soften. "You're a little disturbed."

She smiled again. This time Quentin was struck by the glint in her eyes and felt a surge of passion. But his fervor did not suit the setting. *Soon we'll be home,* he reminded himself. He decided the conversation could serve as a distraction. "More likely they'd join the Indonesian police," he said. "They've got aptitude for making people suffer."

"Why don't you ask them which side they'd choose? Did you see Addison's new shirt? He wore it all over town today. I told him to take it off, and he ignored me."

Quentin turned around to look, noting Addison's shirt for the first time. He was secretly pleased at the thought of his son siding with the indigenous Papuans. "I guess you're right; they'd join the Papuans. Maybe start a village in the rainforest and live on sago grubs."

Quentin glanced around at the other students. At the front of the cabin, Russ and Roberto appeared to be sleeping. Both girls bobbed their heads to music from their headphones. All three younger boys were doing something on their smartphones. A young Indonesian couple sat at the back of the plane, talking intimately together. A policeman whose apparent purpose had been to convince the pilot the Indonesians were legitimate passengers had escorted them onto the plane some minutes ago.

Quentin said, "Whose idea was it to let the students out on their own, anyway?"

Lindsey wiped her smile away, not acknowledging humor in this. "You really don't want to go there right now."

A thud-click broke their thoughts as the pilot slammed and secured the passenger door. The pilot clambered into the cockpit. Both engines started. He revved them up, and the entire plane bucked. An open doorway separated the cockpit from the cabin, exposing the pilot's right side and most of the instrument panel. On the instrument panel was a worn piece of masking tape with a series of marks on it. In what must have been a safety check, the pilot pointed to the instruments one at a time and moved his finger to the next mark on the tape, as if he might lose track of the process. The pilot looked over his shoulder like he was pulling out of a supermarket parking lot, and the plane surged forward onto the airstrip.

In no time, they were rising toward the mountains enclosing the Wamena Valley. Quentin noticed that Miranda was apparently praying. Her cropped blonde hair allowed Quentin to see that her eyes were closed and lips were moving. It was the first inclination toward religion he had seen in any of the students—peculiar, considering they'd been together for over a week. The others watched through the windows as the tin roofs of Wamena gave way to scattered, thatch-roofed huts surrounded by neatly-divided sweet potato gardens.

As they flew north to the peaks of the Maoke Mountains, Lindsey pointed out the road gradually being built from Wamena to Jayapura. Forging a road through hundreds of miles of mountainous and lowland swampy rainforest was beyond Quentin's comprehension. He wished they would give it up, as it seemed like a vicious assault on this remarkable wilderness.

Huts and gardens thinned out and then disappeared entirely, leaving only rainforest and mountaintops to the horizon. Quentin gazed at the expanse. He and Lindsey had traveled here four times but had experienced only the highland area around Wamena. The vast forest below was a different world, dark and mysterious. Other than the atrocious road being constructed, it had changed very little since Alfred Wallace, the first naturalist to set foot in New Guinea in the 1850s, spent several months to the north and published a fascinating account of his adventures.

Wallace's time had been a grand age of discovery, but in all his wisdom, Wallace clearly had not considered the long-term impacts of his contact with the indigenous people. And like Wallace, Quentin's own parents had neglected to appreciate the fact that when people of vastly different cultures met, diffusion of customs and values was inescapable, and they were forever changed. And such changes were not always good.

———

Twenty minutes later, as the mountains gave way to lowland rainforest, the only breaks in the scene below were occasional glimpses of the brown water of winding rivers. Of the students, only Bobby still seemed spellbound by the passing forest, his face glued to the window.

Quentin unbuckled and stood in the narrow aisle facing the three younger boys. "I'm sure you guys have a great story to tell about your morning and why Mrs. Darnell was upset."

Addison didn't even look up from the screen on his smartphone.

Bobby glanced at Quentin and returned his gaze to the window. "Yeah, I guess."

"Well, I want the full story tonight. That'll give you guys a chance to get it straight."

They all smiled at this, even Addison.

As Quentin turned back to his seat, a prickly wave suddenly swept through his body. He nearly toppled over. He reached out to right himself, but his hand found nothing. He looked around and could see nothing. There was only a gray vastness. It was peaceful and demanded no explanation. After an indeterminable time, the gray expanse gave way, returning him to the harsh cabin light. He realized he was gripping his chest with one hand.

A voice came from the side, "Great, what's wrong now?"

Quentin looked at the voice. Addison tapped his smartphone, irritated at something that didn't work. Lindsey's eyes were pinched closed, as if coping with a migraine. As Quentin's equilibrium returned, he watched until she opened her eyes. She seemed as confused as he was.

One of the older boys said, "What the hell was that?"

Bobby's voice screeched, "Mr. Darnell, something's wrong! Look at the engine!"

Quentin leaned over Bobby and pressed against the window. The left engine was mounted on the wing above their heads. Oil streamed from its housing, making a horizontal trail in the air, dashing the wing strut. The oil suddenly caught fire. Flames sputtered wildly in the slipstream. Quentin stared at it for a moment and then turned to the others. The Indonesian couple at the rear of the cabin caught Quentin's attention. They embraced each other as if they were frightened, and he could not see their faces. His eyes were drawn to the man's dark hands, gripping the woman's clean, white shirt. Briefly he thought how strangely beautiful this was.

"Quentin?" It was Lindsey. The students were silent, waiting.

"It's on fire," he whispered, too quietly for anyone to hear. The plane suddenly pitched left. He caught himself on the seat and looked out the window. The engine had shut down, the windmilling propeller creating enough drag to throw the plane into a turn.

"Hey, man, you all right?" It was Russ, shouting to the pilot in front of him. Then he turned to face them. "There's something wrong with him!"

Quentin scrambled to the cockpit doorway. What he saw there

made him freeze. The pilot's back arched, pressing his shoulders against the seat. His legs kicked wildly. Gasping for air, the pilot's breaths came in sickening whines: "HEE, HEE, HEE…" He was trying to remove the headset, but his hands flailed, scratching his face and eyes instead.

With the controls neglected, the plane continued pulling to the left.

Quentin pushed into the cockpit and kneeled by the pilot. "What's wrong? What can I do?" The pilot's arm thrashed out and struck Quentin viciously in the face. Reeling from the pain, Quentin grasped his mouth and then looked at his hand. It was red with blood.

"HEE, HEE, HEE…" The pilot's breathing became even more frantic, and his eyes bulged from his drenched face.

Quentin grabbed the pilot's wrists and held them to the man's chest. He leaned over him, looking into his face. "Listen to me! One of the engines—it's on fire."

The pilot's eyes showed no understanding, only raw pain. "HEE, HEE, HUH, HUH…" His breathing changed from a whine to a gasp and seemed to slow down. His legs and arms stopped flailing and Quentin was able to release him.

"HUH, HUH… HUH…" His breathing softened and then was drowned out by the remaining engine. Suddenly his body arched backward, as if every muscle were straining for air.

Quentin watched the body contract again and again, a gurgle spewing from the man's throat at the peak of each contraction. Finally, the pilot's torso toppled out of the seat, jamming Quentin's legs against the copilot seat. The man's legs struck the control wheel and the plane pitched violently to the side. Quentin tried lifting the pilot, but there wasn't room. That's when he saw the man's feet. His shoes had split apart and pink flesh protruded grotesquely from the rips, as if his feet had exploded.

Quentin pulled his eyes away from this bizarre sight and yelled, "Russ, help me!"

Russ grabbed the pilot's armpit, and together they hoisted the man back into his seat. Outside the cockpit window, the ground was getting closer. They were losing altitude.

"Russ, go back to your seat. Everyone buckle in!" Quentin watched to make sure they responded and then turned back to the now motionless pilot. He gripped the man's head. "Hey, wake up!" The pilot's eyes stared vacuously. Quentin grasped the man's neck for a pulse, but felt only thick, clammy tissue.

"Quentin, we have to do something!" Lindsey cried.

The fear in her voice slapped him in the face. He looked desperately around the cabin. The two girls huddled together, Miranda's head buried in her hands. Bobby stared out the window at the dead engine, as if willing it to life. In the rear, the Indonesian couple still clung to each other. Quentin pushed his way toward the couple.

"We're going to crash! Can you fly this plane?"

The woman remained motionless, her face buried in the man's shoulder, and again Quentin glimpsed dark fingers against her white shirt. The man shouted something in Indonesian, his face creased with terror. He couldn't have been older than twenty.

Quentin turned away from them. "Goddammit!" He made his way back to the cockpit. The forest was much closer, the treetops now a blur of motion. He grabbed the control wheel opposite the pilot and yanked on it, but nothing happened. He leaned over the pilot, grabbed the main wheel, and turned it. The plane responded, banking to the left. Quentin had never flown a plane, but he'd seen pilots in movies pull the wheel up for lift. He pulled hard and the plane's nose pitched upward. He looked out. The trees were not rising as fast, but the plane was still losing altitude. He released the control wheel, and the plane began dropping faster, so he grabbed it and pulled again. It would not stay in place without his hands on it.

Seconds later, the forest canopy was just below them. Quentin saw individual leaves as trees rushed by. The brown surface of a river appeared and then was gone. They were going to crash. He would die. His students and son would die. His wife. Quentin looked back at Lindsey and their eyes met. He released the control wheel and staggered back to her.

"Hurry!" she cried.

He fumbled with the buckle and snapped it into place. Lindsey had been reaching over the seat in front of her, comforting the girls, but now she put her arms around Quentin.

He pressed her head into his shoulder and braced himself for the impact.

THE TREE KANGAROO, known locally as the *mbolop,* made its way up the trunk of a towering klinki pine. The top of the forest often revealed the greatest diversity of living things, and each tree variety seemed to hold its own combination of life thriving at its highest reaches. And so climbing was a good use of its time. The creature gathered information as if it were sustenance, feeding on it in order to live. And still there was so much to be consumed and stored.

Claws pierced the klinki pine's bark, allowing brawny hind legs to propel the creature upward. The tree's limbs became thinner near the top, and the disturbance made them tremble. A raucous group of cockatoos, known to the tree kangaroo as *kékékh,* scolded the creature, their shrieks amplifying as it climbed nearer to them, until finally they blasted out of the canopy, a clamorous white cloud.

As the kangaroo watched them fly upward, a prickly wave passed through its body. It stopped climbing. It discerned immediately what was happening, what the man Samuel had done—a heedless action with unpredictable consequences. But such experimentation was not unprecedented in this place. It was to be expected.

Just as the wave of sensation passed, the flock of cockatoos fell silent. And then they rained down upon the tree they had just vacated. Ruined bodies splattered against the limbs, forcing the mbolop to shut its eyes against the spray of fluids and fragments.

Eyes still closed, the tree kangaroo processed these events. Suppositions and observed facts shifted about on a cognitive puzzle board until they fit together like interlocking pieces. The puzzle was then undone and reassembled, searching for the clearest overall picture.

But the creature's thoughts were again disrupted, this time by a distant sound, a mechanical growl steadily drawing nearer. The mbolop scrambled higher until it could see over the other trees. It spotted the source, a machine hurtling closer and closer, just above the forest canopy. Muscles twitching, the creature prepared to flee. With a deafening roar, the machine passed directly over, close enough that the kangaroo had to tighten its grip to avoid being blown out of the tree by the air wake.

The mbolop turned around in time to see the machine crash into the treetops.

QUENTIN HAD LIVED A MILD LIFE. He had lost a fight when he was a teenager, but adrenaline had prevented him from feeling the pain. He had been in minor car accidents, with no injuries. And he had fallen from a ladder once, cracking his wrist. Never had he experienced anything like the crushing violence of the plane hurtling into the canopy. In a deafening uproar of twisting metal and bursting seams, he was wrenched from Lindsey's embrace. His seatbelt clamped down on his hips, forcing his head to slam the seatback in front of him. Abruptly, the plane skimmed off the tree canopy, and for a moment, there was only the wind rushing through new openings in the cabin. Eleven people were on the plane, but there were no screams, no words—only the whisper of air.

Chaos returned as the fuselage plowed into the canopy a second time. Quentin was thrown to the side this time and then jostled ruthlessly as if the plane were rolling. The fuselage shrieked as sheared tree branches tore into the metal. It then slowed and seemed to stop.

Quentin blinked, but his vision was blurred. He grasped for anything solid and found the seatback in front of him, but it jiggled as if it had been torn loose. He recalled that he should not be alone. Others had been with him. Lindsey! He reached for her and found her arm, her shoulder, and then her hair. Suddenly there was a loud crack and the entire plane rolled to the side. This was followed by an even greater crack, as if an entire tree had been snapped in half. The plane fell. It crashed onto another tree branch and turned on end. For a moment it plunged tail-first like an elevator with a severed cable. The rear of the fuselage impacted an immovable force, throwing Quentin back into his seat and bringing the loosened seat in front of him into his lap. The plane then toppled over, and with one last jarring crash it came to rest. The fuselage groaned and then fell silent.

QUENTIN'S SENSES began to function again. Shapes emerged from the haze. Spasms of pain, starting as mere tingles, intensified from his hips, his neck, and then from everywhere. His ears were the last to surrender. At first, there was only pulsing static, like breaking waves. Then there were voices. The voices intensified, turning nightmarish. They sounded guttural, like animals that were dying.

His students and family were shrieking, gasping for air. He tried closing his eyes, but it didn't stop.

The pain in his hip became unbearable. He looked down and realized he was hanging from his seat. The plane was on its side. Lindsey was above him, her legs pressing against his. She was alive, conscious, pushing against Quentin's thigh and the seatback in front of her. The cabin was dim now, but Quentin saw blood dripping from her face.

"Lindsey!"

She didn't answer. Half her face was concealed by disheveled brown hair. The eye Quentin could see flicked his direction, but blinked confusedly. The students' distressed cries seemed to swell. He had to do something.

"Lindsey, my hip—I have to get out." He pulled on his seatbelt latch and the mechanism popped. He dropped against the left side of the plane, hitting his head on the rim of a window. He pressed his hand where sunlight should have shone through Plexiglas. Instead there was moist soil.

Quentin tried to clear his head, but the girls' cries were persistent and frighteningly intense, making it hard to focus.

"We crashed. Mr. Darnell, we crashed!" Bobby had been seated on the left side of the plane, so he was now against the ground in the seat next to Quentin.

"I know, Bobby. Are you hurt?"

"My head hurts."

Quentin popped Bobby's seatbelt open, allowing him to sit up. Quentin then looked around him. Where a wall once isolated the baggage space at the rear of the cabin, there was now a huge opening. He saw slivers of sunlight against murky foliage. The Indonesian man, slouched in his seat, was silhouetted against the trees. The woman and her seat were gone.

Addison hung limp next to Carlos, who was whimpering and clutching his own bloody hand. Quentin wanted to focus on his son, to make sure Addison was alive. But the girls' cries couldn't be ignored. He turned to them. He saw no movement in the front row beyond the girls, but Russ's head hung loosely from his seat. The opening to the cockpit was now skewed to an odd angle, and through it he saw only twisted wreckage and more forest.

Quentin put his hands to his head. He wanted to fade away into oblivion. But Lindsey rasped above him, pulling him back. He rose from his knees and pressed his shoulder to her chest. "Put your arms around my neck." Her nails dug into his back. He popped the lever on her seatbelt, and her full weight settled onto his shoulder. He collapsed and they both fell.

"Are you okay? Is anything broken?"

She blinked. "I don't know. My head." Blood flowed from a gash above her eye, and Quentin wiped it with his shirt.

"Quentin, the kids."

"I know. You see to the girls. I need to get to Addison."

Lindsey staggered to her feet. Quentin turned to Carlos, who was sobbing and holding his hand. Quentin freed him from his seat and set him to the side so he could reach his son. He turned Addison so he could see his face. His face was even more pale than usual, and a red impact wound covered half his forehead. Quentin gripped his throat and felt a weak pulse. He lowered him to the floor, but was struck by Addison's inertness. There was not a tight muscle in his body.

"Oh God no!" Lindsey was now at the front of the plane. Quentin moved to her side.

Miranda cried over and over, "My leg! Please! My leg!"

But Lindsey's attention was fixed on Russ and Roberto. The gap between their seats and the wall of the cockpit was gone. The wall had crushed Roberto's legs. His head hung to the side at an impossible angle.

Lindsey grabbed Quentin's arm. "He's dead, isn't he?"

There was no doubt of that. Quentin glanced back at Carlos,

who was still cradling his hand but watching intently. Mercifully, he couldn't see his older brother from where he sat. Quentin turned his attention to Russ. The cabin doorway had impacted Russ's head, gashing his temple, exposing several inches of white skull. Quentin felt for a pulse, but found none. Roberto and Russ, both just graduated from high school, their futures full of promise, were dead.

Quentin turned to the girls, his movements becoming mechanical, automatic. He extracted Ashley from her seat, which was now barely attached to the fuselage, and lowered her to the floor. She finally quieted down. Aside from a sizeable cut on her shoulder, she seemed more frightened than seriously hurt. Reaching for Miranda, Quentin felt distant from his own body. The cockpit wall had forced Roberto's seat back, trapping Miranda's right leg. A jagged edge of femur protruded from her thigh, creating a disturbing bulge in her jeans. Lindsey tried to calm her as Quentin released her seatbelt and allowed her weight to settle on him. He started to lower her, but her ruined leg was caught. Her screams had been continuous, but to Quentin they now seemed secluded, unrelated to the task at hand. He twisted and tugged until the leg was free. When he finally put her on the floor, he realized her screaming had stopped.

CHAPTER FIVE

In the minutes or hours that followed, Quentin had no concept of the passing of time. He and Lindsey worked frantically to treat wounds that required skills far beyond theirs. Addison, Miranda, and Carlos needed a hospital with skilled doctors. Quentin, Lindsey, Bobby, and Ashley had minor cuts, which would heal if they could avoid infection. But Quentin was unable to find a first aid kit. The plane didn't have one, or it had been ejected in the crash.

Roberto and Russ were beyond help.

Quentin's mind reeled. Even if they were lucky enough to be rescued without further casualties, nothing would be the same again. He and Lindsey would have to face the parents of students they had promised to care for, but who now were dead, crippled, or emotionally scarred. And if Addison were to die... Quentin forced this thought aside in order to function.

All that remained of the plane was a cylinder of fuselage. Most of the cockpit was destroyed. Even if the pilot had lived until the moment they crashed, he was certainly dead now. His crumpled body lay amidst remnants of the cockpit and baggage from the forward compartment. If Quentin had remained at the plane's controls, he would be part of that debris.

The young Indonesian man seemed mostly unharmed, but he did not offer to help. His girlfriend or wife was gone, her seat ripped from its anchors and ejected. She'd been literally torn from his arms. He wandered aimlessly around the wreck, apparently looking for her. The plane's tail could not have been more than a few hundred meters away, but the forest was dense and no other wreckage was visible.

Miranda's skin was pale and clammy and she was in shock, alternating between unconsciousness and semi-lucid babbling. While she was unconscious, they forced her femur into alignment and tied her straightened legs against one of the plane's seatbacks with a pair of trousers. Ashley bravely helped with these tasks. Ashley had a nasty gash on her shoulder, but they had tied a shirt around her upper arm and she was coping. Addison remained unconscious, and there was nothing they could do for him other than check for a pulse every few minutes.

They set Bobby to work removing the seat cushions and any of the seat frames he could work loose. He seemed to welcome the chance to do something, and he tossed the seats one by one into a growing pile outside the cabin.

Carlos sat at the rear of the fuselage, quietly nursing his damaged hand and staring into the forest. He hadn't said a word, but he'd let Quentin inspect his injuries. Three fingers were crushed, the bones pulverized. Quentin simply wrapped the hand as tight as he dared with a Morning Star t-shirt. When he told him that his brother had died, Carlos shook his head and pulled away, unwilling to listen.

When they had finally met the most pressing needs, Quentin considered the problem of the dead bodies. In the sauna-like cabin, their presence would soon become intolerable. He had to move them. He instructed the others to turn their heads and he carried out the task on his own. He was glad they weren't watching, because Roberto's legs were mostly severed at the knees, and they dangled and flopped bizarrely as Quentin carried the body out of the plane.

Finally he stood some distance from the fuselage, the bodies of the boys and pilot at his feet, mostly hidden from the others by the base of a strangler fig tree. Quentin wiped the sweat from his face and swatted at the cloud of flies around him. The heat was oppressive, and they had no water. He looked up at the forest canopy and took note of what was arguably the largest obstacle to their rescue. The canopy appeared undisturbed. There was no gaping hole through which searchers might spot the wreckage. Would the search planes see them? Had the pilot even been capable of radioing that they were in trouble? Their flight hadn't been a scheduled run. With the chaos in Wamena, dozens of unscheduled flights were leaving the highlands. Their plane may not even be missed yet.

In frustration, Quentin kicked a mangled fragment of the cockpit. The wreckage flipped over and then it caught his eye. The metal appeared to have melted and mushroomed outward. Something about this brought back a scene from the crash Quentin had forgotten. As the pilot was dying, his feet had looked like this—like they had exploded. He stared at the metal for a moment but could make no sense of it.

Quentin searched the debris and failed to find any portion of the instrument panel that might be the radio. The only communication devices they had were their smartphones and one of the walkie-talkies. The other walkie-talkie was in Lindsey's pack in the lost tail of the plane. The smartphones required cellular network access, and the nearest cellular towers were in Wamena and the capitol city of Jayapura. They were probably a hundred miles from either location. Quentin tried his anyway but couldn't pick up a signal. The walkie-talkie had a range of only a few miles. Perhaps they could use it if a search plane flew over. He tried it briefly to make sure it worked and quickly turned it off to conserve the batteries.

They hadn't heard any planes since the crash, which was puzzling considering a steady stream of emergency flights to Sentani would likely continue for some time. He moved farther away from the fuselage and paused, listening. At first all he heard were the incessant flies. Honeyeaters called in the distance, followed by reciprocating calls from other directions. A faint rustling in the leaves above drew his gaze in time to see something move in the canopy. He made out a dark animal, mostly hidden, probably a possum. Then another animal moved, a few meters away but in the same tree. He waited, but there was no further movement.

Other than these natural sounds the area was silent. The crippled Twin Otter must have drifted miles from the Wamena-to-Sentani flight path. Probably to the west, since it was the left engine that had failed. The numb shock in Quentin's mind began to give way to comprehension of the hopelessness of their situation.

He scanned the forest in every direction. It was all the same—murky, emerald-tinted, and textured with buttress roots, twisting vines, and vertical trunks that disappeared into a sea of foliage. He couldn't see more than thirty meters in any direction. The streaks of sunlight penetrating the canopy were now at a lower angle as the day faded away. What would the night here be like? Would Addison be alive in the morning? Overcome, Quentin sank to the ground, just out of view of the Twin Otter. His body shook once, startling him. It had been so long since he'd last cried. But he felt a tidal wave coming. There was no fighting it, but he did make a feeble effort to not be heard by the others.

THE TREE KANGAROO appraised the scene from above. It superimposed images of artifacts scattered about the area over a compendium of objects encountered in the past, but no matches were found. Mannerisms and gestures were likened to a database of known behaviors. Vocalizations, including the man's stifled sobs, ran through audio comparison algorithms but failed to find their counterparts.

The creature categorized the wreckage and survivors as new, unknown. These could be the ones they had been waiting for. Perhaps it was a misguided effort that had brought the strangers here, but that was of little importance.

The tree kangaroo turned to a second creature clinging to a nearby limb, another mbolop. It grunted softly to draw the other's attention and then gestured with one of its forelimbs. The other mbolop loosened its grip on the limb and gestured back an acknowledgement. It then bounded off through the canopy, leaping from one tree to the next. The first tree kangaroo remained, hiding amidst the foliage of the silkwood tree. Its clawed hand raked in a tuft of leaves, shoving them into its mouth. The creature chewed slowly, studying the sobbing figure below.

AFTER DRAINING HIS PENT-UP EMOTIONS, Quentin felt the vigor of renewed resolve. He rose from the muddy ground and was startled by movement in the trees to his right. A human figure made its way through the dense undergrowth.

"Hey!" Quentin stumbled over creepers and roots to close the gap between them. "Hey, wait!" The person paused. It was the Indonesian passenger. The man held one hand over a large bloodstain on the front of his shirt. Flies covered his hand and the stain, feeding on the blood. He looked at Quentin briefly and continued walking.

"Are you okay?"

The man stopped. *"Murni, saya pergi ke Murni. Saya cari Murni."* He was ashen, staring at the ground, and he seemed not to notice the mass of flies. He then walked away.

Apparently he was looking for the woman, named Murni. Her body was probably near the tail portion of the plane. If it were Lindsey, Quentin would do the same. So he watched the man disappear without trying to stop him.

Quentin returned to the plane. With some seats removed, there was now more room in the cabin. Lindsey, Ashley, Carlos, and Bobby sat around the still forms of Addison and Miranda as if waiting for them to wake. The despair in Lindsey's eyes told Quentin that things were no better.

"How long do you think before they find us?" Ashley said.

"I haven't heard any search planes yet," Quentin said. He considered this for a moment. "Listen, there's no way to know how long it will take. It could be in the morning, or maybe not even tomorrow. I want you to remember something: you came on this trip because you weren't afraid. You're all tough. That's why we're going to get through this."

No one responded, so Quentin went on. "In a crisis the first thing to do is care for any injuries. The problem is, we don't have first aid supplies. There had to be a first aid kit on the plane, and we know we have some supplies in our bags in the plane's tail. The second thing to do is to find water and food. Lindsey, what did you have in your bag?"

"I had a few things, a couple of water bottles," she said.

"So we have to find the rest of our stuff. There's not much daylight left. I'll search for the bags and first aid kit. You guys get this area ready for the night. Bobby, we'll need seat cushions arranged for each person to sleep on."

Bobby nodded and stood up.

Quentin considered the mass of flies feeding on the Indonesian's blood and he looked at the torn edges of the fuselage. "If I find the other bags, we might have enough cloth to rig up something to keep the insects out of here." The mosquitoes would get worse as the sun went down. They had taken Chloroquine for the last two weeks to prevent malaria and had planned to continue doses for the next month, but the remaining tablets were waiting for them at home. No other drugs or vaccinations were considered essential for the trip, but now that they were out of the highlands the risk of insect-borne diseases was greater. Besides malaria, there was encephalitis and dengue fever, and probably others Quentin hadn't even heard of. Not to mention the risk of bacterial infection in their wounds, which could lead to gangrene.

Quentin exited the plane and looked at the cracked branches above, trying to determine the plane's path. His eye caught the glint of freshly exposed heartwood some distance beyond the wreckage. That had to be the direction. But the forest was remarkably dense, so he ducked back in and told Lindsey and the kids to listen for his calls.

After moving into the forest he quickly lost sight of the plane. The understory saplings grew so close together in places that he had to force them apart. He made progress for perhaps a hundred meters, trying to keep a straight course. He felt isolated, vulnerable.

"Can you hear me?" At first his call was followed only by the sound of flies.

"Mr. Darnell, we hear you!" It was Bobby, his voice already faint and distant.

He called back to Bobby to keep listening. He then pulled off his shirt, thinking of hanging it as a marker. Immediately the flies descended on the sweaty flesh of his back. This was insufferable, so he put the shirt back on. Scattered on the forest floor were long, rigid leaves of the sago palm. He gathered some of these and set them upright like a small teepee. Moving on, he stopped again when the crude marker was almost out of sight, no more than ten meters. He made a second marker, then moved ahead and made a third. Feeling some confidence, Quentin continued like this, trying to work his way in a straight line.

After the fifth marker, he came upon a small clearing containing four sorted and neatly stacked piles of objects. There was a pile of bright red berries, another of yellow bird feathers, and another of iridescent blue beetle carapaces. The biggest pile contained hundreds of large brown acorns. In the center of the clearing stood an upside-down cone made of thin sticks, resembling a miniature hut. The floor of the clearing was a bed of green moss, meticulously cleaned of all debris except for the piles. For the briefest moment he thought the site might be man-made but then realized it was the bower of a male bowerbird. To convince females they were worthy, males created these impressive shrines of gifts collected from the surrounding forest.

Something in the pile of acorns caught his eye. He stepped into the bower and picked it up. It was a small figurine, carved from a stone, an animal of some kind, perhaps a cuscus or tree kangaroo. It was stylized, like a totem carving, and the craftsmanship was strik-ing. Its oval shape was close enough to that of an acorn that the bowerbird must have collected and classified it as such. Quentin's pulse quickened. There must be a village nearby, perhaps with a radio and an airstrip. Encouraged, he dropped the figurine into his pocket and continued on.

Before long, though, he'd constructed twenty markers and still had not seen the missing wreckage. The light was fading fast. They would have no first aid supplies tonight.

In frustration, he called out, "Hello! Is anyone there?"

A moment later, Bobby called out, "Mr. Darnell, we're here."

Quentin suddenly felt disoriented. Bobby's voice had come from *ahead* and to the right. Somehow he had almost doubled back to the plane. Defeated, he headed in the direction of the voice, leaving his trail of useless markers.

Stumbling through the darkening tangle of vegetation, he called out again. Bobby's reply didn't seem much closer. Then he heard something else, like gushing water, but coming from all sides, and above. A drop hit his cheek and he looked up. Rain was making its way through the gauntlet of the canopy to the forest floor. The pattering became louder, and soon he was in the midst of a deafening downpour. There was no chance of hearing Bobby's still-distant cries.

Rivulets of rainwater ran down his face, reminding Quentin of his thirst. He found a large leaf and held it out flat with the pointed tip in his mouth. The rain gathered on the leaf and flowed onto his tongue. He called out, pushing his voice until it hurt, but he heard only the rain. He pointed at a tree in the direction he had last heard Bobby and then made his way toward it. Halfway to the tree he picked out another directly beyond the first. Then he picked out another beyond that. He continued this way, calling out periodically but hearing nothing in return. The rain only intensified. It became so dark that Quentin could barely see trees just in front of him. He would have to wait for the rain to stop. In nearly total darkness, Quentin found a tree with knee-high buttress roots at the base. He slid to the ground, his back against the tree and his feet pointing to where the Twin Otter should be. He sat there in the mud, waiting.

Exhausted by the most traumatic day of his life, uncertain that their son still lived, and feeling very alone, Quentin drew up his knees and laid his face and arms over them. In only one day his life had been shattered. In spite of this, Quentin felt deep within himself a need to survive. Not for his own sake, because the years of regret he faced were as daunting as this forest. Instead, he needed to live to ensure the survival of Lindsey and Addison, and the remaining students. For this reason, he would not give up.

His guilt and conviction were finally pushed away by the sympathetic veil of sleep. In the gray moments between states of consciousness, Quentin saw his father, kneeling in the forest, sobbing. After years of believing he had brought enlightenment to the Papuans he so loved, he had witnessed the truth. It was the first and only time Quentin had seen him cry.

Dad, I have failed too.

CHAPTER SIX

Bobby awoke thinking someone had called his name. But he heard only birds chattering in the forest outside, and then another of Miranda's moans. The plane's cabin was now gray with the light of morning. The rain had finally stopped.

He wiped his eyes and looked around. The others seemed to be sleeping. Miranda's eyes were closed, but her moans never ended. Carlos was curled up at the front of the plane where his brother had been crushed. He had barely spoken since the crash. Ashley was stretched out next to Miranda. Ashley's wavy hair was clumped and tangled, and Bobby stared at her, wishing he could see more of her face.

Mrs. Darnell slept with her arm around Addison. Addison still hadn't moved a muscle. Maybe he had died already during the night. Bobby was glad Mrs. Darnell had finally fallen asleep. He'd heard her crying through most of the night. They had yelled for Mr. Darnell until they could hardly talk. Then Mrs. Darnell had simply sat down outside the plane, soaked with rain. Finally, Bobby and Ashley had convinced her to move inside.

Bobby wondered what his own mom would do if she were here.

She'd probably be a basket case. She hadn't wanted him to sign up for the trip—said it was too dangerous. But he'd worked hard for the money, and finally she'd given up when Bobby's dad gave him two hundred dollars toward the trip. Bobby's mom gave up on a lot of things, including his dad. *He just wouldn't grow up*, she'd say whenever Bobby asked why she'd left him. Now his dad was going to college, and working two jobs. That seemed pretty grown up to Bobby.

Bobby had to pee, so he rolled to his side and drew his legs up.

"Hey! Are you there?"

Bobby sat up. "Mr. Darnell!"

Mrs. Darnell lifted her head. "Quentin?"

Bobby scrambled out of the cabin. The air was wet but it smelled fresh. Mrs. Darnell came out behind him, followed by Ashley and Carlos.

In a few minutes they spotted Mr. Darnell fighting his way through the jungle. He hugged Mrs. Darnell like he had been lost for weeks. He was soaked and covered with mud and streaks of blood from scratches. But he was back.

Mr. Darnell explained how hard it was to move through the forest, and that he'd slept under a tree. Then he got very serious. "How are Addison and Miranda?"

Mrs. Darnell frowned, and they both went into the plane. Ashley followed them, leaving Carlos and Bobby outside. Carlos just stood there, his normally brown skin looking pale. Bobby fidgeted in silence. He tried not to look, but his eyes kept moving to where the bodies of Russ and Roberto lay. He could see legs and feet, speckled with flies. Carlos was looking at the same spot.

"Sorry about Roberto," Bobby said. "He was nice. Awesome guitar player."

Carlos looked away "Yeah. Maybe I'll get his stuff."

Bobby didn't know if he should laugh and decided not to. He imagined it must be awful to have a brother killed. Bobby had never lost anyone, unless you counted his dad moving out. He had never even had a dog that died.

"How's your hand?" Bobby said.

"Hurts like a son of a bitch. My fingers are fucking smashed."

Bobby changed the subject again. "I'm hungry. Aren't you hungry?"

"Mostly thirsty."

In the night they'd managed to drink some rainwater, but it hadn't been enough. Bobby figured there must be rainwater sitting in pools in the leaves on the ground, maybe even in some of the pieces of the plane. He asked Carlos if he wanted to help collect it.

Carlos shrugged and nodded. "I just got one hand."

They found two zip-lock bags and a plastic rain jacket of Miranda's. Bobby tied knots in the ends of the sleeves so the sleeves could hold water. But finding water that looked clean enough to drink wasn't easy. Water was pooled in the wrecked metal, and they poured what they could into the bags. But the water was brown with dirt and oil. Then they found a jagged piece of the cockpit filled with water that had turned red from hacked-up muscle and skin still stuck to the metal. After that they dumped out both of the bags.

Water was indeed trapped in leaves on the ground, but only small amounts. After tediously collecting nearly a half bag this way, Bobby could see that Carlos's hand was killing him. "You want to take a break? I can do this for a while."

Carlos held out another leaf. "Just hold the bag open."

Leaf by leaf, drop by drop, they worked without saying much more. The first bag filled up and they sealed it and set it at the base of a tree. The clouds disappeared and the forest started to heat up. Water seemed to hang in the air, like rain that wasn't falling.

As Bobby sealed the second full bag and set it next to the first, there was a sudden wave of pattering raindrops. At first he thought the rain had started again, but the pattering lasted only a few seconds, and it came from one place in the trees above them.

"Look at that." Carlos pointed with his mummy-wrapped hand.

Bobby squinted. An animal jumped and sailed toward them to another tree. The branch shook, letting go another shower of rain. The creature eyed them for a second and then launched itself again. Now it was above them, clinging to a tree no fatter than a baseball bat.

Bobby realized it was a tree kangaroo. Its shape was similar to the larger ground kangaroos, but it was the size of a big house cat. Heavy haunches and an arched back made the front part of the animal, the forearms and head, seem small. Its rust-colored eyes were low on its face, just over a short snout, and although its body was mostly dark, its face was golden. Most impressive was its tail, longer than the whole body and mottled with brown and tan fur. The tail hung straight down, like its only purpose was to impress. The creature eyed them, its pointed ears cocked in their direction. Then, clinging to the tree with its forearms, the tree kangaroo pumped its back legs. The tree shook, bringing a shower of rain down on them.

"Hey!" Carlos said, drawing the word out as if scolding a toddler.

Without taking its eyes off them, the creature pumped its legs and showered them again.

Clean rainwater ran from Bobby's hair down his face. "He's trying to help us."

"Probably trying to scare us off," Carlos said.

The creature responded by shaking the tree again, dropping more water on them.

"I'm telling you, Carlos, he's helping!" Bobby pulled out the plastic jacket he had tucked in his pants and spread it out. He didn't have to wait long. The creature shook the tree again and water fell onto the jacket and ran into the knotted sleeves hanging below.

"The water here is gone," Bobby said. "Let's see if he'll do another tree." He moved to a different spot. Carlos grunted and followed. The tree kangaroo scuttled up the tree and leapt from one branch to another until it was above them. It then shook the branch hard, sending a drenching shower onto them and the open jacket. Bobby could now feel the weight of the water.

Bobby shouted back to the plane, "Mr. Darnell, you have to see this!"

QUENTIN WATCHED THE TREE KANGAROO. The creature's fearless behavior could mean humans had influenced it, but perhaps that idea was a manifestation of his need for a connection between the animal and their survival. He pondered this as they stood watching the performance. Suddenly he remembered the figurine he'd found in the bowerbird's nest. He pulled it from his pocket and studied it. The resemblance was unmistakable.

"There must be people around here," he said. "Maybe it's been trained to do this."

"Then there must be a village nearby," Lindsey exclaimed.

Silently, Quentin processed the implausibility of the creature being trained. The only animals domesticated by Papuans were pigs and dogs. Rats lived in close association with them, but even those were not so fearless. Tree kangaroos were marsupials, and he knew of no marsupials anywhere that were domesticated or trained to do any helpful tasks.

The tree kangaroo continued shaking water onto the waiting jacket. As Bobby moved from one spot to another, so did the kangaroo. The animal's behavior was so methodical that Quentin finally allowed himself to believe humans had trained it.

The jacket sleeves filled with water, and Quentin insisted that they all take a generous drink. Astoundingly, the tree kangaroo stopped shaking the trees while they drank, and then promptly started again when Bobby held the jacket out for more.

After returning to the fuselage, Quentin held a bag of water open as Lindsey cleaned Addison's face. His forehead was grotesquely swollen, with concentric circles of blue and black around the impact wound. He had not stirred since the crash, and Quentin feared brain damage. But a pulse could be felt in his neck and wrist, giving them hope.

Miranda, who was in a perpetual state of semiconsciousness, seemed to be faring better. Suddenly, as Lindsey wiped her face, Miranda opened her eyes. "Where are we?"

Lindsey exhaled loudly. "Thank God, honey! We've been so worried."

Miranda tried lifting her head, but then dropped back, moaning.

Quentin said, "Our plane crashed on the flight to Jayapura, Miranda."

"I remember." She squeezed her eyes shut as if the memory hurt. "How long ago?"

"Yesterday," Lindsey said. "We're going to get you to a hospital soon."

Her brows furrowed. "Only one day?" She lifted an arm, whimpering from the pain of movement, and pushed her fingers through her short blonde hair.

Lindsey continued washing Miranda's skin, talking softly to her.

Quentin took one of the bags of water and a reasonably clean portion of a shirt. He found Carlos slumped against a tree, weary from gathering water, and Quentin unwrapped his ruined hand. It was damaged beyond hope of repair, and infection was beginning to set in. Quentin knew that even in a modern hospital they would likely amputate his three crushed fingers. Carlos sobbed but didn't complain as Quentin washed the hand.

"Mʙᴀɪsᴏ!" Bobby said. "That's what we'll call him." He and Ashley, who had taken over for Carlos, now sat on the rotting trunk of a fallen tree. For some minutes they had been discussing the problem of finding the missing tail section of the plane, but Bobby had a hard time ignoring the tree kangaroo.

"Mbaiso?" Ashley said. "Where'd you get that?"

Bobby explained Mr. Darnell's story about the legendary creature, the mbaiso.

Ashley snorted. "Mr. D always tells stories like that. Doesn't mean they're true."

"So what about *him*, then?" Bobby pointed at the animal above them.

"I don't know. Can we focus on finding the rest of the plane? It sounds like your idea might actually work."

Bobby had never talked to Ashley alone. He was fourteen, almost a freshman, and had hardly any friends. Ashley was seventeen, a senior, the kind of girl kids like Bobby dreamed about. She was pretty, and Bobby had always figured she was stuck up. But now things were different. Her sarcasm had mostly disappeared. In fact, she seemed impressed with his plan for finding the rest of their stuff. So they went back and convinced Mr. Darnell to give the plan a try. Soon Mr. Darnell, Bobby, Ashley, and Carlos headed into the forest in the most likely direction until they were out of sight of the plane but still within earshot of Mrs. Darnell. At that spot they posted Carlos, who would stay as a yelling link to Mrs. Darnell. They moved on and then posted Ashley as another link in their voice chain, within shouting distance of Carlos.

Ashley was willing to do this, but she seemed to be hiding some dread, perhaps of being left alone there.

"You gonna be okay?" Bobby asked her.

"Shut up, Bobby. Worry about yourself."

His face flushed. Not willing to give up, he looked up at the tree kangaroo, which had followed them. "Mbaiso, stay here with Ashley, okay?" He pointed at Ashley. The tree kangaroo raised its head and stared, its forelimbs fidgeting while the thicker hind legs gripped a branch. To Bobby's surprise, the creature stayed put as he pushed on after Mr. Darnell.

Over his shoulder Mr. Darnell said, "You call it Mbaiso?"

"I know your story was made up, but that's what he is."

"It's a good name." Mr. Darnell ducked under a vine and then held it up for Bobby. "But I'm hoping our Mbaiso acts the way he does from living with people. If we can find them, they can radio for help." He paused to call to Ashley, who answered right away. Still too close to post another link in the chain.

Bobby glanced to his side and something caught his eye—splintered branches stood out like markers above a small clearing. He approached the spot and Mr. Darnell followed. When they were almost upon it, they froze.

Mr. Darnell whispered, "What the hell?"

The clearing was the size and shape of a Twin Otter wing. But only a small part of the wing was visible at the center of the clearing, protruding from a mound of freshly dug soil.

"It's buried," Bobby said. "Someone buried the wing."

Mr. Darnell moved closer. "What is this?" He kneeled and touched the soil. It was red-brown, different from the black soil of the surrounding area. It was very fine, and the surface reminded Bobby of dark sifted flour.

"It looks like an anthill—like ants buried the wing," Bobby said.

"Yeah, but where are the ants?" Mr. Darnell dug into the stuff with his hand, and Bobby watched, half-expecting the hand to come up covered with angry, swarming ants.

"And why would ants—wait a minute!" Mr. Darnell pushed aside some of the dirt. Then he used his forearm to shove aside an entire armload. Beneath it there was only the forest floor. Mr. Darnell moved to the protruding metal, felt for its edge under the soil, and then lifted the entire piece with one hand. "The wing isn't buried. It's gone."

They stared at the chunk of wing in Mr. Darnell's hand. The soil on the ground seemed dry, but the raw edges of the wreckage shined with wetness. He dropped it and jumped to the edge of the clearing. "Don't touch anything, Bobby!" he wiped his hands on his pants. "The wing has decomposed—or something. Jesus, what is this stuff?" He rubbed his hands and arms like they had acid on them.

Bobby stared at what was left of a Twin Otter wing. It was now upside down, jagged edges turned upward. As he watched, a chunk the size of a penny sagged, dripped to the ground, and then disappeared into the soil.

Bobby and Mr. Darnell watched the last of the wing dissolve. The process reminded Bobby of a time-lapse video he'd seen once of a decomposing rat.

"Hey, you guys! Did you find something?" It was Ashley, calling from her station.

Mr. Darnell shouted, "Yeah, we did. Keep listening for us." He hesitated, looking at his hands like he feared they might melt. Then he turned to Bobby. "The rest of the plane has to be nearby." He pointed to a spot well clear of the disintegrated wing. "You stay there, and I'll search the area within earshot.

Soon after Mr. Darnell left, though, he cried out. As Bobby

rushed to his side, Mr. Darnell grabbed his arm, a silent warning to be careful. Before them lay the tail of the plane, in several pieces. And like the wing each piece was only a small chunk in the middle of a mound of perfect red-brown anthill dirt. To one side was a heap of travel bags, clothing, and other things. Someone had gathered up their stuff.

Mr. Darnell released Bobby's arm and moved away. Bobby followed. Before them was a seat from the plane. It lay on its side—what was left of it. The rest was just soil. Next to the seat, formed to its curves, was another pile of soil. Bobby stared, and then suddenly he inhaled sharply. The soil had the shape of a human body.

"What is that?" Bobby whispered.

"It must have been the Indonesian girl. And I can only assume *that* was her companion." He pointed. Near the dirt figure, as if someone had curled up to fall asleep and then turned to dust, was another mound of soil in the shape of a human body.

Quentin felt ready to burst. He had no answers, but the questions still came.

"I can maybe understand the bodies," Lindsey said. "It's a tropical forest. Things decompose quickly. But the plane wreckage? Where did that go?"

"Not that quickly," he said, after taking several gulps of rainwater. "We've been here less than two days, Linds. Bodies don't decompose that quickly. Besides, the other bodies are still there." Upon returning from their search, he'd inspected the bodies of the pilot, Roberto, and Russ. They'd shown early signs of decomposition, but they were still there.

"Then what could have happened? Are you sure they were

bodies? Maybe the guy found his wife alive and they left together to find a village."

"I don't know!" His voice had an edge that he hadn't intended. "I suppose that's possible." He rubbed his forehead and then glanced at the others. The only conscious person who had not asked the same confounding questions was Miranda. Lying in her makeshift bed, her body broken and weak, she watched the conversation silently.

They sorted through the recovered items. It was mostly clothing and their field supplies: notebooks, binoculars, and wildlife identification guides. Most valuable were Lindsey's first aid supplies and two bottles of Aqua mineral water. Her stash of snacks was mostly gone except for some cereal bars. After setting aside a portion for Addison in hopes that he would wake up, they divided these up and ate them.

There was no medical kit. Perhaps it had turned to dirt with the rest of the wreckage. Lindsey spread out her own first aid supplies. There were bandages, motion-sickness tablets, q-tips, antihistamines, alcohol wipes, two tubes of antibiotic cream, scissors, gauze, tape, a needle and thread, and insect repellant. It was absurdly inadequate, but they decided to use the supplies at once in case they might be able to prevent infection in at least some of their wounds.

As Quentin worked on Carlos's hand, the strange condition of the wreckage gnawed at his consciousness. Their lives were at risk from dehydration, hyperthermia, infection, disease, and blunt trauma. And now, even if they somehow could overcome these threats, an unknown force was at work in this forest, causing people and solid objects to disintegrate overnight.

And then there was the raw and simple fact that they had not seen or heard a single plane or helicopter that might be searching for them.

After depleting the limited supplies, Quentin collapsed and

folded himself up against the fuselage wall. He sat there and quietly stared at Addison's limp form.

BOBBY FIGURED that if Mbaiso had been trained to help collect water, he could probably help do other things. Like getting food. Bobby's hunger was starting to hurt. His small portion of the food they had found only made it worse. And after their success getting water and finding the plane's tail, he was starting to feel he could be useful. Besides, he liked impressing Ashley with his ideas, and she'd been hanging around him all afternoon.

They stood together now in the fading afternoon light, eyeing Mbaiso, who was a few meters away clinging to a tree. A termite trail ran up the tree's trunk, from the ground to somewhere far above. Bobby had seen trails like this before. It was actually a tunnel, a covered highway made on the tree by termites out of chewed wood and saliva. Within the tunnel the termites were protected as they traveled up and down the tree. But Mbaiso had smashed part of the tunnel and now the termites swarmed the area. The tree kangaroo was watching the angry termites and keeping an eye on Bobby and Ashley at the same time.

"You actually think he's going to help us find food?" Ashley sounded skeptical.

"If he can help get water, why not?"

"What are you going to do, just ask him?"

"We didn't have to ask him about the water," Bobby grabbed a vine and pulled it to his mouth like he was eating it. "Wow, I'm hungry. Wish I had something better to eat."

Ashley rolled her eyes and shook her head. She pulled part of the vine to her mouth. "This stuff sucks," she said. "I wish I had some cheeseburgers."

The tree kangaroo stared at them, distracted from the swarming termites.

Bobby moved closer to Mbaiso and pulled another vine to his mouth. "I sure wish I could find—"

He stopped and sputtered. "Ow! Crap it hurts!" His mouth was on fire, like hot needles were sticking his lips. He pushed his hand against his mouth and the pain exploded, hurting so much he fell to his knees.

"What, Bobby? What's wrong?"

"I don't know—Oooogod." It hurt to talk, so he pointed at the vine and then his mouth.

Ashley inspected the vine. "It's covered with little hairs. They must be poisonous."

"Ahhnng gignnnk knoooh."

"Let me see." She knelt in front of him. "Look at me."

Bobby looked into her eyes, only inches away. He could see his reflection against the green of her irises.

"Hold still. Move your hand!"

She was right in his face, the closest he'd ever been to a girl like Ashley. Even after a plane crash and two days of sweating, she smelled good.

"The hairs are stuck on your mouth, Bobby. Hold still."

She bit her lower lip as she concentrated. He felt a pinprick.

"Got it. See?" She held it up, too close to focus on. "There's a bunch of 'em, so sit tight."

A few minutes later she held up the last hair like a trophy. Bobby almost wished there were more. His lips were a little numb, but they felt better.

Ashley settled back onto the ground. "You may be the man-with-a-plan, but maybe you shouldn't put random things in your mouth, especially in the middle of nowhere."

Bobby sat across from her and crossed his legs. He picked at his socks. The morning before, the socks had been white. Now they were brown and red with mud, dried blood, and clinging seeds. Ashley's socks, he noticed, were much cleaner.

From the direction of the plane, they heard Carlos's voice, "No, that hurts!" Then came some calming words from Mr. Darnell that they couldn't make out.

"I hope the doctors can save his hand," Ashley said.

Bobby had seen Carlos's hand. Saving it seemed unlikely. "Me too."

"What do you think is going to happen to us?"

She seemed to want to talk, but Bobby had no answer.

"Do you think they're looking for us?"

"I don't know, but I think maybe we're being watched."

Ashley frowned. "By who?"

"Whoever trained Mbaiso. Whoever did that to those parts of the plane."

Ashley looked around them. There was nothing to see but trees, vines, and mud. "If someone is watching, why don't they help us?"

"I don't know, but I figure they aren't cannibals. They would've come for us by now."

Her brows wrinkled. He shouldn't have mentioned cannibals. He thought hard for something better to say. "Mr. Darnell's parents found a tribe here that had never seen white people before. They made friends with them by trading things, like knives and radios. The Papuans gave them necklaces and food and stuff. Maybe Mbaiso's a present for us."

"Yeah, well that didn't turn out so well for anyone. Mr. D's dad killed himself."

Bobby stared at her. Mr. Darnell hadn't told him that.

Ashley looked around them again and then sighed. "Damn you, Lori, you bitch! I didn't even want to come on this stupid trip."

"Who's Lori?"

"My mother."

"You call your mom Lori?"

Ashley ignored the question. She started picking at debris in her hair. She reached back and swept her long frizzy hair over her head so it hung in front of her face. "God, look at all this crap." She picked at it like she was angry.

"You didn't want to come?" he asked her.

She kept picking at her hair. "Lori talked me into it. Said it would do me good to see how poor some people are. So I would know how lucky I am."

Bobby watched her fingers work. He wanted to reach out and remove the pieces she missed but didn't dare. "You *are* lucky, I think. We both are. We didn't die."

Her fingers stopped.

He went on. "My mom and dad didn't have the money so I earned most of it myself. Took more than a year. I couldn't wait to get here, with the jungle and animals and all."

She looked at him through her tangled hair. "You really are a science boy, aren't you? Mr. Darnell, Junior."

"At least I know what I like, and at least I like something."

Ashley flipped her hair back and looked at him. "That's cool, science boy. I know what I like, too. Most people don't know about it, though."

"What's that?"

"Horses." She eyed him like she was daring him to laugh. "We have four. I like riding them and working with them."

"I didn't know you had horses."

"I don't tell people. So don't go talking or I'll beat you stupid."

"I won't."

"I'm going to have horses when I get my own place. That's one thing Lori and Brent *have* taught me—if you have money, you get what you want."

"I've never been on a horse, but I think it'd be fun."

"Tell you what, then. If you figure out how to get us out of here, I'll teach you to ride."

Bobby heard something approaching in the trees. He looked up and saw the brown-and-gold body of their marsupial friend. He hadn't even realized Mbaiso had left them.

"Shit! What is that?" Ashley jumped up and pointed over Bobby's shoulder.

Bobby turned and suddenly he was nose-to-nose with a strange face. He yelped and backed away. The new creature stood on its hind legs, with smaller forelimbs hanging in front of its chest, like a scrawnier version of the tree kangaroo. It was larger than Mbaiso, but its head was long and thin, and small for the size of its body. Its fur was solid tan except for a white stripe running down the back from head to rump. It raised and lowered its needle-like head. Mbaiso sat quietly above them, watching.

"It's food," Bobby whispered. "I told you he'd bring us food."

"THE INFECTIONS ARE WORSE, and we're out of clean water." Lindsey turned an already soiled cloth over and wiped futilely at the wounds on Miranda's leg. She then swatted at the swarm of flies trying to feed on the stale flesh. Miranda stared vacantly.

"It'll rain again," Quentin said. He was trying to build an insect barrier on the front of the fuselage using natty fabric removed from the seat cushions. He reasoned that if he could create a decent shelter for the others, perhaps he could leave them here and go search for help. If it came to that.

Quentin glanced at the fire. "Hey, Carlos, it's dying down again, pal. Put the rest of that pile on and gather some more." The pile of fuel consisted of anything dry enough to burn, mostly sago leaves. Getting the fire started had taken forever—even with the lighter he'd found on the pilot's body—and he didn't want it going out. A search plane might see the smoke from above. Carlos sat near the fire, his back against a tree. Quentin approached him. "Carlos, you hear me?"

"Yeah, I hear you."

The boy seemed oblivious to the insects on his face and arms. He was becoming more withdrawn. Quentin crouched down beside him. "Come on, pal. On your feet. You've got to keep moving." He pulled the boy up, alarmed at how light he was.

"Mr. Darnell, check this out!" Bobby and Ashley approached from the brush. Bobby carried something in his arms. It looked like a wallaby, but with a very narrow head. "Mbaiso brought it to us. It's supposed to be food."

"That's his opinion," Ashley said. "It just wandered right up to us."

Bobby set it on the ground, where it simply sat on its haunches.

"It looks like a dorcopsis," Quentin said, noting the white stripe on its back. "It's a kind of wallaby. It doesn't seem very afraid." Quentin nudged the wallaby with his foot, thinking it might be sick. Like a dog settling in for a nap, the animal plopped on its side at their feet. With its remarkably narrow head, it struck Quentin as a very stupid looking animal.

"I was starting to think we'd have to eat Mbaiso," Bobby said. "Now we don't have to!"

As the forest began to grow dark, Quentin told the others to move into the plane. There was no need for the fire, as the smoke wouldn't be visible, so Quentin dragged a wrecked piece of metal and glass over the pile of dry fuel in case it rained during the night.

The dorcopsis lay on the ground near the fire, chewing on something. It would be foolish to let it wander off. Bobby was right, butchering the wallaby would go over better than killing the tree kangaroo. At least they hadn't named the wallaby yet. He extracted a length of electrical wire from the wreckage and fastened one end of it around the animal's neck. The dorcopsis shook its head a few times but otherwise seemed oblivious. Quentin scooped it up and placed it next to a tree that was entangled with a thick woody vine at the base. He fastened the other end of the wire to the vine. The wallaby tugged at the wire and then sprawled on the ground.

As Quentin turned away, he detected movement in the forest, beyond where the three bodies lay. He stared, and then nearly stumbled backwards with surprise as his brain processed the dim image. It was an upright figure moving slowly through the trees.

"Hey," he shouted. "Is someone there?"

"Quentin?" Lindsey called from inside the fuselage. "We're all in here."

The truth of this hit him, and suddenly he felt exposed. The figure stopped moving and the forest was too murky to make it out. Quentin walked toward it, reminding himself that no large land predators lived in New Guinea. Suddenly the spot exploded. Quentin pulled back, startled. He could barely make out the movement, but he was almost sure it was a human. Then the rustling of the fleeing figure melded with the sounds of the night and was gone.

CHAPTER SEVEN

THEIR SECOND NIGHT in the rainforest was as fitful for Quentin as the first. The others seemed to sleep fairly well, although Miranda mumbled most of the night. Quentin woke repeatedly, imagining or dreaming that someone was standing at the open end of the fuselage watching him. Finally it began raining, and he drifted into a more restful sleep as the torrent drowned out the other sounds that had kept him alert.

When he awoke, the rain had stopped and the forest glowed with the filtered light of early morning. Every muscle in his body was sore, and he doubted his ability to even sit up. But he willed himself to a vertical position, stifling a groan. The others were quiet, including Miranda. He stared at her for a moment, making sure she was breathing, and then did the same with Addison. With every passing hour, the chances the two would survive grew slimmer.

Once out of the plane, Quentin struggled to rise to his full height. He raised his shirt. His abdomen was one massive black and gray bruise. He looked around, checking the forest for any signs that someone else had been there. He pulled away the wreckage he'd placed over the pile of fuel. Some of it was reasonably dry, so he fished the lighter from his pocket. Before long the fire was burning again, but he would need to find more fuel to create enough smoke to be seen from above.

Quentin didn't have to relieve himself, which meant he was dehydrated. He was also hungry to the point of feeling weak. The dorcopsis was still there, very wet but waiting patiently. They would have to kill and eat it.

But first he needed to bury the three bodies, as they were becoming a health risk to all of them. The light of morning had vanquished his anxiety over the mysterious figure from last night, but as he approached the bodies his courage and composure abruptly melted. In place of the bodies were three mounds of reddish-brown soil, nearly washed into the ground by the rain.

———

Bobby awoke to the smell of cooking meat. His mouth watered before he even opened his eyes, but he was disappointed that he had missed out on the killing and dressing of the wallaby. He sat up and rubbed his bruises. Mrs. Darnell was at the front of the plane, huddled over Addison. Her shoulders shook.

"Mrs. Darnell?" She didn't answer, but her shoulders stopped. "You okay?" Still no answer. This made Bobby uncomfortable, so he left the plane.

Carlos was up and sitting by the fire. Next to him was a pile of sticks and brown palm leaves. A piece of metal from the plane had been dragged over the fire and some chunks of meat hung on the edge of it, cooking in the heat.

Bobby eased his sore butt onto the ground next to Carlos. "Damn, everything hurts. How you feeling?"

There was no answer. Bobby looked at his friend's face, and the air around him seemed to turn cold. Carlos's face had changed. His skin was pale. His eyes seemed to be lighter, almost gray, with red around them. The eyes glanced at Bobby, and then stared into the fire.

Bobby fought the urge to say something about Carlos's appearance. "Where's Mr. Darnell?"

Carlos shrugged slightly.

Bobby nodded at the cooking meat. "That the wallaby?"

Carlos nodded.

"You try it yet?"

Carlos shook his head.

Again, Bobby felt uncomfortable. He gazed awkwardly at the trees.

Mr. Darnell approached them, carrying the raincoat and two plastic bottles filled with clear rainwater. And he was soaking wet.

"Morning, Bobby." Mr. Darnell put the bottles on the ground and then checked the wallaby meat by poking it with his pocketknife.

"Morning. You should talk to Mrs. Darnell. She seems kind of upset."

"Yeah. Maybe we need to give her a little time." He nodded toward Carlos, who was still staring into the fire. "Things aren't going so well, are they?"

Bobby wasn't sure if he was supposed to answer this. "I guess not."

"I tell you what. That tree kangaroo of yours is amazing. I just held out the jacket and he knew what to do. Never seen anything like it. We'll have to write it up for National Geographic or something, eh?" Mbaiso had followed him back and Mr. Darnell looked up at him. "What do you think of that, fella? You want to be famous?"

Bobby knew Mr. Darnell was trying to make him feel better, and it was working. So he decided to go with him to collect more water. With Mbaiso's help, they filled the zip-lock bags. As they worked, they praised the tree kangaroo endlessly.

"Mbaiso, you are a noble marsupial," Mr. Darnell said, after a drenching downpour.

"You're the king of all marsupials," Bobby said. "You're so smart the pythons won't eat you because they can't swallow your brain."

This went on. The stupid diversion almost made Bobby forget his hunger.

Later, they gathered around the fire to share the wallaby meat. Mr. Darnell tasted the meat first. He said it might make them sick if it wasn't cooked enough. It was charred black, so there was little chance of that. Although dry, the meat was tasty, and for some time the only sounds heard were ripping and chewing and the crackling fire. This made Bobby feel like they now belonged here. They were eating a jungle animal, just like the Papuans did. Even Carlos ate some of the meat as Mr. Darnell handed him bite-sized pieces.

Bobby said, "Should we save some food for Miranda and Addison?"

The Darnells looked at each other in a way that made Bobby wish he hadn't asked. But Mr. Darnell nodded and said, "Yes, we should do that."

"Why haven't we heard any search planes?" Ashley asked.

Mr. Darnell sighed. "I don't know. As of last night, they had to know at home that we weren't on the flight to Kansas City. Even if there was confusion at the Sentani airport and they lost track of our plane, they have to know now because your folks are making phone calls."

"Raising hell is what they're doing," Ashley said.

The talking died again, and Bobby thought about this. No matter how mixed up things were at the airport, their parents would do something about it. He thought of his mom and dad. They would have to talk to each other because of this.

He also thought of Carlos's parents. They didn't know yet that

Roberto was dead, or that Carlos might be dying. Their family had been close. Carlos's mom stayed home and didn't work; being a mother was what she did. Bobby pictured her sitting on Roberto's bed, looking at his stuff and crying. Bobby didn't know Russ's family, but he felt bad for them, too. And for the families of the pilot and the Indonesian couple.

Maybe Bobby was the luckiest of all of them. He wasn't badly hurt and he hadn't lost a family member. Ashley was lucky, too. Bobby looked across the fire at her, the image of her face fluttering in the heat waves. Other than a cut on her shoulder, she was okay.

Ashley bit some meat from what may have been a leg bone, and then noticed Bobby staring. Her eyes narrowed. She held up the bone. "I feel like we're eating someone's pet."

When most of the meat was gone, Mr. Darnell cleared his throat. He told them that the bodies were missing, turned into dirt. Everyone got quiet. Bobby felt a chill pass through him.

Mr. Darnell said, "I think we should have a ceremony for Roberto and Russ." He looked at Carlos. "So we can say goodbye."

Carlos just stared vacantly into the fire.

BOBBY STOOD before the three mounds. Three people, clothes and shoes and all—now just piles of dirt streaked with little branching valleys carved out by rainwater.

Mr. Darnell spoke. "Roberto Herrera, Russell Wade, and the pilot of our plane, whose name we don't even know, died before their time." As he talked he swatted at the flies swarming around them. "Roberto, you were one of the smartest students I've known, and you were always willing to share your gifts with others. You were a good brother to Carlos. We could all learn a great deal from your relationship."

Carlos was slouched over, his face pale. Tears filled his eyes finally, which was somehow comforting to Bobby.

Mr. Darnell went on. "Russell, you were a good friend to everyone. You always went out of your way to make the rest of us laugh, and we appreciated this more than you probably knew. It's a tragedy that both of you boys were taken from us and from the rest of the world. When we return home we'll make sure your families know the wonderful things you did in the final days of your lives. Goodbye Roberto. Goodbye Russ."

Mr. Darnell asked if anyone else wanted to speak. Bobby's mind was muddy. He could think of nothing to say.

Mrs. Darnell sighed and wiped her eyes. "Goodbye Roberto," she said. "Goodbye Russ." She rested her hand on Carlos's shoulder briefly and then trudged back to the plane.

Bobby and Ashley repeated Mrs. Darnell's simple goodbyes and then returned to the fire, leaving Carlos and Mr. Darnell staring silently at the piles of dirt.

CARLOS WAS SUFFERING in so many ways, and Quentin wasn't sure what to say to him. They stood quietly for a moment, hearing only the buzzing of flies. Finally Quentin said, "I'm sorry for what's happened, Carlos. Do you want to say goodbye to Roberto?"

"I don't feel good," Carlos said.

"I know you don't. Let's see if we can clean up your hand again, okay?" He steadied the boy with his arm as they walked back to the plane. Carlos's skin was cold. Quentin sat him on the edge of the fuselage and went to find some clean fabric. He sorted through the strips of soiled rags. Most of them had been used at least twice.

"There's none left." Lindsey's voice was flat. "Everything's filthy." She was crouched over Addison and didn't bother turning around.

He rested a hand on her shoulder. "Hang on, Linds. Help will be here soon."

She shook her head almost imperceptibly.

Quentin removed Carlos's wrap and stared at his crushed hand. The flesh was a hundred shades of crimson and violet, and the smell was dreadful. Red puffiness extended up the arm to the elbow. Quentin went through the motions, dabbing it lightly. Flies descended, so he quickly wrapped it back up.

Carlos suddenly wretched. He rolled from the edge of the fuselage and vomited. The dorcopsis meat, barely chewed and undigested, piled onto the ground.

"Oh Christ, Carlos." Quentin rolled him to his side to keep his face clear of the vomit. Carlos's eyes rolled back as his stomach heaved again.

Bobby and Ashley came over from the fire and watched in horror. When Carlos finished vomiting he was unconscious. They moved his limp body inside the plane.

Within minutes, Ashley complained of stomach cramps, and then Bobby joined in. Quentin felt his own stomach clench. They endured several hours of discomfort but nothing more serious.

By midday their cramps had subsided, but Carlos was still unconscious and could now be counted among those who might never wake up. As for Addison, other than drops they'd placed in his mouth, he had taken in no water since the crash—some fifty-five hours ago.

They had kept the fire burning all morning, using up the dried wood and sago fronds in the surrounding area. Each collecting trip took them further away, well out of sight of the fuselage. Soon it would take longer to collect fuel than for the fuel to burn.

They were running out of time.

With sudden crystalline clarity, Quentin knew he had to find a village. There were Papuans near here, he was sure of that. The carved figurine, the tree kangaroo's domesticated behaviors, and the fleeing figure he'd seen last night; there had to be a village. And a village would likely have some way to contact the rest of the world.

"This is stupid, Quentin, and you know it!" Lindsey's eyes were wide with fear. "Our chances are best if we stay with the plane. Survival 101!"

"You and the others *are* staying here with the plane. If a search party finds you before I find the village, they'll get the kids to a hospital. If I find the village first, though, it may save them. Hell, it may save all of us."

"Goddammit, think about this! You're leaving the crash site."

"The rule doesn't apply here! The site is invisible. We can't even keep a fire going." He pointed to the unconscious kids. "How much time do you think they have?"

"How does it help them for you to get lost in the forest again? You already tried this! How far did you get, maybe a tenth of a mile? You'll wander aimlessly until you either stumble on a village or starve to death. Is that your plan?"

She was probably right. But Quentin was going. "I don't want to leave you," he said. "But I don't see how they can find us here." He placed a walkie-talkie into her hand and folded her fingers around it. "There's not much power left, so keep it turned off." He clipped the other one to his waist. "Every half hour we'll turn them on and make contact, okay? I may find a village before I'm even out of range."

That was unlikely. The walkie-talkies supposedly had a range of five miles, but they never lived up to this claim, particularly in a forest. They had charged them the night before their flight, but had used some of the charge while searching for the three boys in Wamena.

Quentin looked at the sun through the trees. "I have to go before it gets any later."

"Maybe one of us should go with you," Ashley suggested. She and Bobby had been tending the fire, trying to ignore the argument.

"Thanks Ash, but the most important thing you can do now is keep the fire burning for as long as you can."

Bobby handed him a canvas bag. "Here's some stuff you might need."

Inside were the two bottles filled with rainwater and Carlos's souvenir machete in its garish sheath. Quentin removed one of the bottles and handed it back. "Thanks. You guys keep that fire burning. If it rains, cover the wood so you can get it started again."

Lindsey had retreated to the fuselage, and Quentin considered going in to face her. He might never see her again, but further fighting would accomplish nothing.

"Lindsey, I'll see you soon, okay?"

After some seconds of awkward foot-shuffling silence, he turned to go.

***

As Lindsey had predicted, Quentin soon had no idea which direction he was going. For a short time Bobby's voice returned his shouts. But that soon faded away, and the only sounds he heard were chattering birds and buzzing insects. Above him there was an occasional rustling from Mbaiso, who had followed him and now moved from tree to tree to keep up.

Quentin found it impossible to maintain a constant bearing without a compass. He was frequently forced to modify his path, moving to the right or left around a dense cluster of saplings, a tangle of vines, or a fallen tree. But he had reasoned that even with an erratic course, he would eventually come across a trail leading to a village. This made sense to him when he had started, but now he was lost and alone and began to question his logic.

After pushing his way through yet another curtain of woody vines, he glanced at his watch. Two minutes until their second radio communication. He pulled the bag from his back, retrieved the water bottle, and took his first drink, downing a third of the bottle. He shook the bottle and gazed at the remaining water. Specks of matter swirled in the vortex. He unclipped the walkie-talkie and pressed the power button. A small battery icon flashed in the corner of the LCD screen—the charge wouldn't last much longer.

"Lindsey? Can you hear me?" There was only static. Quentin sighed and looked around, but the dense forest was the same in every direction. Behind him there were no visible signs of his passage, no trail he could retrace.

The scraping of claws against bark brought his attention to the tree kangaroo, clambering down a tree trunk. "Hey, Mbaiso. You mind if I call you Mbaiso?" The creature appeared not to mind. "Where's the village? Where is everyone?"

"Quentin, are ... there?" The crackling voice startled him.

"Yes, Lindsey, I can hear you."

"Quentin? ... you? ... I can ... hear you. Quen ..."

The flashing battery on the LCD screen had one bar left. "Lindsey, you guys okay?"

"Quentin? I can't ... I hope ... hear me ... Bobby ... people in the forest ... I wasn't sure ... Ashley saw them ... Quentin, they were ... I need ... know you're okay ... the kids ... afraid now ... hear me? ... where ..."

Quentin's throat constricted. "Lindsey, what's going on?"

The broken voice continued, "... what they want, but ... inside the plane ... the kids are ... come closer ... you need to ... back ..."

Quentin jammed his thumb into the talk button to respond.

The unit emitted a warning tone and then shut off. It was dead. He turned it back on and pressed the talk button.

"Lindsey—"

The unit beeped and shut off. It wouldn't come back on.

Quentin stood frozen. The forest seemed to tighten on him, shrinking the already tiny clearing in which he stood. He was a speck in a vast ocean. The clipped echoes of Lindsey's ominous message played in his head. She had been right—he shouldn't have left. He threw his head back and screamed her name, drawing the cry out until the last bit of air left his lungs. When he opened his eyes Mbaiso was clinging to a tree, watching him intently from above.

"What kind of place is this?" he shouted, half to himself and half to anyone who might be listening. "If you're here, why don't you help? Jesus Christ, get out of my face!" He thrashed at the flies, striking his own face in an attempt to kill some of them. Then he plunged back into the tangle in the direction he'd come from.

But everything looked unfamiliar and he was hopelessly lost. Finally he stopped and called out again. Silence. His watch told him twenty minutes had passed since he'd heard Lindsey's broken message. He pulled out the walkie-talkie and pressed power. The batteries had recovered enough to power the unit on. He listened to static and then pressed the talk button. The unit beeped once and shut off. It was useless. Quentin shut his eyes to block the flood of loneliness and fatigue. In a few hours darkness would fall again. He would have to endure the long night not knowing what was happening to Lindsey and the kids.

A sound rose into Quentin's consciousness. At first he thought he imagined it, but there it was again—the sound of moving water. Not a waterfall, but more subtle, like the churning of a slow-moving river. He pushed through the foliage in the direction of the sound and almost immediately came upon a tangled bank of rolling, mud-brown water. Had he not heard it, he might have passed within meters of the river without seeing it.

But it was not the river itself that gave Quentin hope. Running parallel to it was a path. He'd seen numerous animal trails running under low-hanging brush, indicating small mammals or ground birds used them. But this trail was different. In both directions, the foliage over the trail was clear to a height that would accommodate humans.

THE PATH WOULD likely lead to a village. Quentin desperately wanted to return to the others, but there was little chance of finding them by wandering aimlessly. The path gave him a new option. Quentin walked a short distance in one direction, and then the other, but saw no signs that either way was the better choice. After watching the brown water for a moment he decided to head downstream. But first it would be wise to mark where he had found the path. He pulled the souvenir machete from the bag, slid the blade from its sheath, and hefted it in his hand. It looked cheap, but it had some mass to it.

He located a sapling that could be cut up to arrange into an unmistakable marker. He reared back and swung the machete at the base of the tree. The blade sliced cleanly through and continued its arc until it buried itself deep in his left ankle.

Quentin blinked at the machete. It had cut a slice in his trousers and a red stain spread rapidly from the blade. He jiggled the machete's handle, wincing at the pain, but his tibia bone gripped it tight. He yanked hard on the handle, pulling the blade free. Blood spurted from the slice in his trousers and the red stain began spreading even faster.

He crumpled onto the ground and sat staring dumbly at the wound.

CHAPTER EIGHT

I⊤ DIDN'T MAKE sense to Bobby that they should sit inside the plane. It was hot, and it smelled like death. But Mrs. Darnell was afraid of the Papuan men.

If they were so dangerous, they would have attacked when he and Ashley had met them in the forest. At the time they had been gathering fuel for the fire. Bobby was the first to see the dark face watching them and he nudged Ashley. When the stranger realized he'd been spotted, he rose from the bushes to his full height. Another man popped up at his side. Bobby and Ashley just stood there, afraid to speak. The men held sharpened spears, gripping them as if they thought they might have to use them. After a silent stare-down, the men slowly backed away until the forest swallowed them up.

They had returned empty-handed, and the fire soon died. Mrs. Darnell didn't want them leaving the plane anymore, and now Bobby was forced to endure the heat and smell. They hadn't heard from Mr. Darnell in hours, and the plane's cabin was filled with stale air and dread. Was this what it was like to wait for death? Was this what had happened to people he'd read about in books, explorers who were never seen again? Did they sit around like this, watching their friends die, waiting for their turn?

Mrs. Darnell was speaking softly to Addison, stroking his face with a wad of cloth, and Ashley was dripping water in his mouth from a plastic bag. It was all they could do for him.

Bobby thought about his own parents. What would they do? His mom would freak out. But his dad—if he were sitting in this shit-hole with them, he'd try to keep everyone together. Like he did during the divorce. And he would want Bobby to do the same thing.

"Mrs. Darnell," Bobby said, "you know that thing you and Mr. Darnell do sometimes, where you talk about stuff and make things up about it?"

At first she didn't answer, but then she said, "What do you mean?"

"You know, like a game. You make up stories about things, like animals. What they're thinking and stuff. You guys do that."

Mrs. Darnell shook her head slightly but said, "I guess so."

"I remember when I was little, my mom and dad talked like that sometimes."

"Your parents seem like nice people."

"Yeah, but when they're together, you don't even want to be there."

Mrs. Darnell said, "Sometimes people change, even when you don't want them to."

"Maybe Mr. Darnell found the Papuans' village."

"Maybe," Mrs. Darnell said quietly.

"I think they're a lost tribe, like the tribe Mr. Darnell's parents found," Bobby said. "That's why they aren't helping us."

Ashley snorted. "So now we're all lost."

Bobby thought for a moment. "And Mr. Darnell found their village. They think he's from the future or something. He's trying to tell them we need to get to a town. But they don't even know about towns."

Ashley opened her mouth like she might chime in, but then she just leaned back silently.

"They're probably getting ready to have a feast for us," Bobby said. "All kinds of food we've never tried before."

This wasn't working. Mrs. Darnell held her eyes shut as if his attempts at optimism were giving her a headache.

Suddenly a dark figure filled the cabin's opening. For a second, Bobby thought Mr. Darnell had come back. But it wasn't him. They all stared at the stranger.

The man crouched, holding a spear in front of him. He was a Papuan tribesman, maybe one Bobby and Ashley had seen earlier, but he was much closer now. Green parrot feathers stuck out from his hair in all directions. Bobby couldn't tell how old the man was. The skin on his face was smooth, like a boy's, but the confidence in his eyes was that of a grown man.

Mrs. Darnell's voice was a whisper. "Don't do anything to threaten him."

The man inched into the opening. Bobby turned to Mrs. Darnell for help, but his eyes were drawn to a hole in the unfinished insect barrier above her head, where a second Papuan peered in at them. This man's eyes, set high on a smooth black face, had the same cool, assured gaze, and Bobby felt a chill when they looked directly at him. And then the face pulled away and was gone. Bobby spun around and the second Papuan appeared next to the first. The green-feathered man looked from Bobby to Ashley, and then to Mrs. Darnell and the still bodies at her side. He bobbed his head from side to side as if to see into the shadows more clearly.

"*Gu mbakha-to-fosu le-bo? Mba-mbam?*" The Papuan's voice was higher than Bobby expected, almost musical. The man stepped into the cabin and then moved toward Mrs. Darnell. "*Walukh, khomilo?*"[3]

Bobby saw Ashley tense up, and he feared what she might do. The man passed by within arm's reach. Bobby stared at the dark-stained point of his spear. Above the darkened tip, rows of symbols and shapes were carved into the wood. There were rectangles, triangles, spirals, loops, and many more, and for some reason the carvings seemed oddly familiar to Bobby.

"*Walukh, khomilo?* Dead?" The man pointed to Addison, Carlos and Miranda.

Mrs. Darnell's eyes widened. "You speak English? You understand me? *Toktok Inglis?* Uh... *saya dari Amerika. Dari mana?*"

The Papuan kneeled next to Carlos and pointed at him. "*Khomilo?* Dead?"

"They're not dead, but they're hurt. Can you help us? Do you speak English?"

"English. Samuel *neni fo* English." The Papuan touched Carlos's arm and ran his finger down the red and gray flesh. He started removing the wrap from Carlos's hand.

Mrs. Darnell pushed his hand away. "We need to get to a hospital. Can you help?"

The man turned to Mrs. Darnell. Bobby couldn't see, but he must have given her a convincing look, because she let him remove the wrap. He looked at the rotting hand and then reached into a pouch that hung from his neck. He pulled out his hand, his fingertips covered in gray globs. He spoke to Mrs. Darnell in his musical chatter.

"Thank you," she said. "But that's not what we need."

The Papuan reached for Carlos's face, forced open one eye and smeared the stuff onto his eyeball. Bobby's stomach went tight.

Mrs. Darnell pushed the man's hands again. "Stop that!"

The second Papuan rushed past Bobby and held his spear in Mrs. Darnell's face. This man's spear was also covered with vaguely familiar symbols and shapes.

"Please," Mrs. Darnell said. "There's nothing wrong with his eyes. He needs a hospital."

The man spoke to her again. They were soft words, and they made Bobby believe the men did not want to hurt them.

Ashley said. "Just let them do what they want so they'll leave!"

Mrs. Darnell backed away and watched.

The man with the pouch crawled from Carlos to Miranda. He examined her broken leg and then scooped out more gray sludge and forced open her eyelid. She moaned as he smeared the stuff against her bare eyeball. Mrs. Darnell whimpered and turned away, helpless.

Next he moved to Addison. The man touched his face and chest, and felt his neck.

"Yu le khomilo-mbo," he said. *"Khomilo.* Dead."[4]

Mrs. Darnell wheeled around. "He's not dead!" She moved toward them, and the second man brought his spear up again, but she ignored it. "His heart is beating, see?"

The man looked at her silently, his face close to hers. Bobby had always thought of Mrs. Darnell as pretty, but next to the Papuan her face seemed old, and very white.

She was sobbing now. "He's breathing."

The Papuans looked at each other. They talked in their high voices back and forth like they were trying to decide something. The man then reached to Addison's face and rubbed the stuff into his eye. The second man frowned and shook his head at this.

Both men left the plane, and again stale air and dread filled the empty space.

QUENTIN LIMPED ALONG THE PATH, cursing his recklessness. He paused and gazed down at his leg. Blood still flowed from the gash in spite of his efforts to stem it. He'd knotted one of his socks around his ankle, but the sock and lower leg of his trousers were now saturated with blood. The blood had seeped into his hiking shoe, and his foot slid inside it with each step. It was getting harder to walk. He had to find a village before losing consciousness. So he trudged on.

The path still followed the river. Occasionally it would cut away and Quentin would lose sight of the water, but soon it would reappear. Finally he could stand the pain no longer, and he stopped. He turned and looked back the way he had come. The forest seemed darker than before. For a moment he forgot which way he had been walking, and he rubbed his face in frustration. Only a small amount of water remained in the bottle, and he drank it down, reveling in the sensation of moisture in his throat. Grunting, he hobbled to the river's edge and knelt by the water. He submerged the empty bottle. The water looked like chocolate milk as it gurgled into the bottle. No doubt it contained microbes that would have a heyday with his system. But what difference did it make now? This thought struck him as funny, and he laughed out loud and took a long drink from the bottle. The water tasted like mud and algae.

He pulled the bag from his shoulder and peeled off his shirt. He pushed aside the tangled vegetation and waded into the river. A red stain curled away from his blood-soaked trousers and moved slowly downstream. He splashed brown water over his head and body.

Feeling somewhat renewed, he pushed on. The path continued, but seemed to narrow. Sometimes the way was blocked by a riot of new growth, but when he fought through it the path continued on the other side. With every step he heard himself grunt, but it seemed like the voice of a stranger.

The forest grew dark, and the stain on his trousers was now black. Quentin could hardly see the path, but he pushed on anyway, feeling only pain and hearing only the continuous grunting. He no longer knew or cared whether he was making the noise himself. He cared only about taking another step, and then another.

Finally he could go no further and he stopped. For a moment he stood watching the shadows swing back and forth as his body swayed. With a final grunt he buckled and sat down on the trail. He just needed to rest. Then maybe he could start again.

———

THERE WERE voices talking in the blackness—small, funny voices Quentin didn't understand. He willed himself to open his eyes and look. A few stars peeped through the canopy, and he realized he was on his back. Two figures, silhouettes of blackness, stood above him. He tried to speak but the words jumbled themselves. The figures stopped talking.

He focused his efforts and tried again. "Help...we need help."

One of the figures spoke, *"Gu mbakha-to-fosu le-bo?"*[5]

Quentin tried to concentrate. "I don't understand."

"Nu pesau im-le. Pesua." The speaker crouched by him. "Friend, *gu* spirit *lai-ati-bo-dakhu. Lele-mbol-e-kho-lo? Laleo?* Spirit?"[6]

Suddenly Quentin was more alert. "Do you speak English?" He struggled to sit up. The figures moved and there was a sharp pain. The men were holding spears against his chest.

"What are you doing?" He collapsed. "Jesus!"

"Mbakha lekhen, Jesus? *Laleo khop."*[7]

Quentin's mind groped. Were the men even real? He raised his head again. They were still there. One was taller. Strands of light-colored objects encircled his neck, forming a wide loop over his shoulders and chest. Each of the men wore a headdress of some kind.

"I need to go to your village and radio for help. Do you have a radio?"

"Gu laleo-lu de-te-dakhu, Jesus," the taller man said.[8]

Quentin tried to get up again but the weapons snapped to his chest. He shoved the spears aside, gripping one of them in his hand. "Look, I need—"

The spear was yanked from his hand and he felt a fire in his chest, and then another. He fell back, clutching the pain. Looking down he saw two dark spots on his shirt.

"You stabbed me! Shit!"

A calm grayness descended upon Quentin. "Lindsey, I didn't…"

As he faded away, the voices followed him into the grayness. *"Gu mbakha-lekhe wa-mol-mo, dodepa-le* Lindsey? Lindsey *gekhene mbakha mo-mba-te?"*[9]

IN THE DARKNESS, the tree kangaroo watched the men from above. Their present behaviors intertwined with a long history of observed behaviors, allowing a reasonably accurate prediction of the scene's outcome. Rarely was the mbolop allowed to intervene in the unfolding of such events, but it now seemed likely that the potential role of the new outsiders would have no chance to play itself out.

With a drawn-out grunt, the tree kangaroo unfolded itself from its restful perch in the fork of a *yawol* tree and clambered to the ground. This drew the attention of the tribesmen, and they turned to stare at the approaching creature. In the sultry darkness of the trail beside the river Méanmaél, paws and claws moved with precision. The men watched the movements, nodding their heads in understanding. Soft words were exchanged between them, a dispute ensued, and chewed pandanus nuts were spat with disdain onto the ground. Finally, one of the tribesmen turned and departed, making his way on the trail in the direction the one called Quentin had been walking. The other stayed behind, pacing in circles around the crumpled figure, his spear held ready. The mbolop returned to its comfortable perch to wait.

———

THE CABIN WAS DARK NOW, and somehow this seemed better to Bobby. He felt almost safe lying next to Ashley. Mrs. Darnell was still awake. She was trying to be quiet but he heard her crying. And the Papuan men were still there, moving around outside the plane. Occasionally a dark shape appeared at the opening, as if checking on them.

He whispered, "Ashley, you awake?"

"How the hell can I sleep?" she hissed. "It's like we're prisoners and I have to pee."

"I don't think they want to hurt us."

"Maybe not, but if they were trying to help us, they'd call for a rescue helicopter. In case you haven't noticed, we're dying off here."

Bobby didn't have anything to say to this. Eventually he closed his eyes and slept.

———

QUENTIN WAS AWAKENED BY VOICES. Someone was poking his leg and chest. He fought his way to consciousness. The forest was still dark, and several figures crouched beside him.

"What...what are you doing?" he managed to say.

"Ah, very well, then," a man at his side said. "Perhaps our verdict was premature."

Quentin blinked and lifted his head. He tried to sit up but was too weak.

"You would be obliged to rest, young man," said the stranger.

Quentin tried to think clearly. "You speak English. Thank God."

The man was doing something to Quentin's leg, tugging at the cloth of his trousers. "Having yet to know me, you might do well to withhold your thanks to God."

"Our plane crashed and some of my students are hurt."

"I was told there were young people in your company. Students, you say? Curious."

"Do you have a radio?"

The man gazed at his own hand as he rubbed something between his fingers. "No doubt you will find this uncomfortable. Steady yourself." In one swift motion he gripped Quentin's face, pried open one of his eyes, and roughly smeared something onto his eyeball.

Quentin recoiled. "Ow—shit! What is that?"

"Shit." The stranger pronounced the word as if he had never heard it before. "It has always been my opinion that a man in distress is an honest man. Your words expose your state of civilization, sir."

Quentin rubbed his eye and after a moment the initial pain subsided. "What the hell did you put in my eye?"

"You should not worry over that. You will thank me for it soon enough. It is time for questions of my own. From whence have you and your companions come?"

"We're from the U.S."

"The U.S. Where might that be?"

Quentin looked at the man, trying for the first time to make out his features. Although it was dark, Quentin saw that he was oddly dressed. What appeared to be a light-colored vest covered his upper body. Over his crotch was a loosely cut pair of shorts. His legs and feet were bare. His accent was not Australian, which was how Quentin described the inflections of all English-speaking people in this part of the world. Instead, it sounded British—a Masterpiece

Theatre sort of British. He sounded and looked like a fairly young man. His dark hair was cut short, and he appeared clean-shaven.

"The U.S. The United States," Quentin said.

"The United States, of course. Tell me, if you will—what do you call this place?" The man held his hands out, indicating their surroundings.

"New Guinea? Papua? I don't really understand what—"

"Papua? Curious. What brings you here? And with students, no less."

The man's questions seemed irrelevant. "I'm sorry, but we need help. My students, my wife, we need to get to a hospital."

"Do you mean to say that you have brought your wife to this place?"

"Yes. My wife and I survived the plane crash, but some of our students died. The others are hurt. Our son may be dead by now. They need a hospital."

The man stared at Quentin for a moment. "Sir, you should not worry over them any longer. Their fate, and yours as well, is no longer in the hands of God. I fear your wife and students have perished."

Quentin stared, but it was too dark to see the man's eyes. "What do you mean?"

"I mean that you can do nothing to save them." He motioned to two Papuans standing at Quentin's feet. "These indigenes, within whose territory you find yourself, fancy their privacy in a way you could scarcely imagine. You will not be leaving this place."

Quentin suddenly felt weak. He slumped onto his back on the ground. This couldn't be real. He wasn't lying injured in the mud in a black forest. He was in his bed, cool dry sheets over him, Lindsey's smooth skin against his side, the smell of her hair in his face. They would wake up together. He would share the dream he'd had with her, and she would listen.

Quentin heard himself moaning. It was the same voice—his

voice—that had followed him on the path. He wanted it to stop, so he pulled Lindsey's body closer and fell asleep.

QUENTIN WAS FLOATING IN SPACE. Stars were everywhere, all around him, above and below. The stars appeared to be passing by in the vast distance, as if he were moving at unimaginable speed. A cold loneliness washed over him, a sensation that he'd been alone for a long, long time. Quentin noticed one particular star growing larger as it approached. It continued to grow, until he had to look away from its blinding light.

"WAKE YOURSELF, sir. It seems you are to persevere another day."

Someone gripped Quentin's shoulders and lifted him to a sitting position. The forest was no longer dark. A Papuan man stood above him, armed with a spear. Kneeling beside him was a white man, wearing a peculiar gray vest and little else. Quentin focused on the man's face—thirtyish, smudged but clean-shaven. The eyes were very light brown, almost gold. Quentin's mind fought to connect the face before him with the shadowed specter of the night before. Then the words the man had spoken came back with ruthless lucidity. He pushed himself up, gripped the man's vest, and flipped him onto his back. Quentin was on top of him in an instant.

"What have you done with my wife? And my kids?"

There was a flash of movement as the Papuan jabbed his spear to Quentin's chest. *"Yu Khentelo! Yu beben!"* The spear punctured Quentin's skin, but he ignored it.[10]

The man beneath him spoke calmly to the Papuan, *"Yu khentelo tekhen. Khedi belen. Khedi belen."* He looked at Quentin. "I assure you that I mean no harm to you or your fellow travelers. I have, in fact, returned to you to seek a remedy."[11]

"You told me they had perished. What did you mean by that?"

"My conclusion was premature. Our situation has changed. With my assistance, you may yet save them. Please yield, sir."

Quentin looked up at the Papuan and was struck by the man's appearance. His face was that of a mature Papuan man, but his skin was smooth and flawless. It lacked the markings of disease and wrinkles that were characteristic of tribal Papuans. And this man's dress suggested a most traditional existence. Other than a short penis sheath, he wore nothing but three cords around his neck, each strung with small white objects. The Papuan smiled, flashing a row of perfect white teeth, and then suddenly wrenched the spear to the side, tearing Quentin's flesh.

Startled, Quentin released his grip on the Englishman's vest. He retreated to one side and sat on the ground, clutching his new wound.

The white man rose to his feet and smoothed his vest. The material shimmered strangely, and it occurred to Quentin that the vest had felt extraordinarily light in his grip.

"Do be wary of Noadi," said the Englishman. "Whatever schooling you may have had, you can scarcely comprehend the chasm between his morality and your own. Presently it is sufficient to note that he is but a savage, with savage ways. Tell me, sir, have you the want of seeing your wife again?"

"What'd you do to them? Where are they?"

"Their locality is unknown to me. I have hopes that you will lead me there."

Quentin shook his head. "Last night you said you knew about them, that they were... dead." The word dropped from his mouth like a stone.

"But I had not the opportunity to confirm the claim." He gestured to the Papuan. "It is the brothers of Noadi who have frequented the area where your flying vessel ran aground. As is their custom with strangers, they had determined to kill you all. But I only recently learned that they have, curiously, stayed their hand. Your wife and students may yet live. I have come to you so that we might save them."

Quentin glared at him. "I'm listening."

"If you would pause for a moment and consider your condition. Mere hours ago you were scarcely living, with copious bleeding and fetid injuries. You have made an astounding recovery, would you not agree?"

Quentin inspected his shin. By now the deep slice from the machete should have been festering, infected with microbes from the river and from his own filth. Amazingly, the gash was partially healed. Instead of red and swollen, it was pale and smooth.

"How long was I asleep?"

"Your rest was brief, I assure you. What of the wounds on your chest? My friends were rather vigorous in restraining you."

Quentin pulled up his shirt. There was a ragged gash from Noadi's savage gesture only moments before. On either side of it were two nearly-healed wounds where the spear points had pierced him during the night.

Quentin stammered, "I don't understand."

"Don't you?"

Quentin tried to grasp the situation. He was sure the stranger was not lying, that it was indeed only hours ago that he lay wounded and delirious, perhaps near death. Suddenly he remembered the man rubbing a gritty substance into his eye. "What did you treat me with?"

The man raised his brows. "Pray tell me, are you familiar with ointments or poultices with such powers to heal?"

Quentin's answer was immediate. "There is no such substance."

The man stared for a moment, his face blank. "Curious."

"What I mean is, there isn't—"

The man interrupted. "Perhaps later there will be time for this discussion. Let us, for the moment, agree that your recovery surpasses your expectations, and return to the fate of your companions. Clearly your strength is returned. Are you prepared to travel?"

Quentin felt stronger than he had in days. Even his hunger and thirst were diminished.

"Yeah, let's move."

***

Bobby forced himself awake. Something wasn't right. Wetness struck his face and he wiped it away. Through sleep-crusted eyelids he saw the green light of morning above him. Something struck his face again, and then his arm. He squinted. The stuff on his arm was reddish-brown and moist. He propped up on an elbow and hit his head. His confusion turned to fear. The roof of the plane's cabin was less than a meter above the ground.

Bobby looked at the floor beneath him. It was covered with fine soil, concealing his ankles and part of his legs. Ashley and the others were half buried where they lay. Bobby shook Ashley's shoulder. She moaned.

"Ashley, wake up! Mrs. Darnell, wake up!"

Mrs. Darnell responded immediately. "What's wrong?" She had been sleeping on her side, and her body was partly buried. She sat up, striking her head on the ceiling, which seemed even lower now than it did only moments before. The soil fell away from her body.

"Mrs. Darnell, your clothes!" Bobby tried to look away, but couldn't. Most of her shirt was gone. Where the fabric had touched the soil, only bare skin showed.

Bobby realized his own shirt had fallen into his lap. He lifted what was left. The entire back was gone. He grabbed his jeans and pulled. Only the front remained, and they lifted easily from his legs, leaving him naked. The heel portions of his shoes were gone, and the remains covered only his toes. The soil was eating everything around them.

"We need to get out!" Mrs. Darnell cried.

QUENTIN LED the Englishman along the riverside path, retracing his steps. The Papuan, Noadi, was no longer with them. Apparently he had serious misgivings about the crash site and survivors.

As they walked, Quentin was astounded at his own dexterity. His machete wound was all but healed. The pain in his hip from the plane crash was gone. His lacerations, which had been infected, were now aseptic and dry. Even the bites that had pockmarked every inch of his exposed skin were nearly gone. And now the insects had apparently decided he was no longer fair game. They buzzed near him briefly and then left, as if he were distasteful.

"What did you give me last night?" he asked. The path was wide here, and they walked side by side. "Are you a doctor—a shaman or something?"

"I am no doctor—medical, magical, or otherwise—although I have learned much about healing as a guest amongst the indigenes."

"What tribe are these people? Are they Yali, or maybe Korowai? They don't look like Papuans I've seen before."

The man hesitated, as if his choice of words were very important. "What they call themselves is of little importance, as I assure you they are unknown to you."

"And you," Quentin said. "Why are you here?"

"I am a naturalist, devoted to studying the fauna and the flora of this land."

"Well, whatever you gave me healed wounds that should take months to heal."

The Englishman was silent.

Quentin tried again. "This is an immense medical discovery."

Silence.

"Who are you?" Quentin asked. "How long have you been here with these people?"

"My name is Samuel Inwood."

Samuel wore no modern clothing, only a pair of shorts and a strange vest. The shorts were made of animal leather, supported by a strap tied around the waist. The vest seemed to be hand woven and stitched, perhaps from hair or silk. The only item that was plainly not from the forest was a peculiar amulet, made of twisted gold wire and hanging from a cord around his neck.

Quentin asked again, "How long have you been here, Samuel?"

"Perhaps we shall have the opportunity to become better acquainted. As for now, I have learned a good deal from your words regarding the state of society beyond this forest. Your surprise at the healing nature of my treatments, for example, tells me that my discoveries here have not been duplicated elsewhere." He paused. "But I have yet to learn your name, sir."

"Quentin Darnell. I'm a teacher. I teach Eighth graders—about fourteen years old."

"And you have brought with you here your young students, from the United States. Remarkable. Tell me Quentin, what is your age?"

"I'm thirty-six. Why?"

"Thirty-six years. Yes, you have the appearance of a man of that age."

Quentin was wondering how to respond when they came upon the marker he had arranged on the path after slicing his ankle. "This is where I found the trail," he said. "I may have walked in circles for hours before that."

"You must recall your route, Quentin. I am aware of but the general direction."

Quentin felt panic surfacing. He should have made an effort to mark his path from the crash site. He had carried a machete in his bag; he could have cut markers. The others might die simply because he hadn't thought to do that. He took a deep breath, trying to flush his doubts. With Samuel's help, they would find the others and save them. And then perhaps Samuel's medications could be used on them. Quentin glanced at the listless brown water of the river. He would need to hydrate before leaving the trail.

"Samuel," Quentin said, "I need some water. Is this safe to drink?"

Samuel was busy scattering the sticks that made up Quentin's marker. "You may drink without ill effects," he said.

Quentin no longer had his water bottle, so he waded in to drink with his hands. "Good, I drank from it yesterday."

Samuel tossed the last stick away. "Yesterday was an altogether different matter."

Quentin had scooped a handful of brown water to his face, but he paused. "It's safe today, but it wasn't yesterday?"

"It is not the river which has changed, Quentin. It is you."

Once off the path, Quentin could discern no sign of his passage. "I can't do this. I came too far."

Samuel pointed ahead. "It is somewhere to the east. But without your assistance, we may not find it. The lives of your party are at risk. I am not deceiving you on this point. The indigenes are intent upon killing all intruders. I learned only this morning they have not yet committed murder. For what reason and for how long, I do not know."

"If they told you that, why aren't they guiding us to the plane?"

"They have not invited me to go there. I am but a guest among them."

Quentin's fists clenched. "Then why didn't you ask them not to hurt my family?"

Samuel gazed at him with patient eyes. "You must understand that their savage ways have been gradually embedded, with no intelligent eyes to observe them, and no civilized mind to reason with them. The habits of countless ages cannot be so easily set aside. So I have come to you in hopes that we might together find your party and prevent violence."

In spite of the irrationality of the very existence of the half-naked white man in this place, Quentin sensed for the first time that he could trust Samuel.

A motion in the trees above caught their attention. Quentin glanced up in time to see a brown shape complete an arch through the air from one branch to another. It was the tree kangaroo. It jockeyed for a stable position and then turned to stare at them.

Quentin watched the Englishman to see his reaction, but Samuel only glanced at the creature and then looked away as if it were as common as a honeyeater.

Quentin sighed. "Mbaiso, how do we get back?"

Samuel's brows folded with interest. "Mbaiso, do you say? I presume you are referring to the mbolop, the tree kangaroo?"

"Mbaiso is the name one of my students gave it. It's from a story I told them."

"Why did you speak to it in such a way? Does the creature answer you?"

Quentin gave him a sidelong glance. "Just wishful thinking. It's been hanging around us. It helped us gather water, and it followed me here from the crash site."

Abruptly the Englishman turned to the tree kangaroo, clicked his tongue in rapid succession, and gestured at the animal with both his arms. In response, Mbaiso backed down the tree by reverse-jumping, claws noisily scratching bark, and hopped to the two men.

Samuel began gesturing with his hands, a series of motions as elaborate as any sign language. He was clearly trying to talk to the tree kangaroo. It hadn't occurred to Quentin until now that this man may simply be insane.

Mbaiso watched until Samuel finished his extraordinary performance. Then the creature rolled back onto its haunches and began gesturing in return. The tiny forearms weaved, folded, and gyrated with miniature motions as controlled and precise as Samuel's. Samuel responded, as if clarifying the finer points of his first discourse. Then the conversation suddenly ended. Mbaiso hopped away and scuttled up a tree.

Samuel turned to Quentin. "If you had but told me sooner of your acquaintance with the mbolop, you may have saved us some consternation."

Quentin could think of nothing coherent to say. "I didn't think it was—"

For the first time, Samuel's eyes showed what might have been a sparkle of humor. "Once again, sir, your response reveals much."

"I, uh, have some questions for you," Quentin said.

"And I have questions as well. But now the mbolop will lead us to your vessel." Without another word he turned and followed the tree kangaroo, which now bounded from tree to tree.

BOBBY CHECKED that all his body parts were still there as he fumbled with the remains of his clothing. He tied his jeans around his waist, covering his front but leaving his butt exposed. Ashley and Mrs. Darnell were struggling with the same problems, and it might have been funny if a mass of steel were not collapsing above their heads.

"We have to get them out!" Mrs. Darnell said to Bobby and Ashley as she tied a knot in her shirt. She grabbed Addison by the armpits and tried pulling him to the front of the cabin. The rear ceiling was nearly touching the ground, so this was the only way out.

Bobby moved to her side to help. Ashley gave up trying to knot a scrap of her pants and tried to help too, but there wasn't much room. Mrs. Darnell squirmed out the opening. She tugged on Addison's arms, while Bobby and Ashley pushed from inside. As Addison inched through the opening, the remains of his clothing were torn from his body. His skin was pale, almost gray, and Bobby tried not to look at it. Addison's head rolled to the side and his face pressed against Mrs. Darnell's arm, forcing one eye open. The eyeball was gray and lifeless.

Addison was finally through and Bobby crawled out to help drag him clear of the wreckage. As they turned back to the shrinking doorway, Ashley's voice came from inside. She was talking excitedly, but not to them. Bobby and Mrs. Darnell looked at each other. They crawled back through, and there was Carlos, sitting upright.

"They're awake!" Ashley said.

"What's going on?" It was Miranda. She was propped up on her elbow.

Mrs. Darnell paused only briefly. "We need to get you out. Carlos, can you crawl?"

Carlos looked at the shrinking opening. "No problem, Mrs. D." Then he edged past them and through the hole.

Mrs. Darnell glanced at Bobby again, her eyes wide, and then grabbed Miranda's arm. "Miranda, honey, this is going to hurt, but we have to move you out of here too."

"Wait a second." Miranda pulled away the remains of the bloody jeans that had held the splint in place. The splint had disintegrated. She bent the leg, bringing her knee to her chest, and then slapped her thigh. The sound filled the tiny space of the cabin.

Mrs. Darnell put her hand over her mouth. "Miranda!"

"It seems okay now," Miranda said, as if announcing that cookies were ready to come out of the oven. She pulled at the remains of her shirt and it fell from her body, exposing her breasts. "Can someone tell me what in the name of Elvis is going on?"

Before anyone could answer, a portion of the plane's fuselage gave way, and the structure dropped another few centimeters with a thunk. The doorway was now smaller than ever.

Carlos's voice came from outside. "I think you guys should get out. Like now."

Ashley grabbed Miranda's shirt and pushed it to her chest. "C'mon, I'll help you."

"I told you I'm fine." Miranda used both legs to push herself through the opening.

Bobby and Mrs. Darnell followed her out just before the gap closed.

They watched the last of the Twin Otter disappear into a heap of soil. Their shelter was gone. Everything was gone. They didn't even have a single complete item of clothing between them. There was barely enough to cover their privates. Bobby had already glimpsed more female body parts than he had seen in all his life. He sat on the ground against a tree, mainly because he had not figured out a good way to cover his butt. Trying not to stare, he watched Ashley as she talked to Miranda. Somehow the girls had managed to tie their clothing together to cover their breasts and waists, somewhat like bikinis. Miranda walked back and forth as they talked, bouncing like she was eager to run but had no room for it. Bobby had seen the broken bone sticking out of her leg. Now she was walking around like it had never happened.

Carlos was seated on the ground. He had removed the wrap and was staring at his hand. The fingers looked swollen and lumpy, but he was opening and closing his fist. He grinned and held his hand up for Bobby to see.

It seemed like a miracle, except for Addison, who was no better than before. Mrs. Darnell held Addison's head in her lap as she watched Miranda bounce around.

Suddenly the girls saw something and stopped talking. Bobby turned. Three Papuan men stood side-by-side without moving, like ghosts in the trees.

"Don't do anything to threaten them," Mrs. Darnell said. She lifted Addison's head from her lap so the men could see him. "He's not better," she called out. "Can you help him?"

Bobby recognized two of the men from the night before. They still held their spears with darkened tips and patterned shafts. The man with the green-feathered head was the first to approach. He glanced at a piece of wreckage on the ground and pointed to it. One of the other men reached into his pouch and smeared the pasty miracle-cure stuff onto the chunk of metal. The spot immediately began gleaming with wetness as the wreckage dissolved.

"Our clothes, and all our stuff," Ashley said. "They're the ones who did this!"

Mrs. Darnell shushed Ashley. She raised Addison's head again. "Can you help him?"

The green-feathered Papuan kneeled, looking closely at Addison. *"Yu le khomilo-mbo. Khomilo.* Dead."[4]

"He's still alive," Mrs. Darnell said. But her voice was quiet, like she wasn't sure.

The man rose to his feet. *"Khomilo."*

Mrs. Darnell pointed to the pouch hanging from his neck. "Your medicine. Maybe it can help him. Maybe he needs more."

"*Ané kha-fen.*" He pointed away, into the forest. "*Ané lai-m.*" With his spear he motioned for her to get up. Mrs. Darnell didn't move, and he repeated the words. The two other men were smearing paste onto small leftover parts from the plane. They stopped what they were doing, approached Bobby and Carlos, and waved their spears for them to go.[12]

"Mrs. Darnell, they want us to go with them," Bobby said. "Maybe they want to help."

"Or maybe they want to eat us," Ashley muttered.

The green-feathered man shoved his spear tip under Mrs. Darnell's chin and forced her to stand. She waited for the spear to be withdrawn and then grabbed Addison by the armpits, trying to lift him.

"Bobby, Carlos, you'll have to help me carry him."

The Papuan's foot shot out and pushed Addison out of Mrs. Darnell's hands. Addison's head thumped the ground.

"*Khomilo!*"

QUENTIN DIDN'T RECOGNIZE any landmarks, but the tree kangaroo moved with such purpose that he was reassured. And Samuel followed the animal, asking Quentin no more questions concerning direction.

"Do you think they're still okay?" Quentin asked as he caught up for the third time. Physically, Quentin felt great, but he lacked Samuel's practiced agility.

"With any good fortune. Nevertheless, we will soon know."

Quentin's anxiety over Lindsey and the kids was like a crushing weight, so he tried thinking of other things. "What is the medicine you rubbed in my eye?"

"I wondered if you might inform me that such things had been found elsewhere. It appears, however, that my own discoveries are more important than I had supposed."

"But what is it? Is it from a plant?"

"No, most certainly not a plant, nor from insect or beast. Soon enough, Quentin, you may understand. Assuming our indigene hosts allow it."

"Why haven't you reported what the stuff can do to the rest of the world?"

"There is much about my discoveries you have yet to learn. Can you be quite sure that your society is prepared for such things?"

"What do you mean?"

"Tell me, are you a Christian man, a follower of God?"

This caught Quentin off guard. "I don't know. No—not really."

"Is this also true of others you know? Is this true of your society?"

"No. There are plenty of religious people. Christians mostly, where I'm from. Why do you ask?"

The Englishman stopped walking. Mbaiso moved ahead, leaping from tree to tree. Samuel clicked his tongue and the tree kangaroo stopped and turned, waiting. A few flies buzzed Quentin's head but then left without biting.

Samuel spoke. "In my younger life, Quentin, I was a man of Christian principles. Those principles served as a guide for my actions and judgments. While many naturalists were driven to find in nature the evidence that might disprove the hand of God, I was inclined to see God's hand in all of the wonders of the world—in the elegant design of the butterfly's wing or in the restless winds of the tropical seas. In my eyes, God's wisdom was to be found in all of nature. Do you understand, Quentin?"

"I know people who look at things that way."

"Then you might understand my consternation upon discovering that, in this place, God does not preside."

Quentin frowned. "What are you saying?"

Samuel paused, as if uncertain. "Forgive me, for I have rarely had occasion to express such thoughts to another man. They are bitter on my tongue. It will suffice to say that God is not here—because something else rules in this place."

Quentin eyed him. "Something else?"

Before Samuel could answer Quentin suddenly held up his hand. "Do you hear that?" They stood motionless, listening. There were voices in the distance. "It's them," Quentin said. "They must be okay!" The voices rose again. Now they were shouting, followed by a scream. Quentin's stomach lurched, and then he was running headlong through the tangled forest.

"Lindsey, I'm here!" he shouted. "Bobby, can you hear me? Hold on!"

SOMETHING ABOUT THE PAPUANS' calm willpower scared Bobby. They didn't say much, but their message was clear—they wanted the Americans to go with them. And it was also clear they wanted to leave Addison here, probably to be dissolved into soil like everything else. Mrs. Darnell would not leave him, and that scared Bobby even more. She and green featherhead were in a standoff.

"He's not dead." Mrs. Darnell's voice was low, and her eyes glowered with piercing intensity. "And he's coming with us."

"*I mbakha? Yu le khomilo-mbo. Ané lai-m.*" Again he motioned for her to walk.[13]

Mrs. Darnell spoke firmly. "I have to take him with us. He is my son, my family." She grabbed Addison again to lift him.

The man shoved her back with his foot and stepped between them. "*Khomilo!*" He then began kicking leaves and soil over Addison, covering his pale face.

Ashley exploded forward and swung at the Papuan. "You pygmy bastard!"

The man ducked and she struck his shoulder. They all raised their spears and moved in on her before she could swing again. Three spear points converged on her neck.

"Ashley, stop!" Mrs. Darnell cried. "Let me handle this."

Ashley's fists were trembling. "They're going to kill him!"

"I won't let that happen."

Ashley glared at the men. Suddenly she released an earsplitting scream of anger. In the seconds of shock that followed, the forest seemed to echo with the scream.

Bobby swallowed his fear and rushed in. He grabbed two of the spears, trying to hold them away from Ashley. "Please, you guys, just let us—" Before Bobby could finish, one of the spears was yanked from his hand and thrust into his chest.

The words stuck in Bobby's throat and a bubbling sound came from his mouth. Suddenly he was sitting on the ground, looking up. Ashley screamed again and charged the Papuan man, who now had no spear. Mrs. Darnell grabbed hold of another man's spear to wrestle it away, and she called to the others for help. Bobby thought he should help, too, but it was hard to breathe. A shaft protruded from his chest. It looked strange hanging there, and his eyes again were drawn to carved symbols he had seen somewhere before. The forest was darker now. A gush of prickling heat rose from his chest and filled his head. As he collapsed onto his back, he thought he heard Mr. Darnell's voice calling to him from far away.

—————

CHAPTER NINE

Quentin fought through the trees with Samuel at his heels. He stopped running in order to hear the voices again and adjust his course.

Samuel passed him without stopping. "We are near. Remain behind me."

The voices rose again—screaming and cursing. Quentin sprinted after Samuel. Suddenly the others were before them and they stopped short. Lindsey, Ashley, Miranda, and Carlos, all of them only partly dressed, faced off with three Papuan men. Quentin's eyes were drawn to two figures on the ground. One was Bobby, a spear embedded in his chest. The other was Addison, his pallid face and nearly naked body partially covered with dirt and leaves. Both boys lay still, as if dead. Samuel raised his hands to the Papuans, speaking their language firmly. This seemed to draw their attention and they turned away from the fight.

"Quentin!" Lindsey cried. She rushed over and embraced him. "They've hurt Bobby."

As Samuel held off the Papuans, Quentin and the others

converged on Bobby's still form. Quentin felt the spear. It was embedded deep. He held his ear to Bobby's mouth.

"Is he dead?" Ashley asked.

There was breathing, raspy and wet. "He's alive, but he doesn't sound good." Quentin looked to Lindsey. "Addison?"

"I don't know," she said. "His heart was still beating, but..."

Still crouched over Bobby, Quentin glanced at Addison's colorless skin. It was clear Addison was dying. The truth of this nearly crumpled Quentin's fortitude. Why in the hell had he brought them here? They'd all be safe at home if he hadn't. Quentin turned to the survivors. Was there even a chance of saving any of them? Suddenly he straightened up. "Miranda? You're walking! And Carlos, you're awake!"

"They used some kind of medicine on them," Ashley said matter-of-factly. "But it didn't work with Addison."

Quentin rubbed the mostly healed spear wounds on his chest and eyed the Papuan men, who now appeared to be negotiating with Samuel, perhaps regarding killing all the Americans. Was this about the medicine contained in their pouches? Were they trying to keep it secret?

Quentin's eyes drifted again to Addison's form. Addison's right hand protruded from the dirt and leaves that partially covered him. The skin on the hand was pale gray. Suddenly the hand turned and flattened against the ground. Quentin blinked. Addison lifted his head and stared back at him. His eyes were the color of storm clouds.

"Jesus Christ!" Quentin said, nearly stumbling backward over Bobby's body.

Addison was now sitting up. All commotion stopped.

"Laléo-khén! Laléo!" said one of the Papuan men.[14]

Quentin regained his composure and approached his son. Addison's eyes followed him, but his deathly face showed no expression. Quentin knelt and touched his shoulder. Addison's cloudy eyes showed no sign of recognition.

"*Laléo-khen!*" the Papuan repeated, and then he stepped forward, raising his spear. Samuel held the man back and spoke to him. Finally the Papuan nodded, as if in agreement.

Quentin touched Addison's face and felt cool, unfamiliar flesh. "Are you okay?"

Lindsey came to Quentin's side. "Addison, can you see us?"

Ashley's cry came from behind them. "Someone help! Bobby's choking!"

Gurgling coughs came from Bobby's body. Quentin looked to Samuel for help. "Samuel, can that medicine of yours help him?"

"I will do what I can. Do not fear the indigenes. They will not harm you, for now." Without further explanation, Samuel turned his attention to Bobby. The Papuan men gathered around Addison, uncomfortably close in Quentin's opinion.

"Addison, can you speak?" Lindsey said. He turned his head to face her, and she clutched Quentin's arm. Addison's face was that of a corpse.

Addison's eyes shifted from one of them to the other as they spoke, but milky corneas shrouded his pupils. A garbled sound came from his throat and then turned into coughing.

"It's okay, son," Quentin said. "Don't try to talk."

Something brushed Quentin's elbow, and there was Mbaiso. The creature pushed past him until it was nose to nose with Addison. Mbaiso sniffed him a few times, and Addison's eyes seemed to focus on the animal as the snout almost touched his lips. Quentin started to push the tree kangaroo away.

"*Fano! Mbolop manop.*" One of the Papuans handed his spear to the others and motioned for them all to back away from Addison and the tree kangaroo. The man did not seem threatening, and Quentin took note of his appearance for the first time. Like the Papuans he'd seen with Samuel, his face was smooth. He wore traditional adornments, but his most striking feature was the array of green feathers woven into his hair, flaring out like an emerald pincushion.[15]

The tree kangaroo sniffed at Addison's face again, pushing higher onto its haunches. Addison tried once more to speak, which led to more coughing. Mbaiso sat back, as if studying the situation. And then its diminutive forearms began moving. They danced with graceful movements that could not be mistaken for random, unthinking motion.

"Quentin," Lindsey hissed in his ear. "What the hell?"

Quentin nodded. "It can talk."

"It can talk," she repeated.

Addison watched with a stony face as the kangaroo continued gyrating its arms.

Ashley's voice rose from the group gathered around Bobby. "Oh God, Bobby!"

Quentin pivoted to see Samuel set a bloodstained spear onto the ground next to Bobby's body. Samuel's hands were also red. Quentin hesitated for a moment, and then turned his attention back to Addison.

The Papuan men squatted side by side, intently watching Mbaiso. The creature paused its hand motions, but Addison only stared. Mbaiso sat back, apparently giving up. It scratched at its abdomen with the nails of both forepaws, as if digging at fleas.

"*I mbakha!*" the green-headed Papuan said, pointing at Mbaiso.[16]

The kangaroo's digging claws punctured its own flesh. And they kept digging, working their way deep into the abdomen. The claws suddenly pulled a chunk of flesh loose. Mbaiso eyed it for a moment, as if inspecting it. The glistening flesh quickly turned dark, leaving a formless brown mass. With a very human gesture, the creature extended its forepaws, offering the substance to Addison.

For the first time since awakening, Addison demonstrated a purposeful behavior. He grabbed the chunk of Mbaiso's body, shoved it into his mouth, chewed, and swallowed.

Lindsey started forward. "Quentin, he's—"

"*Mbolop manop,*" interjected the Papuan. His tone was firm.

Quentin looked at Mbaiso's abdomen. There was no gaping hole and no blood.

Addison's emotionless gaze slowly drifted from Mbaiso to the assortment of people surrounding him. When his eyes met Quentin's, the gray clouds were rapidly vanishing.

As THE SUN heated the under-canopy into a sauna, the white noise shifted from the chatter of morning birds to the drone of midday insects. Quentin had begun to believe that the clockwork regularity of this pattern could drive a person mad. But today he hardly noticed. The insects still would not bite him, the heat was less stifling, and the morning's events were more extraordinary than any past experiences of his life.

Bobby was alive, in spite of the enormity of his chest wound. His pulse and breathing were strong, though he was unconscious. Samuel insisted on leaving the wound open to the air, and during the last few hours the tissue had grown together, healing itself before their eyes.

Quentin chewed the last meat from the dorcopsis leg bone in his hand. After Bobby had stabilized, Samuel had instructed Mbaiso to gather food. Within minutes, Mbaiso had herded two dorcopsis wallabies into their midst. The Papuans had promptly killed and butchered the creatures with a shaft of bamboo and their bare hands, and then cooked them over a low, nearly smokeless fire. They'd all devoured the meat as if it were a Thanksgiving turkey, giving little thought to the stomach cramps incurred the last time they had eaten dorcopsis.

They now sat around the extinguished fire, staring at the slight remains of the wallabies. Quentin wrapped one arm around Lindsey, thankful to have her back. Addison sat to his other side. Addison's skin had regained its color, and his corneas had cleared up. But his pupils were dilated to enormous size, making his eyes appear black. He had barely acknowledged their attempts to talk to him. But he was alive. And the other students were as energetic as ever, including Miranda, who by all accounts should have been immobile for weeks or months.

Minutes earlier, Samuel had disappeared into the forest with the three Papuan men. He now returned alone and settled to the ground across from Quentin. "When we arrive at the village of my hosts, I shall see that you are properly fed. A preponderance of flesh from the *soyabu* may produce abdominal distress."[17]

"We found that out already," Carlos said. He had nevertheless eaten his share.

Lindsey asked, "Where did the others go, Samuel?"

"They have returned to their village to discuss matters. It seems your presence here utterly confounds them. We shall venture there when your companion wakes." He motioned to Bobby, lying beside Lindsey. "The boy shows every appearance that we haven't long to wait. You should ready yourselves."

"We have nothing to get ready," Lindsey said. She explained the events of the morning—why they were left with nothing but the scraps of clothing tied to their bodies.

"The loss of your belongings is regrettable." Samuel said. "My hosts have little concern for possessions and contrivances."

"What is it they want from us?" Lindsey asked. "If they don't have a radio or an airstrip, why are we going to their village? We need to get these kids to a hospital."

"Do they not seem to you to be healthy, madam?"

"Yes, but I don't understand why. Does this miracle cure have side effects?"

"The poultice will result only in unreserved benefits to you all."

Lindsey wasn't giving up. "So if you're all about helping us, you'll help us get to civilization?"

Samuel hesitated. "We will soon be departing. You should ready yourself."

"I have *nothing* to get ready. I would like to know our plans!"

As Lindsey spoke, she routinely brushed flies from her face and exposed skin. Quentin looked at the students. While everyone else's arms were still, Ashley swiped at flies buzzing her face. Lindsey and Ashley, the only two not treated by Samuel's medicine.

Quentin got up and walked over to the remains of the plane. For a long moment he pondered the mound of soil that was once the Twin Otter's fuselage. The stuff Samuel and the Papuans carried in their pouches could turn the fields of medicine and chemistry on their heads. But the world had no knowledge of it. This was not a lost tribe, yet to be discovered. The tribe *had* been discovered, possibly over and over again. But the world had no knowledge of this substance because no one had ever left this place to tell about it.

Quentin turned back to the group. Physically, he felt more vigor than he had in days. But his mind was fatigued, staggering to keep pace with an unprecedented string of enigmas and disquieting revelations. He eyed Samuel, noting the Englishman's apparent good-natured grace with Quentin's family and students. Was Quentin capable of hurting such a man in order to protect them? At that moment he decided that he was. He would get his group out of here and back to civilization, even if he had to kill Samuel or anyone else who tried to stop them.

CHAPTER TEN

As if waking from a dream, Bobby was suddenly aware. But the dream continued. The sky was filled with stars, and there was no ground beneath him. The stars were endless, and Bobby sensed a deep loneliness. One star was closer, growing steadily larger. It swelled until he thought it might blind him. Near it was another object—a planet, with wisps of white and blue. He turned from the bright sun to watch the planet draw nearer, until his vision was filled with clouds and water and ice and land.

Abruptly Bobby was back in the steaming forest. Mbaiso was there, leading him somewhere. The creature turned and waited for him to catch up and then went on. Finally, Mbaiso stopped next to a massive tree and turned his snout upward. At first Bobby saw nothing unusual, but then he made out a darker leafy area. Like a spirit leaving its body, he rose from the ground. A slit in the foliage appeared, and he entered. It was darker inside, but he could see that he was in a room, with walls and floor made of living branches and vines. A thick trunk of the tree protruded through the floor. The trunk split into two limbs at chest level, and both limbs rose up and out the ceiling. The trunk was swollen at the split, like a large termite nest. As Bobby stared, a feeling of knowing washed over him. It was definitely not a termite nest.

———

SOMETHING SQUEEZED Bobby's hand and pulled him out of his dream. He opened his eyes, and the grip on his hand tightened.

"Hey, he's awake!" It was Ashley. Her curly hair framed her face as she looked down at him.

He blinked at her. "Ashley? I saw stars."

"I bet you did. You okay, science boy?"

She dropped his hand as other faces appeared above him—the Darnells, Carlos, Miranda.

"I saw stars," he told them. "I was in the sky, then I came here."

Suddenly, memories flooded Bobby's mind: Addison, Ashley, the Papuans—a spear in his chest. Bobby gasped. "He stabbed me!" He looked down at his chest. A scar was there, but it looked old. He turned to them. "I'm not dying?"

Mr. Darnell smiled. It was a good, truthful smile.

"This guy, Samuel, fixed you up," Miranda said. "His medicine fixed all of us."

Bobby tried sitting up, and found that it was easy. "Addison's okay, too?" He looked and there was Addison, upright and awake. "Hey, Addison."

Addison looked but didn't smile. There was something different about his eyes. They were darker. And then Addison spoke. "Tell them, Bobby."

Everyone seemed surprised by this and they all turned to Addison.

"Tell them what?" Bobby said.

"About the stars."

"Addison, what are you talking about?" Mr. Darnell said.

But Addison didn't answer. He just waited.

Addison's stare made Bobby nervous, so he looked away. "It was my dream."

Mr. Darnell said, "You had a dream about stars, too?"

"I dreamt about stars," Miranda said. "There were stars, then the Earth, and then the jungle."

"I had that dream," Carlos said. "There was this thing, like in a tree."

"Perhaps I might help elucidate these visions." The voice was new to Bobby. A strange man emerged from behind the others. He was dressed like he lived in the forest but was not black like the Papuans and was not Indonesian. "The dreams are peculiar to your medicinal treatments." He patted a pouch at his waist. "The poultice I carry possesses healing qualities, but is not without curious effects. I myself had the very dream of which you speak, long ago."

"Bobby, this is Samuel," Mr. Darnell said.

"Pleased to meet you, Bobby." The man talked like he was reading lines from a play.

"How could we all have the same dream?" Mr. Darnell said.

Mrs. Darnell frowned at him. "You had this dream too?"

Mr. Darnell nodded. "This morning. I was surrounded by stars. It seemed incredibly real. But then Samuel woke me up."

Samuel said, "Then the vision may revisit you, Quentin, until you have witnessed its conclusion. The vision will lead you to the very destination for which we are bound today."

Addison's black eyes still stared directly at Bobby. "It will speak to you," he said. "You should listen."

Mr. Darnell put his hands on Addison's shoulders. "Son, what does that mean?"

The black eyes turned to Mr. Darnell. "You won't understand it."

For a moment no one spoke.

"Curious," said the half-naked white man named Samuel.

THE TREE KANGAROO STUDIED THE HUMANS' activities from a snug depression between two rotting logs where damp soil cooled it belly. Events were unfolding rapidly but in unpredictable ways. The recently arrived strangers displayed novel attributes, indicating they were yet another step in an accelerating progression. But yet some of them revealed impulses that could disrupt this progression. The tree kangaroo had observed such disruptions before—somewhat interesting although devastating to those who were unfortunate to be in the vicinity. Now, the behaviors of the one they called Addison could prove to be interesting as well.

AGAIN THE AFTERNOON sun gave way to clouds, and everything faded to gray. The forest made it impossible to walk side by side, so they hiked in single file as Samuel and Mbaiso led the group toward the village of the Papuans. Bobby brought up the rear. Mr. Darnell had asked him to, and this made Bobby feel important. Physically, he felt great. No more sore bruises, oozing cuts, or bug bites. He even had a belly full of wallaby meat. He felt like he could walk all the way to Jayapura.

But they weren't going to Jayapura. They were going to the Papuans' village. Being stabbed by a spear was still fresh in Bobby's mind. He wanted to believe it had been a mistake—perhaps if they had spoken the same language, the fight wouldn't have happened. But he still feared what might happen at the village.

As they pushed on, the group became quiet and gradually spread out. Like Bobby, the others seemed to have their own thoughts. Carlos began humming a familiar song that Roberto's band used to play in their basement. It cheered Bobby up to see him acting normal again.

"Hey Bobby, what did the kangaroo say when someone cut off his tail?"

"What?"

"It won't be long now. And Addison, where did he go to get a new tail?" There was no answer. "To the retailer, man."

"You're so funny that I wallaby your friend," Bobby said.

Carlos stopped to poke at a covered termite trail running up the trunk of a tree. He broke a hole in the tunnel. "Look at those little mothers," he said. "Probably think I'm their god or something." He flicked one of the termites off the tree. "You will obey me!"

Bobby laughed. "Bite him, guys! He's not koala-fied to be a god."

"You insulted their god, man. You gotta pay." Carlos held out his hand, fingers hooked and thumb straight up. "This hand was busted to bits. Think you can beat it?"

The hand looked almost normal, but Bobby wasn't sure he should mess with it. He looked ahead to see if the teachers were watching. He saw only Addison, looking back at them, so he grabbed Carlos's hand, ready to thumb-wrestle. Addison walked back to where they stood, and Bobby released Carlos's hand. Addison looked at the termites on the tree.

"Those are my subjects," Carlos told him. "They worship me."

The termites were now swarming around the hole in their tunnel. Suddenly Addison rubbed his hand on the tree, killing them. Then he licked the smashed bodies from his palm.

"Now they worship me," he said.

"What the hell's wrong with you?" Carlos said.

Addison stared at his palm and then licked a few termites he had missed.

Bobby said, "Addison, your mom and dad are worried about you. We are too."

"Why?"

"Because you may have brain damage," Carlos said.

"Do you remember things?" Bobby asked him. "Things before the plane crashed?"

"I remember flying. And I saw the other plane. Then we crashed."

"You're messed up," Carlos said. "There was no another plane."

They were interrupted by Mr. Darnell's shout. "Hey, you guys, is Addison okay?"

Bobby looked at Addison. "Well, are you?"

Addison licked his hand again.

Bobby shouted back, "Yeah, I guess so. We're coming."

THE THREE BOYS stayed together as they walked. As Bobby looked ahead he got a glimpse of Mbaiso jumping between trees. "I feel like I know just where we're going," he said.

Carlos leapt into the air, trying to touch a pair of seedpods hanging from a tree. "I know, too. It's from our dream."

Bobby jumped at the seedpods, easily grabbing one loose even though they were at least a meter above his head. His chest wound tingled a little, but it didn't really hurt.

Carlos nodded toward the other seedpod. "Your turn, Addison."

"Can't eat those," Addison said.

"I don't want to eat them. I just want to see if you can jump."

Bobby held up the green seedpod. "How do you know we can't eat these?"

Addison's black eyes seemed to stare through Bobby, like they were looking at something behind him. "*Kembakhi*," he said.

Bobby looked at Carlos, then back at Addison. "Huh? Kim-backy?"

"*Kembakhi*," Addison said again. He pointed to the pod. "Inside."

Bobby snapped the seedpod in two. From inside, a swarm of black ants rushed out and onto his hands. The ants were mad, and Bobby felt stinging bites. He flung the pod away and wiped his hands against his thighs. They both looked at Addison.

"*Kembakhi*," Addison said. Then he turned away.

EVENTUALLY THEY REACHED A DIRTY-BROWN RIVER. There was a footpath by the river, the first sign of human impact that Bobby had seen since the plane crash. Mrs. Darnell said she was tired and needed to sit down, so they decided to rest. Ashley said she was tired, too. The flies were really swarming and biting the two of them, but no one else.

They all waded in to cool off. Samuel said they could drink the water, except for Ashley and Mrs. Darnell, because they might get sick. Mrs. Darnell grumbled something about the miracle medicine and just washed her face. Ashley drank some anyway. Bobby didn't blame her. He was thirsty, and he drank a lot, even though it tasted like mud. Then he noticed Mr. Darnell trying to talk to Addison.

"... and then we'll get you out of here, and we'll go home," Mr. Darnell was saying.

Addison looked at Mr. Darnell the way he'd looked at Bobby, like he didn't really see him. "We can stay here," he said.

"Addison, we're getting you home as soon as we can."

"We can stay here," Addison repeated.

Mr. Darnell looked around like he didn't know what to do.

Bobby spoke up. "Mr. Darnell, do you know what kim... backy is? Kimbacky?"

"*Kembakhi*, did you say, young man?" It was Samuel. "The

indigenes here speak that word. You have heard them speak it, no doubt?"

"No. Addison said it. What does it mean?"

"The word makes reference to Hymenoptera. Ants. Aggressive, biting ants, to put a sharp definition to it."

Bobby turned to Addison. "How did you know that?"

Addison's eyes looked through Bobby. "*Kembakhi* live in the *lepun melun*."[18]

"Young man," Samuel said. "How can it be that you know words spoken by the indigenes if you have awakened in this place only today? *Anggufa diabo?*"[19]

"*Nu khomile-lé-dakhu khosü kha-lé*," Addison said. "But I'm better now. *Khi-telo*."[20]

Bobby's skin turned cold. Addison had said the words without even slowing down, like he'd been talking that way all his life.

"Do you know what he said?" Mr. Darnell asked Samuel.

Samuel's eyebrows were wrinkled, and this was the first time Bobby had seen him look completely baffled. "Very curious, indeed. He said, 'I have died and have gone there.'"

"Gone where?" Mr. Darnell asked. His voice had an edge of fear.

"To the place of the dead."

ADDISON STOPPED SPEAKING AFTER THAT, so Bobby looked for something else to do while they rested. Mbaiso was drinking at the edge of the river, so Bobby and Carlos sat on the footpath, coaxing the kangaroo to come near them. Soon Ashley and Miranda joined them. Mbaiso approached their group, but then he climbed a tree to watch them from above.

Ashley said what was already on Bobby's mind. "Do you think we should be listening to this guy?" She waved a hand toward

Samuel. "He seems like a nut job to me. What kind of British guy would want to live in this creepy, hotter-than-hell place?"

Miranda had been quiet, but she spoke up. "If he's taking us to the place in my dream, then I don't think we need to be afraid."

Ashley said, "It was just a dream, Miranda."

"But we all had it," Carlos said, like this proved Ashley was wrong.

Bobby looked at Ashley. Her face was red, and flies were trying to get into her eyes. "Not all of us," Bobby said. "Ashley didn't get the medicine."

Ashley swiped at her face for the zillionth time. "If it gets rid of the damn bugs, I'll take some. But I'm waiting to see if it's turning you guys into monsters or something." She pulled her hair over her face to keep the flies at bay.

After a moment of silence she shoved her hair back. "I'm really starting to feel left out. You all have this dream, right? It's at night and you can see the stars, and then you go—"

Miranda interrupted, "It's not really at night, Ash. It was like being in the stars, flying through space. For a long time, it seemed like."

"It's the thing in the tree," Bobby said. "It's trying to tell us how it got here."

Ashley sneered. "You mean you think it's an alien. Great."

Bobby paused, embarrassed. "In the dream there was something there—on the tree but not part of it. It was telling me not to be afraid."

Ashley said, "What if it just wants you to think that, so you'll come closer?"

No one answered.

THE FOREST GREW DARK AGAIN, and Quentin could scarcely

believe this would only be their fourth night since the crash. They had suffered enough for a lifetime. And now, as they approached the Papuan village, led by an eccentric Englishman and a talking kangaroo, Quentin had no idea what awaited them. Getting straight answers from Samuel was like pulling teeth from a toad, and the Papuans had shown a fondness for jabbing their spears into people.

Quentin had tried concocting escape plans, but they all had similar outcomes: they would either be killed for trying or they would succeed, only to find themselves lost in the remote rainforest. If it was twenty miles to the nearest airstrip, it might as well be a thousand.

Lindsey walked the path in front of Quentin. She had become quiet. She stumbled on something, and Quentin grabbed her arm. He brushed away the mosquitoes biting her neck. With evening setting in, the flies were resting and the mosquitoes were taking over.

Addison would hardly speak unless pressed to, and Quentin feared what might come out of his mouth next. Should he rejoice that Addison now seemed healthy, or agonize that the medicine he'd been given had somehow changed him forever? Addison could now speak a second language, something that would make most parents proud. But the language damn sure wasn't French or Spanish. And most kids don't learn a language while they are in a coma.

Lindsey stumbled yet again, this time falling to her knees. Quentin helped her up. It appeared they were no longer on the footpath, and it was difficult to negotiate the vegetation in the growing darkness.

Quentin called ahead, "Samuel, why aren't we on the path?"

Samuel turned to wait for them.

"I need to rest," Lindsey said. She settled onto the ground. The kids did the same.

"As I have told you, Quentin, the indigenes value their privacy.

Would it not be to their advantage to conceal the path near to the village itself?"

"So how do they get plants to grow more on the most heavily used part of the path? Wait—don't tell me. The same way they get animals to talk and airplanes to turn to dirt, right?"

Lindsey said, "Maybe he's not taking us to the village."

Samuel frowned. "My Papuan hosts are stewards of a most unusual phenomenon. In their low state of civilization, they are ill-equipped to understand it, but they value and guard it nonetheless. In all the years since I arrived here, there have been few allowed near their village. But you are to receive this privilege. I assure you, the village is our destination."

Quentin said, "There isn't going to be an airstrip, is there? Or a radio?"

"I am not acquainted with either, but I fear not."

Lindsey had been rubbing her ankles, but now she stopped. "Samuel, how long have you been here? Please give us a straight answer."

He sighed, as if giving in. "I was once an eager young student of natural history, with interminable wanderlust. As I resided in London, and frequented the proceedings of the Linnean and Royal Societies, I was fortunate to attend a reading by an esteemed naturalist, Mr. Wallace, whom I greatly admired, regarding his studies of the flora and fauna of this region. He was a student of the entire Malay Archipelago, as a matter of fact. His tales of the great island of New Guinea particularly seduced me. I persuaded him to give me advice, so that I might travel to this land to discover living things new to science. In his time here, Mr. Wallace only explored the northern coasts. This determined me to forge inland, to collect species new even to Mr. Wallace's substantial collection."

Quentin held up his hand. "Wait. It sounds like you're talking about Alfred Wallace."

"Ah," Samuel said. "I am pleased that you know of him. A great man of science, surely worthy of such recognition. Upon Mr. Wallace's counsel I assembled supplies and funds for my own journey. Unfortunately, my resources were—"

Quentin interrupted again. "Alfred Wallace is long dead. He lived back in the eighteen hundreds. When Charles Darwin lived."

"Mr. Darwin was also an esteemed naturalist. But I hadn't the occasion to meet him."

Quentin stared. "That was over a hundred and fifty years ago."

"Lift your shirt, Quentin," Samuel said. "Examine your wounds there."

Quentin felt his chest. There was no pain. The wounds were healed.

"Examine your own son, Quentin, and your students who have reaped the benefits of our medicine. Do you find it so difficult to believe?"

Quentin sank to the ground, overwhelmed. He held his head in his hands.

A voice came from behind him. "We're there now, father."

Quentin turned. "What did you say?" Addison had always called him *dad*.

"We're there now. *Khosükhop, khaim.*" Addison pointed up.[21]

"He is correct," Samuel said. "We have arrived at the village."

Quentin turned. Around them was forest, no different than everywhere else.

"As your son attempted to tell you, the village is there." Samuel pointed up.

Quentin looked. He could see only dark foliage.

"There, Quentin!" Lindsey pointed and he followed her finger —still only darkness. In fact, the place where she pointed was especially dark, with no gaps where the sky peeked through. He looked around and saw another spot that was too dark, and then another. The Papuans' village was far above them, hidden in the rainforest canopy.

Quentin turned back to Samuel. "You've got to be kidding."

THE KIDS BECAME VERY quiet as they followed Samuel. Quentin tried estimating the height of the tree houses, but the darkness made it difficult. He sensed a slight rustle from the trees above. Something was moving up there. If these were indeed huts, the people in them were keeping to themselves.

He poked Samuel and whispered, "Do they know we're here?"

"Your excessive noise long ago declared our approach. They are a deliberate people, and there is little they do not observe. You will also find them exceedingly shy. Do not anticipate a welcoming party. You have been allowed to come here, but most assuredly not for a social visit. That concept is unknown to them. You may not see the women at all. Even I am not certain I have seen all of their women, and you are now privy to the duration of my stay here."

"Privy to your claims, anyway," Quentin mumbled.

Samuel turned. "As I've said, Quentin, my hosts are aware of your presence. Whispering is without warrant."

"If they won't show themselves or talk to us, why are we here?"

"You ask too much of me, sir. As a visitor, I am not told all things." Samuel stopped, resting one hand on a massive buttressed tree. "We have arrived."

Quentin had hoped the hut prepared for them was actually touching the ground. Almost afraid to look, he gazed upward. If there was a tree house there, it could have been ten meters above them or fifty.

"We don't have to go up there, do we?" Miranda said.

"Sinanie has returned before us to prepare this hut," Samuel said. "I trust you will find it adequate." Samuel clicked his tongue repeatedly.

There was movement in the foliage above. Something swooshed by Quentin's ear, and he ducked involuntarily.

"There we are." Samuel reached for a rope that had evidently been dropped for them.

"We have to climb that thing?" Lindsey's voice had an edge.

"It is quite safe, I assure you."

Quentin took the rope from Samuel. It was absurdly thin and light. Loops had been tied in it every half-meter or so, like rungs in a ladder. Quentin tugged at one of the loops, which were held open by rigid cross-weaving so hands and feet could grip them. The rungs were woven into the main rope rather than knotted on—an impressive piece of handiwork.

Ashley said, "I guess there's not going to be a shower up there, is there?"

Samuel grabbed the rope ladder. "I will demonstrate. Please follow me when I call out. The *yebun* is sturdy, but it is unwise to burden it with more than one climber." With that, he swiftly climbed up the rope until he became a murky gray shape above them.[22]

Quentin held the end of the rope, feeling it jerk about as Samuel climbed. Finally the rope was still, and Samuel called down for the next climber to begin. Several of the kids immediately volunteered, but Quentin wouldn't let them climb the rope without testing it himself. But he also didn't want to leave Lindsey to climb on her own in her weakened state.

"I'll climb up first and make sure the tree house is safe. Then I'll come back down and the rest of you can climb up." No one argued with this.

Climbing the rope ladder was harder than it looked. Whenever Quentin let his hands bear too little of his weight, his foot would push the rope away from his body, and he would end up dangling horizontally. But soon he found his rhythm and began making steady progress. It was difficult to judge the distance to the ghost-like faces watching him from below, and he was glad it was dark. Finally he approached a mass of foliage. But the rope passed through it, and he climbed even higher. "Samuel! Where are you?"

"Just above you," came the reply. But Samuel's voice was still distant.

Quentin could no longer see the ground. Suddenly the rope seemed ridiculously thin. One weak spot would send him falling to his death, perhaps even landing on Lindsey or one of the kids. His arms were now shaking, but still he kept climbing. Finally he entered another darkened mass of foliage, and there was Samuel's face, like a pale beacon above.

"You were lying," Quentin puffed. "You were not just above me."

"One's notion of height shifts while living among the trees. I intended no deceit."

Quentin climbed through a black opening, and Samuel helped him step from the ladder to a solid surface. He sensed that he was in a room, but it was very dark. The air was extremely humid and smelled faintly of wood smoke. Quentin felt around him. Two walls of entwined fibers or vines joined to form a corner near the opening in the floor. The rest was black, empty space. He hopped up and down, testing the surface beneath his feet. The walls of the room rustled from the movement, and the floor bounced like a stiff trampoline.

"These huts are remarkable achievements of structural design and of cultivation," Samuel said. "They are quite safe."

"It's the climb that worries me most. I don't think—"

At that moment a figure appeared in the opening.

"Welcome, young Addison," Samuel said.

Addison climbed nimbly into the hut. "Hey *n-até-o*."[23]

Quentin was sure Addison had not started up the rope while he was still on it. He would have felt the weight. "Why didn't you wait, like I asked you to?"

Addison moved away into the darkness of the hut. "I can climb the yebun, my father."

Quentin gazed at his son for a moment then decided to begin his descent. Most difficult was finding the rungs with his feet, particularly with his cumbersome hiking shoes. It was no wonder the Papuans and Samuel went barefoot. Just before reaching the ground, he heard something. He paused. From above, the sound grew, like a soft ocean wave. It was raining. *Perfect—as if this weren't hard enough.*

Bobby climbed the ladder next and made it safely to the hut, followed by Carlos, and then Miranda. But in their weakened state, Ashley and Lindsey would need help. Maybe he could tie the end of the rope around their waists. But this wouldn't stop them from falling.

"Hey!" It was Bobby's voice, from far above, almost drowned out by the rain. "We have a plan. Ashley, get on the rope and hold on."

Quentin realized what they wanted to do, and he wished he had stayed in the tree house to help. He ran the scenario through his head. There were five people up there, but Samuel was the only adult. How much help would the kids be?

Ashley shoved her foot into the lowest rung, pulled herself up, and placed her other foot in the next rung. Then she was on her way up, rising at a surprising rate.

As she receded into the gloom, she yelled, "If you guys drop me, you're dead!"

"Just hang on, Ash." Miranda's words were punctuated by the effort.

Quentin held his breath, trying to transfer his own strength to the arms of his students. At last there was faint laughter from the tree house, and Quentin sighed forcefully.

"Major Tom to ground control. It's your turn, Mrs. D. Look out below!"

The rope snapped the air beside them. Lindsey mounted the two lower rungs as Ashley had. Her face was pale even in the darkness, and Quentin sensed her trepidation.

She said, "We'll laugh about this someday, right?"

Quentin forced a smile. "The time Lindsey was at the end of her rope." He turned to the canopy and shouted, "Ground control, ready! Guys, please don't drop my wife."

Lindsey whispered something unintelligible as she rose into the darkness.

STARS SURROUNDED QUENTIN. He'd been here before, in another dream. The long aloneness returned. The stars passed by him, and he waited, knowing one would grow brighter. And there it was, distant but beckoning. As the star swelled, the planet appeared like a tiny blue sapphire. The sun grew and passed by him, and the blue planet filled his vision. Something about the planet was familiar, but not quite right. The continents were misshapen, and mostly desert brown. The planet drew nearer, engulfing him in its vastness.

And then he was in a forest, surrounded by foliage and steaming wetness. On the ground before him a familiar tree kangaroo sat on its haunches. Mbaiso led him to the village of the Papuans, their tree houses veiled in the branches far above. They stopped at an exceptionally large tree, and Quentin suddenly floated from the ground and entered a tree hut, smaller than the one in which he was sleeping. The room was dominated by something clinging to the large, splitting trunk of the tree. Quentin reached out to its gray-brown surface. It was soft, like moist clay. His fingers molded the surface, and he pulled a portion of it free.

The stuff spread over his fingers and palm. It glistened with movement, as if thousands of tiny particles were at work. Abruptly it was gone, absorbed by his flesh. His fingers tingled. The sensation moved through his arm to his shoulder. He stood motionless, allowing the tingles to spread through his entire body.

Quentin awoke. He lay in the dark hut listening to tree frogs and crickets, still feeling the sensation of the substance coursing through his system. Something within him was different. Memories, rich in detail, steadily began flooding his mind.

He was sprawled on his belly under the summer sun, peering at the water's edge. Two green turtles returned his stare. Their yellow-striped legs paddled gently in the clear water to keep their heads above the surface. He wanted to catch them and take them home. "Quentin, let's go!" He turned and saw his father, looking very young, with a fistful of fishing poles in one hand and a metal tackle box in the other.

Quentin hadn't thought about that day in a long time. And there were others—long forgotten scenes, accessible as if they'd occurred only moments before. Many of them were gratifying, notable events of his life. Others were more dismal.

The jet engines' roar made it easier to concentrate and draw. Quentin's picture of a Papuan hut was almost finished. He'd already drawn on sixteen pages and he wanted to fill the whole pad before they landed in California. He held the pad up. "Look, Dad. It's a cooking hut. See the fire hole?" His dad just stared out the window. "Dad, see my hut?" Quentin's mom turned the pad so she could see. "Nice job, kiddo. Why don't you let your dad rest for now? He's not feeling so good." Quentin looked at his dad. "I liked them, anyway, Dad. Even if they're not the same as before. I liked Gupy, and Amius too. They're still nice." His dad just stared at the clouds.

CHAPTER ELEVEN

BOBBY AWOKE. The tree house was quiet. Morning light pierced the walls and ceiling, speckling the sleeping bodies. His night had been full of dreams—the stars again, the forest and Mbaiso, and then the tree. But this time there had been more. He had dreamt he touched the object on the tree, and part of it had soaked into his body as if that were its purpose. Bobby rolled onto his back and stared at the tangled vines of the hut's ceiling. He rubbed the scar on his chest. It didn't even hurt. His mind drifted to the fight with the Papuan tribesmen the day before. Without warning the violent scene erupted in his mind with horrifying clarity. Startled, Bobby squirmed and then bolted upright. He was still in the silent, darkened hut. But for just a moment it had been like he was there again, confronting the tribesmen, seconds away from being stabbed with a spear. He sensed that it had been no more than a vivid memory. So he tried conjuring up another.

The frog sat on his hand, looking back at him with round eyes on a flattened face. Its skin was turquoise, almost blue, and kind of dry for a frog. It looked like a plastic statue of a cartoon character. Bobby loved it. But his mom wrinkled her nose at it. "Mr. Darnell gave it to me," he said to her. "He's going to give me a male, too, so she can have babies. She can have a thousand tadpoles. This is a White's treefrog and pet shops in the city will buy them for ten dollars each." "Well, I can't imagine why," she said. "But I guess it might teach you some responsibility." Bobby looked at the frog in his hand, the most wonderful thing he had ever owned.

Back in the tree hut, Bobby smiled to himself. He could remember every detail. He tried it again, thinking of when Ashley pulled the stinging vine hairs out of his lips. Her face had been so close to his that he could smell her. He realized he could slow the memory down, and then he watched Ashley's face as she worked at the task in slow motion. He saw details in her eyes and mouth he had completely forgotten.

But then Addison's voice broke his thoughts. "No... no. *Gu laléo-lu.* You need me."[24]

Addison was talking in his sleep. Bobby crept over to where he lay.

"*Senggile-lé.* No... They'll all die. *Yanop khomile-lé-dakhu.*"[25]

Addison's voice faded to a whisper, and Bobby leaned closer, his ear only inches away.

"Don't. *Gu laléo-lu...* I'll make you help me..."

"Bobby? What's wrong?"

Bobby drew back, startled. It was Mr. Darnell, sitting up on the other side of Addison.

"I don't know. Addison was saying weird stuff is all."

Suddenly Addison cried out. Bobby nearly fell over backward. The utter rage in Addison's scream made Bobby want to cover his ears and purge it from his mind.

Mrs. Darnell sputtered awake. "What? Quentin, what?"

"What's wrong with him?" Miranda said. The others were awake now.

Mr. Darnell reached for Addison to hold him, but then pulled back like he was afraid.

Addison crawled away to a corner of the hut and then sat quietly watching them as if nothing had happened.

Mr. Darnell eyed his son. "Did you have a bad dream?"

Addison's face was blank. "Dreams are real now, my father."

Mrs. Darnell groaned and pushed to one elbow. "They're not real. They're only dreams." She fell back to the floor. "Oh God, Quentin, I don't think I can get up."

Mr. Darnell felt her forehead. A beam of sunlight from a hole above fell directly on her face, and her skin was red and sweaty.

"Addison's right," Bobby blurted out. "Our dreams are real. I dreamed that something got into my body and was changing me. And now I can remember everything."

These words shut everyone up. As Bobby waited for them to try it, a flock of parrots screeched in the distance. A snicker came from the back of Carlos's throat, and Miranda whispered, "Oh my God."

"Jesus, it *is* real," Mr. Darnell said.

Mrs. Darnell was still lying on her back. "What's real?"

"We can remember stuff," Bobby said. "Everything that ever happened to us."

There was a moment of silence, and then she said, "What?"

A movement at the floor's opening caught Bobby's eye. Mbaiso climbed through. The kangaroo circled the opening to where the rope ladder lay coiled on the floor, turned away from it, and with a kick of his hind legs sent it tumbling. For a moment the rope hung loose from the ceiling, but then it went tight and the tree house shook from the weight of a climber.

Bobby crept to the edge of the opening and watched. It was Samuel. Bobby looked at the tree kangaroo. He reached out, palm down, like he would to a dog. "Hey, boy. Mr. Darnell says you can talk. Can you teach me?"

Mbaiso simply stared, and then moved out of the way as Samuel's head appeared.

"Sinanie claims that you are the noisiest creatures of the living world. I am inclined to agree." He climbed the last few rungs into the tree house, and the rope ladder went tight again as someone else started climbing. "I trust you had adequate rest," Samuel said.

"We slept well," Mr. Darnell said. "But we had dreams again, and this time—"

Samuel held up his hand. "Explanations will come. Of particular concern now is your health." He eyed Mrs. Darnell, still lying on the floor, and then Ashley, who was still sleeping. "There are two among you who yet suffer. You should allow them treatment. I offer the same ointments that have proven beneficial to the rest of you."

Mrs. Darnell moaned and said, "No, I don't know what the stuff is."

Mr. Darnell frowned. "Lindsey, you're getting worse."

"Don't try to make me."

Mr. Darnell sighed and shook his head at Samuel.

Samuel seemed as if he were about to argue with this. Instead he hoisted a swollen bag from his shoulder to the floor. "I have brought food." He pulled something the size of a person's head from the bag. It was wrapped in green leaves, which he peeled away and laid flat on the floor. The stuff inside was mostly white and looked like oatmeal. "You may find *khosül* to be rather tasteless, but I assure you it contains sufficient nourishment."

"Looks like sago," Miranda said.

"Indeed, young lady. Sago paste is the foundation. But only the foundation, for khosül contains animal matter from the sago beetle larva. It is more palatable and nourishing."

Miranda's shoulders slumped. "Grubs. We're eating grubs."

"Thank you for the food, Samuel," Mr. Darnell said.

Just then the other climber's head appeared. The now familiar pincushion of green feathers indicated it was Sinanie. Almost against Bobby's will, a vivid scene appeared in his mind: Sinanie's confident face and grunt of effort as he plunged a spear into Bobby's chest. Bobby gasped and forced the memory from his mind.

Sinanie climbed through the opening, removed a container that hung from his neck, and set it next to the khosül. It was a gourd, wet from water that must have spilled during the climb. Sinanie moved to the only corner of the tree house not occupied. He squatted there and quietly watched them. His eyes met Bobby's, and he flashed a white smile. Bobby tried to smile back.

Samuel nodded to Ashley, whose eyes were still closed. "May I treat the young lady?"

Mr. Darnell nodded. "Please."

THE KHOSÜL WAS ALMOST TASTELESS, but Bobby was hungry enough to eat mud. The others didn't seem to mind it either, and they all ate in silence. Bobby knew another reason they weren't talking. They were busy with their own memories. Giggles and murmurs of surprise were mixed with eating sounds as they relived forgotten experiences. In his mind, Bobby saw his mom and dad long before the divorce. For the first time he realized they were never very happy together. When he was younger he couldn't have known. They had laughed and played with him and he felt safe. But now he saw that they laughed only with him, never with each other. There was something between them—a coldness.

"Holy crap, I can remember right after I was born!" Carlos said.

This was followed by more silence as the others tried it. But Bobby had done that already. The visions were blurry, with voices he didn't understand and shapes he didn't recognize. Memories from infancy were too baffling to make sense of.

"Oh, you're kidding me!" Everyone turned to Miranda. "I found my journal," she said. "My baking journal—like a diary but with all the recipes I invented. I lost it a year ago, and I just remembered I hid it in the wall in my closet."

"You're such a Barbie, Miranda," Ashley said. Ashley still looked pale, but apparently she was already feeling better.

Carlos was frowning. Finally he said, "When I was four, Roberto got sick. He was gone for like two weeks, and I didn't know what my parents were talking about then. But now I know. His appendix burst and he got infected. He almost died. No one ever talked about it after that." Carlos laughed quietly like there was something funny about that.

"Maybe we forget some things for a reason," Mr. Darnell said to Carlos. He then turned to Addison. "Son, do you remember anything?"

"I had two mothers," Addison said, his dark eyes staring at the wall.

"What do you mean, two mothers?"

"Two mothers when I was *abül*, a boy. Lindsey was my mother. And Koina was my mother. She brought me to be with the *yanop lop*."

"*Yanop lop*?"

"The people of the trees. Koina brought me from the place of ancestors to live with the *yanop lop*."

Mr. Darnell frowned. "You think you have a mother named Koina?"

"Quentin! We have to go!" It was Mrs. Darnell. Every few minutes she would wake up and say something like this. She was getting worse.

For some time they all sat in silence. Bobby scooped another handful of khosül and shoved it into his mouth. He felt something hard. He worked the object out of his mouth and onto his palm. It was a shiny black oval the size of a quarter. He turned it over, and his stomach tightened at the sight of two large mandibles. It was the head of an insect. The head alone was larger than any beetle he had ever seen.

"What you got there?" Carlos asked.

Bobby couldn't answer. He dropped the black head onto the floor for Carlos to see. Samuel had told them the khosül contained sago grubs. But Bobby had seen sago grubs in the market in Wamena, with their tiny black heads. An image popped into Bobby's mind of an enormous white, legless, squirming sago grub with a head this huge. This was too much. He barely made it to the hut's opening in time. He heard his vomit strike the ground just as he finished retching. Bobby sat back, panting from the effort. He had just ejected nutrients that he desperately needed. He would have to start again.

SAMUEL HAD LEFT, saying that he would talk to the village elders about their situation. While they waited for his return, Bobby had eaten what he could and decided to explore every inch of the tree house. He even climbed the walls. There wasn't really a ceiling. Instead, the walls sloped inward until they came together to form two points. He pushed his hand through the sticks and living vines of the walls and felt a rope above each point. The hut seemed to be hanging by these two ropes. Although thicker than the rope ladder, the cords seemed too thin to support the weight.

Mrs. Darnell was getting worse, while Ashley seemed to be improving. After Samuel had treated her with his medicine, Ashley had slept. She awoke after a short time and reported having the same dream, about stars and the forest and the thing in the tree house. This got everyone talking about it again.

"Do you think they'll take us to the dream-tree?" Carlos asked.

Mr. Darnell said, "It was a dream. It may not even exist."

"But the dream felt real," Bobby said. "It's like someone is trying to show us where it came from, and where it is now. The stuff came from space. It ended up here in the jungle. Maybe the Papuans found it and hid it in a tree so no one would take it."

"Guys, you're not thinking like scientists," Mr. Darnell said. "We shouldn't consider the most bizarre explanation first. It's the simplest that usually turns out to be true."

"Like what?" Carlos asked. They all waited for his answer.

"Like maybe it's a medicine the villagers mixed together from things they got from the forest. That could happen. People are creating new drugs from rainforest products all the time."

"When was the last time they found one that fixes broken legs?" Miranda said.

"And makes you remember your whole life," Bobby added.

"And keeps people alive who should be dead," Carlos said. He then looked at Addison.

Addison regarded Carlos without expression. But Bobby thought he saw something menacing in the blackness of his eyes. Although barely noticeable, it made Bobby avert his gaze so Addison wouldn't look at him in such a way.

Mr. Darnell broke the silence. "I don't doubt that we've been given an amazing medicine. And obviously it does more than heal wounds. That doesn't mean it's from space."

"Perhaps soon you will have answers." Samuel had returned. He climbed the last few rungs and stepped onto the floor of the hut. He spoke to Mr. Darnell. "You are to accompany me. Perhaps you may satisfy your curiosities while the indigenes satisfy theirs."

"Lindsey is weak," Mr. Darnell said. "She can't climb down the ladder."

"*Your* presence is sufficient at this time, Quentin. Your wife will be safe here."

Mrs. Darnell tried to sit up. "Quentin, don't leave."

Samuel said, "Lindsey, you are as safe here as any place upon this world. The villagers demand to see your husband. There would be consequences should he refuse."

Mr. Darnell hugged her and whispered something in her ear. He stood and faced the rest of them. "I'll be back as soon as I can."

As Mr. Darnell climbed down the ladder, Samuel waited in uncomfortable silence.

"Samuel, what's going to happen to us?" Mrs. Darnell asked. "The truth."

"The truth, Lindsey, is that I do not know."

"What will it take for them to help us get home?"

"That would require the merciful hand of God himself. But as I've told your husband, God does not inhabit this place." He gripped the rope ladder, but Mr. Darnell was still climbing.

Mrs. Darnell didn't give up. "Samuel, you seem like a civilized person. Why won't you help us?"

"You misunderstand me, dear Lindsey. It is for the sake of the civilized world that I believe you should not leave this place." The rope ladder went limp, and he stepped into a rung. "You should not judge me too harshly. Nor should you judge the Papuans. The civilized world, which you speak of so fondly, would be a changed place were it not for their secretive nature. It may not be wise to reveal what they hold secret."

And then he was gone. Bobby watched the rope twitch as Samuel descended.

"He won't listen." Addison spoke so quietly that Bobby almost missed it.

"Who won't?" Mrs. Darnell said.

"Father won't. The *Lamotelokhai* will talk to him, but he won't know how to listen."

Carlos said, "What's the lamb-oh tell-oh kye?"

Addison turned to him with eyes as cold and black as space. "The Lamotelokhai talks to you when you sleep. I know how to listen. I should be the one to see it, not my father." Then Addison looked directly at Bobby. "You know how to listen, too."

Bobby felt his face flush. "What do you mean?" He looked around at the others. "What about them?"

"They don't matter."

"Screw you, Addison," Ashley said.

Carlos spat on the floor. "He's brain damaged."

Mrs. Darnell said, "Stop it! Addison's not well. We need to get him home." She eyed Carlos. "Can you understand that?"

Carlos shrugged. "Sure."

Addison stared at them, but something about his eyes made it seem like he didn't really see them—or didn't care. "I am staying," he said.

Mrs. Darnell closed her eyes. "No, Addison, we're all going home."

"It is wrong to go home now."

Miranda spoke up. "How can it be wrong? Our families are worried about us. At least you have your parents with you."

"They won't want you there," said Addison. "Not now."

The back of Bobby's neck tingled.

Mrs. Darnell said, "Sweetie, you're scaring everyone."

"Mother, you can't remember." Addison's voice was louder now. He turned to Bobby and the others. "But they can."

Mrs. Darnell looked like she might cry. "You're not making sense. Please stop."

Addison didn't stop. He stood and approached Carlos. "You can remember. Before the *pesua* crashed. *Gekhené pesua im-le.* You saw the other airplane."[26]

Carlos's hands were fists. His brows scrunched up, like he was trying to remember. He closed his eyes. When he opened them they were wide with terror. "No!" he cried. "Roberto! He's not..." His words turned into sobs, and he crumpled to the floor. He sat in the corner, crying and holding his hand like it was smashed all over again.

Addison turned away from him toward Bobby. "You can remember," he said. "You'll see." He came nearer.

Bobby felt trapped. He backed up and almost stepped into the opening in the floor. He grabbed the rope ladder to keep from falling.

Suddenly Ashley was between them. She pushed Addison, saying something about how they'd be better off if he'd go back into his coma.

"You can't remember," Addison said to her. "But Bobby can."

Bobby started climbing down the ladder—to hell with Addison and all the fighting.

Ashley's face appeared in the opening above him. "Bobby, where are you going?"

"I want to be alone." He heard Mrs. Darnell's voice, protesting. "I'll be back. Tell her not to worry." He didn't look up again.

After reaching the forest floor, Bobby sat at the base of a tree and rested his head on his knees. Why did Addison want him to remember the plane crash? Why was he talking about another plane? There was no other plane, and they hadn't seen or heard any since the crash. He pulled up the memory, and like all other memories, the events appeared in complete detail. He was sitting in the hot plane, waiting to take off, hoping he wasn't in trouble for making everyone late. Then they were flying over the mountains. He was talking to Mr. Darnell.

Bobby knew what would come next, and panic swelled in his chest. It was no wonder Carlos had freaked out in the tree house. Bobby tried to calm down. The plane crash was in the past. There was no reason to be afraid now. He swallowed hard and went back in time.

He stared out the window at the jungle below, listening to the engines. Mr. Darnell said, "I'm sure you guys have a great story to tell about your morning." Mr. Darnell was kneeling in the aisle. "Yeah, I guess," Bobby said. "Well, I want the full story tonight. That'll give you guys a chance to get it straight." And then it happened. Bobby's vision blurred and everything went blank. The next thing he knew, he was staring at a stream of brown stuff streaking out of the plane's engine outside his window. "Mr. Darnell," he cried, "something's wrong!"

It felt so real that Bobby was shaking, so he opened his eyes. He hadn't remembered blanking out like that before. Intrigued, he took a deep breath and went over it again in his mind. This time he remembered more. There were strange shapes moving in front of his eyes. He couldn't tell what they were. So he sat up straight against the tree and clenched his fists. He closed his eyes and put all his effort into the memory.

"...That'll give you guys a chance to get it straight," Mr. Darnell said. Bobby smiled, staring out the window. And then the blankness washed over him. It felt like that instant of dreamlike feebleness at the top of a roller coaster just before the plunge—helpless and barely aware. There was a shape there, just outside the airplane. It was confusing because the shape seemed so close. A flash of white; a curved edge of something dark; some bits of blue, maybe they were letters; several dark oval shapes in a row. And within one of the ovals Bobby glimpsed another shape. It was a face.

Bobby bolted upright, hitting the back of his head against the tree. Addison was right; there had been another plane. And someone in the plane had been staring right at him.

Muddy water of the Méanmaél churned past as the tree kangaroo made its way along the river's bank. It emerged from the brush and stopped before eleven small mounds of soil and plant material arranged in two parallel rows. One row contained five, conspicuously missing the one mound that would balance the two rows. The mbolop relaxed its forelimbs, releasing a collection of sticks, bark, and leaves onto the ground. A second tree kangaroo appeared beside it and dropped a similar collection. And soon a third joined them, adding more collected items. The creatures pushed the loose pieces together, arranging them into a mound that completed two rows of six. The other two kangaroos hopped to the water's edge, pushed their snouts under the surface for a moment, and then returned and let fly streams of water from their mouths onto one of the mounds. They returned to the river repeatedly to do this for the other eleven mounds. The first kangaroo, known now to the newcomers as Mbaiso, dug into its belly and pulled free a chunk of its own flesh. This it dropped onto one of the mounds. It methodically moved to each mound and did the same thing.

Finally, the tree kangaroos sat back and stared at the mounds. While the other two sat perfectly still, Mbaiso fidgeted. It understood the need for the task at hand, to periodically replenish the local *Aiyal,* the creature Samuel called a bandicoot. But Mbaiso's thoughts were engaged with other matters. The new visitors were turning out to be surprisingly diverse, each of them revealing exclusive behaviors and abilities. This made it difficult to generate predictions. Any one of them could alter the course of events in so many ways, making for a most interesting and volatile situation.

The younger one called Bobby was proving to show some promise. Perhaps it would be allowable to push him in directions that could reveal more of his potential.

Mbaiso signaled for the other tree kangaroos to follow, and they left behind the twelve mounds, which were just beginning to change their shape.

CHAPTER TWELVE

SAMUEL LED Quentin to another tree house, and they climbed a rope ladder. Quentin removed his hiking shoes this time, and the climb was easier although this hut was even higher than where they had slept. Waiting for them there were two Papuan men Quentin had not seen before. One had multiple coils of white objects strung around his neck, making a wide collar that covered his shoulders and upper chest. The other had only a few strands of cord around his neck, with dark objects hanging from them. But in his hair were dozens of white cockatoo feathers, sticking out in all directions, similar to the green feathers worn by Sinanie. Both men wore short, functional penis gourds that were intricately painted or carved.

After appraising Quentin's appearance, the men began questioning him. The questions came rapidly, and some of them seemed irrelevant to Quentin. Surprisingly, Samuel did not seem to have full command of the tribe's language. He would hesitate often, apparently querying the tribesmen to decipher their meaning. In Quentin's opinion, this was a strike against the credibility of his claim of living with these Papuans for a hundred and fifty years.

"*Gu laleo lai-ati-bo-dakhu. Lele-mbol-e-kho-lo?*" the men asked for the third time. By now Quentin knew what it meant: "How are you coming to us, as a man or a spirit?" He had already told them he was a regular, living man.

"They believe your son, Addison, to have risen from the world of the dead," Samuel said. "And they surmise, therefore, that you are, one and all, spirits."

"Addison was cured by their medicine. They're the ones who gave it to him. Why would they think he has come from the dead?" Even as he said this, Quentin remembered that Addison himself had said he had been to the place of the dead.

"Sinanie applied the ointment as a kindness to your wife, who was distraught over your son's death. They believe the boy was already dead at the time."

Quentin eyed Samuel. "Do you believe that?"

"I have seen many things I once believed impossible. But notwithstanding my opinion, I fear they believe you are a spirit, Quentin. Perhaps no amount of arguing will convince them otherwise. It might benefit you to simply concede."

"Will it help us get to civilization if I'm a spirit? If so, then fine, I'm a spirit. We're all fucking spirits." So far Quentin hadn't given a single answer that seemed satisfactory to them.

They asked if Quentin had come because of the Lamotelokhai. Samuel explained that the Lamotelokhai was the source of the ointment. Quentin answered that he had no previous knowledge of the stuff. They asked if he were the creator of the Lamotelokhai. Quentin told them no, he had no idea what it was or where it came from.

The questions continued, and Samuel translated.

"What message from our ancestors have you brought us?"

Quentin repeated that he was a real man, and had no message for anyone.

"You have brought hurt with you. Did you come to kill us?"

Samuel explained that shortly before the plane crash, one of the Papuans had been hurt and another killed.

Quentin said he knew nothing about that, and he meant them no harm.

"Can you be killed?"

Quentin answered yes.

"When we kill you, will the world end?" Samuel explained that the end of the world was a concept deeply rooted in their belief system. They believed this event to be inevitable.

Quentin said, "Are they waiting to kill us because they think it might end the world?"

"Quite the contrary," Samuel said. "The one man who will end their world is the same man they will most definitely allow to live."

Quentin shook his head at this illogical answer. "Help me out here, Samuel. How can I convince them to let us leave?"

"I believe there are two ways that you may be safe. The first would require you to be the very man they believe will someday come, the man who would end their world. I doubt that to be the case. The second would require you to remain here, as I have. And there are ample doubts regarding that, considering the size of your party."

Quentin felt panic beginning to well up from his center. "Then we'll find our way out of here on our own. We won't tell anyone about this village."

Samuel shook his head, frowning. "They would not run such a risk. Surely you can see that. Consider the great lengths they have taken to remain concealed."

Apparently they would have to escape without the Papuans' knowledge. This seemed impossible, but again Quentin began running assorted scenarios through his mind.

The questions continued. The Papuans wanted to know if they themselves would now grow old. They wanted to know if more spirits would come. And they wanted to know if Quentin was an ancestor of Peter.

Samuel explained. "Peter was a poor fellow who ventured up the river perhaps half a century ago. He was a brave man, whom the indigenes spared for a short time before ultimately deciding his fate." Samuel shifted uneasily.

"I thought you said we were the first ones allowed to come to this village besides you."

"I was reluctant to discuss Peter. His was an unfortunate circumstance."

"What happened to him?"

The Papuans addressed Samuel before he could answer. Samuel frowned, and as they talked, he became increasingly distressed. Were they debating killing them? Quentin eyed the opening in the floor and considered making a run for it. But he would never get Lindsey and the kids safely down from the tree house and out of the village if the Papuans truly meant them harm. He was at their mercy.

As they talked, Quentin focused on an object hanging from the white-feathered man's neck. It was familiar. It was a carved animal, similar to the one he had found the day of the crash. Though he was uncertain of what effect the action might have, he pulled the figurine from his pocket and held it out to them. "I found this. I think it might be yours."

The Papuan men stared at the figurine and made no move to accept it.

Samuel's voice grew tighter than before. "Quentin, I do not know how you obtained that, but it will not—"

"*Nu lefaf! Yu be-khomilo-n-din-da. Ya nokhu wola-maman-é. Nokhu solditai imoné khomilo.*" The white-feathered man spoke with such force that Samuel became quiet.[27]

Samuel turned to Quentin. "This council is concluded. We must now go."

BOBBY TRIED, but he could pull no more detail from his memory of the other airplane. It had happened so fast. And he seemed to have fainted or blacked out at the time. Was the other plane the cause of their crash? Bobby was pretty sure a mid-air collision would do more than just cause an engine to leak and then catch fire. It didn't make sense. He rose to his feet to return to the tree house before Mrs. Darnell blew a circuit. There was movement in a nearby patch of saplings. Bobby saw two brown eyes gazing at him from the brush.

"Mbaiso! Where've you been, boy?" He held out his hand.

The tree kangaroo stayed put. Then out of the brush came a second tree kangaroo, which Bobby recognized as the true Mbaiso. "Whoa, you brought a friend?"

Mbaiso hopped to his hand and sniffed it. Bobby tried petting his head like he would a dog, but Mbaiso ducked to the side. Suddenly there was a third tree kangaroo. The two newcomers sat a few feet away, watching him. Bobby settled onto the ground and crossed his legs, face to face with Mbaiso. "I know you can talk. Can your friends talk too?"

Mbaiso scratched an ear with his hind leg.

"Parrots can talk, but they don't know what they're talking about. But you do, don't you? If I could just understand, maybe you'd tell me what the hell's going on here."

Mbaiso settled back on his haunches. His two companions moved a little closer.

"Can you teach me?" Bobby moved his hands in a nonsense attempt at sign language.

Mbaiso cocked his head, watching Bobby's hands. And then he began moving his front paws. The movements were controlled and definite.

"How'd you learn to do that?" Bobby tried repeating Mbaiso's signs. Because of the shape of the creature's hands, there were no finger movements. The memory of the sequence ran through his mind on demand, and he simply copied it. It was easy.

They continued this way—Mbaiso showing, Bobby repeating. The new kangaroos moved closer until they sat just behind Mbaiso.

Bobby finally dropped his hands. "I have no idea what you're saying."

Mbaiso tried again, but Bobby just shrugged. Mbaiso's forepaws began digging into the fur on his belly, as if scratching an itch. He scratched deeper. Bobby stared at the digging claws as they pushed their way through the skin. One paw disappeared. Bobby looked into Mbaiso's eyes, but the creature seemed unconcerned. Finally the paw appeared again, holding a wet lump of pink innards.

Bobby's voice was a whisper. "What did you do?"

Mbaiso held the lump of flesh out, and it quickly changed from pink to tan. Mbaiso held the stuff toward Bobby's face.

"What? What do you want me to..." But Bobby knew, and Mbaiso confirmed it by leaning forward and touching the lump of flesh to Bobby's mouth.

Not a good idea, Bobby told himself. But before he could talk himself out of it, he pinched it up from Mbaiso's paw and dropped it into his mouth. He chewed it a few times. It had the texture of gritty mud, with a bitter and metallic taste. Not what he expected from animal flesh. So he closed his eyes and swallowed.

"Okay, now what?"

QUENTIN DESCENDED THE ROPE LADDER, put on his shoes, and waited for Samuel.

"Your presence here has disturbed my indigene hosts more than I dared to believe," Samuel said when he reached the forest floor. "Tell me, Quentin, how is it you have come to possess an mbolop talisman?"

"I found it in the forest, in a bowerbird's nest. The day our plane went down."

"Your choice of occasion to produce this find is unfortunate. I wish that you would have consulted with me beforehand."

"I thought they might want it. So what do we do now?"

"It is not you and your party that concerns me so much now." Samuel seemed to struggle for the right words. "You must understand that these indigenes, as with other lower civilizations, have deeply-held beliefs that, although unrefined to us, guide them in their lives."

If Samuel was lying about his age, he was going to great and offensive lengths to be convincing. "That would be considered an old-fashioned attitude in my world," Quentin said.

Samuel raised his brows. "Would it?"

"We've come to realize that the people of unrefined cultures are just as intelligent as anyone else—more intelligent when it comes to some things."

Samuel seemed to contemplate this. Then he waved his hand dismissively. "Regardless of their inherent capabilities, uncivilized peoples subscribe to doctrines based upon their beliefs. This is true throughout the world. But here—here among the indigenes to which we are both now bound—there is a force at work. It is a force I can scarcely hope to understand after many years of study. Savage tribes of the world believe supernatural forces are at work in their daily living. Commonly these notions are simple and unwarranted. Our Papuan hosts, in contrast, believe in the supernatural because here it is real. I assure you of this. Whether the force is of nature, or from beyond the natural world, it is one of great magnitude. And so the indigenes' beliefs should not be ignored. Matiinuo, the elder with whom we have just met, has told me with the firmest conviction that he believes the world is coming finally to an end. Never before have I witnessed such passion in his words."

"But you know better," Quentin said. "You know the world isn't ending, so what difference does it make?"

Samuel held his gaze without answering.

"Don't tell me you believe him."

"Perhaps not. But if the people of this tribe decide that their world will end, then I fear not only for them, but for all the peoples of this world."

Samuel began walking, and Quentin followed.

"Why?" Quentin asked. "The substance you've found here will help people beyond anything I can imagine."

Samuel cleared his throat as if preparing to say something important. "Quentin, are you familiar with the consequences of introducing uncivilized peoples to the civilized world?"

This took Quentin aback. "There are few people who understand it better than I do."

Samuel gazed at him for a moment with raised brows. "Is that so?"

"My parents were anthropologists. They studied indigenous people here in New Guinea, and I know exactly what you're referring to. People know of poverty because they have learned about personal possessions and money. People know shame because they were shown clothing. They live in fear because they were given modern weapons."

Samuel nodded. "Consider the acts of missionaries. Their mission, so to speak, is to bring uncivilized peoples into the light of God and the civilized world. In doing so, such peoples are changed, never to be the same again. Some would argue this is for the savages' own good. But I have come to realize that this is good only if one accepts that the indigenous state is inherently bad. Do you understand?"

Perhaps Samuel's ideas were not so outdated. Quentin nodded. "As I said, better than most."

"Suppose that we turn the situation about. Suppose that we—you and I, and the civilized peoples of this world—are the poor subjects of the missionaries. Suppose that we live our lives in such a way that suits us quite well, praying to our Gods, adopting rules by which to live in harmony, improving ourselves with scientific pursuits. And we are most content with this existence. In fact, there are some of us who would sacrifice much to preserve it."

Quentin felt a tightness building in his throat. "You think the medicine you've discovered is meant to change us?"

Samuel nodded. "It is a gift."

"A gift from who? God? I thought you said God had nothing to do with this place."

"It is not a gift from God. God provides us with limits, and with humility. With the Lamotelokhai, there are no limits."

Quentin stared at him. "No limits?"

Samuel nodded, his face grim. "Quentin, you must never leave this place, even if the indigenes decide you are the one to do so."

THE SENSATION STARTED in Bobby's gut. It wasn't painful. It was more like the tingles you get when your foot falls asleep and then slowly wakes up. The sensation crept to his chest and up to his neck before he became frightened.

"What'd you give me?" he said to Mbaiso. The feeling entered his face, prickling his lips and warming his eyes. "What is it?" he nearly yelled.

As the feeling rose to his scalp, Bobby pressed his hands to his face. And then the wave of tingles stopped. He peeked through his fingers. The tree kangaroos were still there, watching him. Mbaiso raised one foreleg, moved it as if drawing the letter L in the air, and then repeated the action with the other foreleg, but like a reverse L.

This was a sign Mbaiso had shown him already. But this time, as the gesture ended Bobby saw something strange. The lines of Mbaiso's body melted away, and an image of the kangaroo pulled free from his own body, rose from the ground, and hung in the air just in front of Bobby. It happened quickly. Mbaiso's image floated there briefly, and then faded away.

"What the hell?"

Mbaiso signed again. Both arms moved at once, one of them drawing a letter L, the other drawing what looked more like a J with an extra coil at the bottom. Immediately Bobby saw another hallucination. This time one of the kangaroos behind Mbaiso popped up and floated before his face, then vanished. Suddenly it made sense. They were introducing themselves.

"No freakin' way!" With shaking hands, Bobby copied the two opposite Ls and pointed at Mbaiso. He made the other sign and pointed at the second kangaroo. Finally, he pointed at the third kangaroo and waited.

Mbaiso's forepaws drew another pair of signs in the air, this time a letter L and a circle with a squiggle through it. A likeness of the third tree kangaroo popped up and then vanished.

"I get it," Bobby whispered.

The kangaroo named *L and curly-J* hopped forward and made a new sign. It ended with the two paws together, as if praying, and then slowly moving them apart several inches. As soon as the paws stopped, another hallucination appeared. The tree kangaroo's likeness moved away from Bobby a few meters. The kangaroo repeated the sign, but separated his paws even farther. The creature's likeness hopped away again, but farther than before.

Bobby copied it, but he spread his hands apart until there was a foot of space between them. There was no hallucination, but all three of the kangaroos hopped away into the brush and stopped about ten meters out. On a hunch, Bobby made the gesture again, but this time he passed his hands over each other and reversed the direction of separation. The tree kangaroos obediently returned to him.

Bobby smiled. He was learning their language.

QUENTIN AND SAMUEL made their way around enormous sago and eucalyptus trees. The immense trees must have been why the Papuans had chosen this location for their village.

"Samuel, how did you end up in this place, anyway? If you started your life with these villagers as long ago as you say—what, back in eighteen sixty or something like that?"

"Eighteen hundred and sixty-eight, actually."

"If you started living with them then, how did you get here, to this location? There weren't many explorers who penetrated the interior back then."

"At that time their village was far to the north, near the port of Hollandia where I made my residence. I first encountered them on a collecting trip. An assistant of mine, Charles Newman, accompanied me. The young man had only recently arrived from London. We had chanced to hear stories of a place the local villagers rarely entered. They told us that those who visited there never returned. As a naturalist, this interested me. I gave no thought to their superstitions. I saw an opportunity to collect specimens rare even to the locals themselves. And so we set out to enter the region. With three of my boys, whom I employed to assist in collecting and carrying, Charles and I ventured inland, making our way along the river. We traveled six days, as we were instructed to. When we approached our destination all signs of mankind gave way to a pathless wilderness. The area appeared to be uninhabited."

"But it wasn't."

"Correct," Samuel said. "Upon entering the area, we encountered creatures that were most assuredly new to science. My assistant Charles shot several *aiyals*: bandicoots, which seemed to hold no fear of man. And then he shot a tree kangaroo. That is when our good fortune expired. We found ourselves surrounded by indigenous Papuans, quite unlike any I had seen before, who proved to be as dangerous as they were silent. Almost immediately, they murdered poor Charles. My boys tried to run but were stabbed to death without so much as a word spoken. I feared for my life and kneeled to them, determined on appearing agreeable.

"And then something astounding happened. The mbolop, which I was certain was shot dead by Charles, awoke, and it approached me as I kneeled in the mud waiting for my death. This may seem difficult to conceive, but sure as I attribute the death of my companions to the shooting of the mbolop, I also attribute my own survival to that very creature. The tribesmen I faced were much influenced by the tree kangaroos, as they are to this day."

"Which is why they make these figurines of them," Quentin said, pulling the troublesome object from his pocket. "I suppose I insulted them somehow by having one?"

"It is not that you insulted Matiinuo so much as you confused him. The talisman you hold once belonged to him. It is a possession that an Elder does not readily give up. But he did give it away, and soon after it was lost under the most unfortunate circumstances."

"What circumstances?"

Samuel hesitated. "I have told you of the poor fellow, Peter."

"Yes. Who exactly was Peter?"

Samuel sighed. "As I have said, Peter found his way to the village of my hosts, quite by accident. He was allowed to live for some time. The villagers held hopes that Peter could understand the Lamotelokhai. Matiinuo even gave him the mbolop talisman, a sign of the highest regard." Samuel looked at the ground. "Peter became a friend to me. But then he insisted on leaving the village."

"The Papuans killed him, didn't they?"

Samuel responded only with a blank stare.

"So they let you live, and you remained here for all these years? Why?"

Samuel leveled his gaze at Quentin. "I quickly learned that the indigenes possessed a substance with extraordinary medicinal qualities. When they shared it with me, I experienced the most pleasing advantages. As with Peter, they held hopes that I might understand the Lamotelokhai, and that I might communicate with it." With these last words, Samuel gave Quentin a guarded look. "You see, the indigenes will not themselves communicate with the Lamotelokhai. Long ago they determined that to do so results in misfortune and bereavement. But they do wait for a man to come who will assume the obligation of doing so. And to some extent I could. But evidently I was not the one they had been waiting for. I faced the dilemma of becoming useful to them or suffering the same fate as the others in my party. I had no more freedom to leave this tribe than you now do. Or that Peter did. I chose to be useful, and to devote my scientific efforts to ascertaining the potentials of the Lamotelokhai. For all the answers that I uncover, however, more questions are revealed. The Lamotelokhai is most mysterious, and very dangerous."

"What do you mean, dangerous?"

"In recent years, my questions concerning the substance's capabilities have become more earnest, and the results of my investigations more pervasive and treacherous. I have concluded that there will be, quite literally, no limits to the capabilities of the man who unlocks the particulars of its true nature."

"And you want to be that man. You're helping them hide this thing, aren't you?"

"You think me to be self-interested. But I know I am not that man. My indigene hosts believe a man will come who will converse with the Lamotelokhai in ways that I cannot, and will then take it from this place, essentially bringing their world to an end, or turning the world upside down, as they put it. They accept this as inevitable truth. I suspect that they believe *you* may be this man, which explains why you are alive at this moment. But I am not so convinced as they are. I mean no contempt, Quentin, but you and those in your party do not lead me to believe that society has progressed to such a state of civilization that the Lamotelokhai's properties would be utilized safely and sensibly."

Quentin regarded him. "You decided this after knowing us for two days?"

"As I said, I mean no contempt. When you have learned more of the Lamotelokhai, I trust you will agree that it should remain hidden from those who would suffer its temptations. So strongly do I hold this to be true that I convinced the tribe to migrate far inland to avoid inevitable encounters with civilized peoples. In the fifty years after my capture, I moved with my hosts to no less than four new home territories, each one more remote than before. At last we settled here, a place I was sure would not yield to strangers. Wandering souls of Papuan descent, yes. But for many years no civilized men, until Peter—and now your own party."

"But you must have known civilization was closing in on you, from all the planes flying over." Quentin recalled again that he still hadn't seen or heard a plane since the crash.

"I have indeed seen such things. A means of travel long anticipated by imaginative thinkers. But until now these vessels passed over us harmlessly."

Abruptly, Samuel stopped walking. He gazed into the forest ahead of them and then spoke loudly, "Noadi, *gu mbakha-lekhé wa-mol-mo?*"[28]

Quentin followed his gaze. Noadi, the Papuan who'd pierced Quentin's chest with his spear, stood in their path. Noadi approached them cautiously. He was not carrying his spear. Instead he held what appeared to be a cord strung with white teeth.

"Gu mbakha-lekhé wa-mol-mo, Noadi?" Samuel repeated.

"Nu if-e-kha misafi gup-tekhé fédo-p. Nokhu-yanop-tu." As he spoke, Noadi nodded at Quentin, and then at the string of teeth in his hands.[29]

Samuel frowned. "He would like for you to see something he has made. This is most unusual. It is rarely moved from its place of security."

Noadi stopped before Quentin, looking him squarely in the eye. He grinned broadly.

"Nokhu-yanop-tu," Noadi said. His singsong voice held no threat. He pulled the string of teeth open before Quentin and spoke rapidly. The cord was long, with perhaps two hundred teeth. The teeth were quite large, probably taken from crocodiles since no other large predators were found in New Guinea. At one end of the string the teeth were much larger, some of them ten centimeters in length—too large for even the most impressive crocodiles Quentin had seen. Noadi held the string of teeth closer, and Quentin saw that they were each etched with a picture. Intrigued, he moved closer and reached for the strand.

Samuel cleared his throat. "Quentin, I wouldn't..."

Noadi's eyes grew wide, but then he handed it over. *"Nokhu-yanop-tu."* Noadi sat on the ground and gestured for Quentin to sit across from him. As Quentin settled onto the ground, Samuel exchanged words with the Papuan.

"Noadi believes it is important to show this to you. I lived among these people for many years before I was allowed to see it."

Quentin looked closer. The level of detail of the etched images was astonishing. "What exactly is it?"

"It is an account of the history of the tribe. Each tooth shows an event of significance."

Noadi pointed to the larger teeth at one end of the cord and spoke rapidly. The first tooth showed three people in the forest. Beyond them was water, perhaps the ocean. They appeared to be hunting, carrying weapons and game. The image wrapped around the back of the tooth and Quentin lifted it to see underneath. The hunters were confronting a palm tree with a large bulge in the trunk.

Quentin looked at the next tooth. The image was unmistakable. It was a Papuan man, suspended against a background of stars. Quentin turned it over. There was the Earth, drawn in great detail, standing out prominently against the stars. The image even revealed continents, misshapen in the same pattern that Quentin remembered from his dream.

"The dream!" Quentin said.

"Indeed," Samuel said. "A consequence of the Lamotelokhai."

"I've never seen artistry like this, Samuel, not unless it was created with the help of microscopes and lasers. How do they do this?"

"These are a people of extraordinary patience, as they do not grow old. I have known Noadi to labor for eight years on the design of one tooth. The pictures represent hundreds of years of efforts, and the events they show occurred throughout thousands of years. I believe that the tribe discovered the Lamotelokhai on the northern shore of New Guinea ten thousand years ago, perhaps more."

"Ten thousand years? What evidence do you have of that?"

"It could be much more. But details I have assembled from their narratives suggest this. Also, observe the crocodilian teeth before you. Notice how the teeth decrease in size from one end to the other. It is not only a record of depicted events, but also a record of the species of crocodiles available to the artist. Such significant change requires many thousands of years."

Quentin's mind reeled. Papuans were thought to have traveled in boats to New Guinea at least forty thousand years ago, one of the oldest cultures isolated from the rest of the world. To think that this was a detailed pictorial history of such a span of time was beyond belief. If so, the value of the string of teeth before him would be immeasurable.

"I have scrupulously pieced together a scanty picture of historical events," Samuel said. "But these people are very shy, often unwilling to discuss matters at length, if at all. And the elder, Matiinuo, whom you have met, is the only tribesman living today who lived when they discovered the Lamotelokhai. Matiinuo is notoriously difficult to talk to."

Quentin stared at him. "You're not trying to tell me Matiinuo is ten thousand years old."

"No," Samuel replied. "Most likely much older. Ten thousand is only a moderate guess." He returned Quentin's gaze without faltering.

"Jesus Christ," Quentin muttered. He looked more closely at the teeth. There were depictions of hunting and fishing, and what might have been a marriage ritual. One image near the beginning of the string caught Quentin's eye. It showed a frightening creature that resembled a man, but with longer arms and a stooped posture. In one hand the creature held what appeared to be a human head, and the ground around it was littered with bodies. Gazing at the tiny scene, Quentin felt a chill.

He pointed at the creature. "What is this thing?"

Noadi simply stared at the tooth grimly, but Samuel said, "That tooth depicts an event that has shaped the villagers' beliefs regarding the Lamotelokhai. The powers of the Lamotelokhai intoxicated one of their tribe. He apparently ran amok, madly killing fellow tribesmen before being destroyed. It was this event which induced the indigenes to never again communicate directly with the Lamotelokhai." Samuel touched the next tooth on the string. "And which induced them to employ the mbolop in communicating with the substance."

Quentin looked closely. The tooth showed a villager engaged in a sign language conversation with a tree kangaroo.

Near the middle of the string was a scene of the ocean shoreline, with jungle and water. Men in canoes were on the beach. He turned the tooth over and saw that the boat people were being killed by Papuans with spears. Beyond this tooth were more images of battle, each with bodies on the ground, killed by tribesmen with spears. Quentin glanced from tooth to tooth. The second half of the string contained dozens of scenes of killing. Scattered among them were pictures of such activities as building tree houses and hunting. Quentin was witnessing an account of the populating of the island of New Guinea over the centuries, reflected by increasing encounters with outsiders.

Quentin looked at Noadi, who grinned back at him. "Which of these pictures did you make, Noadi? Samuel, can you ask him that?"

"There is no need," Samuel said. "Noadi created them all. He has witnessed all the events shown, but for the first ones. Matiinuo described the first encounter with the Lamotelokhai to him. Noadi is nearly as old as Matiinuo, as are other members of this tribe."

The string of teeth was the most stunning artistic achievement Quentin had ever seen, and it looked oddly out of place lying in the leaf litter and mud. "Why have you shown me this?"

"An excellent question," Samuel said. He exchanged words with Noadi.

The Papuan pointed at the teeth, running his finger from one end to the other, and then jabbing at the last few. "*Nokhu-yanop-tu. Wolakholol lembu-té-n-da.*" He then pointed at Quentin. "*Yu nggulun. Yu manop. Gu di mbolombolop.*"[30]

"Most distressing," Samuel said. "It appears that Matiinuo's dismal view of the tribe's fate is shared by Noadi, and probably the rest of the tribe. He would like you to know that his people have lived an existence worthy of respect, or perhaps reverence."

"*Nokhu-yanop-tu,*" Noadi repeated, pointing to the last few teeth on the string.

Quentin looked. There was a scene with men wearing clothing. One of them lay dead on the ground. The other kneeled with his hands up. Quentin turned over the tooth. A tree kangaroo sat between the kneeling man and his attackers. "This is you, isn't it?"

Samuel nodded, his face grim.

The next tooth showed a man who was plainly Samuel, no longer fully clothed, but wearing his unmistakable vest. He was pointing to what looked like a fallen tree with numerous holes in it. There were several small animals in the scene as well.

The second to the last tooth showed another clothed man. He was on his knees, a spear protruding from his body, facing his attackers. Quentin presumed this was Peter.

The last tooth was unfinished, an image only roughly outlined and not yet etched into the surface. But there was no doubt what it was—the fuselage of the Twin Otter, twisted and on its side. Beside it stood several people, with more lying on the ground.

"*Maf lebil lefu-manda*," Noadi said. From his pouch he pulled out another tooth and held it out to Quentin.[31]

"Curious," Samuel said. "Noadi says that this tooth will be the last."

Quentin accepted the tooth from the child-like hand. Unlike the image of the plane, this one was detailed, etched into the surface as if it were completed long ago. Quentin stared at it. He turned it over. It was the same on both sides—nothing but stars. He held the tooth up to Samuel. "What does it mean?"

Samuel frowned at the tooth. "It is all that they believe will soon remain. After the world is turned upside down."

CHAPTER THIRTEEN

Mʙᴀɪsᴏ sɪɢɴᴇᴅ, drawing a T in the air with a curl at one end. Bobby promptly saw a vision of a tree kangaroo scampering up a tree and then a rope ladder falling and hanging there, ready to be climbed. The vision faded. Mbaiso signed again, followed by another vision, this time a tree kangaroo bouncing on a wet branch, releasing a shower of rainwater.

And so it continued. The pace of the lesson picked up, until Bobby thought his brain might boil over. At first, the signs had mostly to do with things the tree kangaroos did to help people. But soon the lesson shifted to human actions such as climbing, making things, and even killing. There were signs for objects such as spears, rope, and carving tools. And there were plants and animals that Bobby had never seen before. When Mbaiso paused the rapid-fire lesson, Bobby easily recalled everything he had learned.

"If we ever get home, school is going to be a breeze from now on," he said aloud.

Suddenly the kangaroos sat up straight and twitched their ears.

Bobby looked around, but saw nothing. "What is it, guys?"

The two newer kangaroos scurried off, leaving Mbaiso and

Bobby alone. Mbaiso signed, and a matching vision appeared: something moving through the trees. Mbaiso kept signing and the vision changed. A body—a Papuan—lay in the mud. The body was mangled, but it suddenly opened its eyes, sat up, and then struggled to its feet, a twisted, broken man standing before him. Then the vision vanished.

Bobby looked at the trees around him. He whispered, "What are you trying to tell me?"

"Maybe it's telling you I am here."

Bobby jerked around. "Addison. I didn't see you."

Addison's black eyes did not blink as he moved closer.

Bobby stepped back. "Why'd you leave the tree house? Your dad will be back soon."

Addison stopped just in front of him but didn't speak. His silence was unnerving.

"Why did you scare Carlos like that?" Bobby said.

"I wanted him to remember."

"I remember the other airplane now, like you said. Is that what you mean?"

Addison actually blinked. "Did you see what he saw?"

"What who saw?"

Addison looked confused for a moment, and then he said, "The boy, Addison."

Bobby frowned. "I saw the other plane. I even saw people in it."

"Yes, people," Addison said. "Do you know who?"

Bobby frowned even more and didn't answer.

"You don't remember. Keep trying, then you'll see." Addison turned to walk away.

"Addison, did you die? Back at the airplane?"

Addison stopped and turned around.

"I can talk to the tree kangaroos now," Bobby said. "Mbaiso showed me this dead guy that got up, and then you showed up. And the Papuans, they tried to bury you. And you said so yourself. You said you went to the place of the dead. What happened to you?"

Addison approached until he was close enough to touch. Bobby braced himself for a bad odor, but all he smelled was wet soil and humid air. He whispered, "Are you still Addison?"

The dark eyes stared through him. "I know about Addison."

Bobby wanted to step back, but he held his ground. "What does that mean?"

Addison held up his hands, looking at the palms. "I am someone else, too. He is Ahea. I have his memories."

"How can that be?"

Addison rubbed one hand on the other, like there might be something hidden under the surface. "I don't know. But I will find out." He turned away again. "You should go to it, too. You can listen to it. The others won't know how."

Bobby moved to catch up with him. "Listen to what? I don't know—"

Mbaiso jumped in front of them. He bleated, almost like a sheep, a sound Bobby had not yet heard him make. Both boys stopped walking. Then Mbaiso signed with his tiny arms. The movements came so fast that Bobby could not follow them. He saw visions, but they were quickly swept away by new ones. There was the lump of stuff in a tree—the Lamotelokhai—and tree kangaroos near it. They were touching it, maybe talking to it.

Suddenly Addison shouted, "*Ané kha-fén! Nokhu ima-fon khüp Lamotelokhai!* I will see it myself." Mbaiso didn't move. Addison lunged at him. Mbaiso jumped, but Addison caught his tail. Before Bobby had a chance to stop him, Addison lifted Mbaiso with both hands and swung him over his head. Mbaiso bleated once more before Addison smashed him to the ground. The kangaroo bounced, rolled over, and was still.[32]

Bobby's skin prickled. Static filled his ears like a TV signal suddenly cut off. He stared at Mbaiso's broken body. "You bastard!" he cried. "Why'd you do that?"

"It made me mad," was all Addison said. And then he walked away.

Bobby ran in front of him and shoved his chest as hard as he could. "He didn't do anything to you! What's wrong with you?"

Addison threw himself at Bobby, driving him to the ground. Bobby tried punching at the face above him, but Addison grabbed his wrists. His grip was too tight to pull free, so tight that Bobby yelled from the pain. Addison stared down at him.

Bobby's anger turned to fear. "Let go, Addison! Really, it hurts!"

Addison didn't budge.

Bobby tried to think. "I need to help Mbaiso. You might have killed him."

Addison's faced changed a little, into what might have been a smile. "Killed doesn't mean anything anymore. You know that."

"You smashed him—hard."

"He made me mad. Now you're making me mad. The mbolop isn't dead."

Bobby turned his head to look at Mbaiso. "He looks dead."

"The mbolop doesn't die. I know, because Ahea knows." Addison's grip grew even tighter, and gray veins appeared through the skin of his forehead. "The other airplane, Bobby—remember, or I'll make you!"

Bobby tried to turn onto his side so he could push himself up. But it was no use. "Okay, will you let me up if I try? I want to help Mbaiso."

Addison was silent, waiting.

Bobby squeezed his eyes shut. And then he was back in the plane again. *Mr. Darnell was talking to them. "That'll give you guys a chance to get it straight," he said. Bobby smiled at this and stared out the window. And then his vision started to blur. There was some-*

thing there. For a moment he saw only shapes and surfaces. Then the other plane moved away. He saw the wing, and windows in a row, with shapes beyond them. And then the plane was gone.

Bobby couldn't remember anything more. It had happened too fast. He opened his eyes. "I saw the plane, Addison. People were on it. That's all I remember. Now let me up."

Addison's face changed. At first Bobby thought he was going to laugh. But the grin grew larger, until it looked like his cheeks might split open. Addison's breathing was wet and loud, and his tightened mouth trembled. Bobby pushed against him, trying to back away, but the ground held him in place.

"*Nu khén-telo! Gekhené pesua im-le!*" Addison's voice was shrill. "I'll make you remember!" Addison let go of his wrists and grabbed Bobby's face. He yanked Bobby's head from the ground until it was inches from his own.[33]

Bobby struggled. He struck Addison's face, but Addison didn't even flinch. Finally he stopped fighting. "Okay, I'm trying!" He could feel Addison's wet breath, and he held his eyes shut so he wouldn't have to see him. He tried slowing the memory down.

He was on the plane. His vision faded, and he saw the shapes. The other plane was so close that he could have touched it if he could have reached through the window. Bobby slowed the memory down, almost to a stop. *The plane slowly moved away—the windows on the side—the shapes beyond them. The shapes were dark, except for the last one, near the rear of the plane. The shape was a person's head. It was lighter than the others because it was turned to the window, looking out. The face seemed familiar.*

Bobby paused the memory and strained for more detail. Suddenly he recognized the face. There was no mistaking it. It was Addison, looking back at him with wide eyes.

Bobby snapped his eyes open. "What the hell? What the hell Addison?"

"What did you see?"

"There was someone on the other airplane. He looked like you."

Addison let go of Bobby and rolled off to the side. Bobby jumped to his feet, but all he could think about now was what he'd seen. "How the hell could you be on two planes at once?"

Addison rose to his feet. "I am going to the Lamotelokhai. You should too."

Bobby watched him go until Addison's form was lost in the trees. He rubbed his ears where Addison had held him. He knelt by Mbaiso, afraid he might find spilled intestines. But Mbaiso was in one piece. Bobby rolled him over. "Oh shit. You poor guy."

Mbaiso's face was the wrong shape. It was flat on one side, and the eye was popped most of the way out of its socket. Tears welled up in Bobby's eyes, blurring Mbaiso's shape even more. He put his hand on the kangaroo's chest to feel for signs of life. Something inside moved. Bobby jerked his hand away, and then put it back. There was something. Not breathing, exactly, but solid things moving inside. As he stared, Mbaiso's head changed. The flattened side slowly took shape again, and the popped eye pulled back into its socket. Bobby rolled back on his heels, watching in wonder as Mbaiso put himself back together.

After what seemed like an hour, Mbaiso's chest began to rise and fall.

"I knew you could do it!" Bobby said aloud.

Mbaiso's whole body stretched, like a cat waking from a nap. His head turned Bobby's way, his brown eyes bright with life. He rolled to his haunches and sat there as if nothing had happened. The tiny forehands began to make signs in the air.

Visions appeared to Bobby: Papuan faces that he didn't know, the Lamotelokhai in its tree, men running through the forest, disturbing scenes of men fighting—fighting to the death. Bobby closed his eyes, but the scenes were in his mind, and he couldn't hide from them. The visions kept coming. There was a Papuan man walking in the forest. The man changed and became Addison. Addison walked, looking into the trees, searching for something. Other Papuan's appeared. They carried heavy clubs. Without any warning they attacked Addison. They beat him, knocking him to the ground. They kept beating him, even when he was clearly dead. They didn't stop. The beating went on and on. The clubs smashed Addison's body until there was nothing left but a pulverized mix of leaves, soil, and blood on the ground.

Finally, the vision ended. Bobby stood there, shaken, in the middle of a dark forest full of perils he did not understand. He realized he was crying. "Why did you show me that?"

Mbaiso signed again, and one more vision appeared. As Bobby watched, a lump rose in his throat, one he could not swallow.

He saw the gory soil where Addison's body was pulverized. But it was not Papuan men standing over it. It was Bobby. And in his hand was a club, stained red.

CHAPTER FOURTEEN

Samuel stopped at the base of a large sago palm. "Perhaps, Quentin, you would care to see my own contributions to the welfare of my indigene hosts. I have not, after all, been idle for all these years."

Quentin said that he was interested, but he should return to Lindsey and the kids.

Samuel shrugged this off and pointed to the tree. "The sago palm provides sago paste, a staple food for the indigenes. To add to their worth, the fallen trunks of dead sago palms provide food and shelter for another important source of nourishment, the larva of Rhynchophorus, the Capricorn beetle. I have discovered that a simple combination of these two foods serves as nourishment of the most remarkable quality. You have eaten khosül yourself."

"You showed them how to mix sago paste and grubs. That's your contribution?"

There was some frustration in Samuel's frown. "Allow me to continue. Because Capricorn beetle larvae were difficult to gather, this food was limited. Collecting the larvae required perseverance, with comparatively small return for months of preparations and many hours of labor. Through my study of the Lamotelokhai, I was able to perfect an efficient system of cultivating Capricorn beetle larvae. And as well, I increased production by breeding more superlative individuals."

Quentin was curious. "More superlative?"

"Allow me to show you." Samuel placed his hands on the massive trunk and moved them over the overlapping palm fronds that covered it, feeling for something. "Ah!" he said. He pressed against the surface, and it split open as he forced his way into a hole that was slightly larger than his hand. His arm disappeared into the trunk to the elbow. "Ah!" he said again.

Samuel pulled his arm out. He held a large squirming creature. After a moment trying to comprehend what he was looking at, Quentin exhaled with surprise and disgust. It was a sago grub. But it was enormous. The gleaming black head was easily as big around as his thumb. The writhing white body was like a fat banana. As it squirmed, veins and organs shifted beneath the translucent skin. Samuel held it out to him, but Quentin made no move to take it.

"It is quite harmless, I assure you," Samuel said.

Quentin was content to observe without holding it. "Okay, I'm impressed. How did you make that? Selective breeding?"

Samuel smiled. "I had some help from the Lamotelokhai."

Quentin cautiously poked at the larva. "The object we've seen in our dreams made these?"

"In a manner of speaking. But under my direction." Samuel felt the tree again and found another spot where the bark seemed paper-thin. He pressed, forcing the bark inward, but not far enough to break it. "You see, here is another. There may be a hundred in this tree alone. Capricorn beetle larvae naturally feed upon the pith of dead sago palms. I have persuaded them to feed upon living sago trees. Likewise, I have persuaded the sago trees to provide sustenance for them, as well as a safe refuge in which they may live." He pointed to the gaping hole where he'd found the oversized grub. "If a hollow such as this one is left open, a female beetle will soon lay her eggs inside. The tree will then grow a protective covering over the hollow, leaving it practically invisible to hungry intruders. In time, the larvae grow as large as this one."

Quentin said, "Interspecies relationships like that take thousands, maybe millions, of years to develop."

"As I have said, I have not been idle. At the time that the indigenes took me in, they were but hunters and gatherers, expending much energy and time. It is true that they had domesticated a few game animals: the *soyabu*, which you have had the occasion to eat, and the *aiyal*, a species of bandicoot. And although not developed for eating, you know of the mbolop. But it was I who taught them the true cultivation of food."

Samuel gripped the grub with both hands. He wrenched the head off with a pop and tossed it away. The body still writhed in his hand as whitish fluid flowed from the open wound. He placed his mouth over the hole where the head used to be and squeezed the body, causing his cheeks to inflate with sago grub juices. He swallowed as if it were a shot of fine scotch. Again he held the grub out. Quentin simply shook his head, not trusting himself to speak.

Samuel then led him to a place where smaller trees grew close together, reminding Quentin of the nearly impenetrable area where their plane had crashed. Most striking, though, was that all the trees were flowering at the same time. Yellow, white, orange, and red blossoms splattered the foliage, and the sultry air was sweet with the smell of nectar. This was unusual, as rainforest trees typically flower at different times to better attract the attentions of a limited supply of pollinators. Countless insects swarmed among the flowers above them.

As they came to a stop, Quentin caught a stray thread of spider web with his face. He brushed at the strand, but it only grew tighter and did not break. He then grasped it with both hands and pulled until it finally broke. He'd used fishing line with less tensile strength than this.

Samuel was now several meters above him, climbing with the agility of a tree kangaroo. He snatched at something Quentin couldn't see and then descended to the ground using only one hand and his feet. Obviously proud, he held a wriggling creature aloft for Quentin to examine. Again Quentin was stunned. It was a spider with an abdomen the size of his fist. Its long legs flailed helplessly in the air.

"Another source of nourishment," Samuel said. "And much more." He grabbed the strand of silk trailing from the spider's abdomen, which was still connected to the web above them. "I have developed in these orb-weaving spiders characteristics that benefit the tribe, particularly the silk you see here. Woven together, this silk possesses immeasurable strength." He pulled down on the silk strand, and it grew tight but did not break.

Quentin looked closer at the silk. "This is how you made the rope-ladders. And your vest."

"Indeed." With his free hand Samuel fingered his vest. "This garment is nearly the last reminder of my former life."

"I wondered about that," Quentin said. "It doesn't seem very practical in this heat."

"There are certain needs that outweigh practicality. Keeping a few items to remind me of the man I once was, for example." He lifted the object that hung from a cord around his neck. "This serves a similar purpose. I was once a rather feeble being, with poor vision, among other imperfections. I required spectacles to see clearly what was just before my own face. Now I have no need for such contrivances."

Quentin had thought the object was simply a ball of twisted wire. Now he saw that it was shaped with great care—a beautifully crafted ornament made from a one hundred fifty year-old pair of eyeglasses.

"WHY DO I NEED A CLUB?" Bobby said. "Are you telling me I need to kill Addison?"

Mbaiso sat on his haunches without responding.

Bobby sighed. "I don't want to hurt anybody. I just want to go home."

He decided he'd had enough of the language visions for now. He considered looking for Mr. Darnell but had no idea where to start, and he definitely wasn't going after Addison. So his only option was to go back to the tree house.

Bobby was not afraid as he climbed the ladder. He figured if he fell, he probably wouldn't die anyway. Maybe he would never die. His eyes adjusted to the dim light as he entered the tree house, and he saw Ashley looking at him. Mrs. Darnell, Carlos, and Miranda were all sleeping.

"Welcome back, science boy," Ashley whispered as he sat beside her. "Addison left after you did. I wasn't sorry to see him go."

"Yeah, I ran into him." Bobby said no more about it, and he was glad she didn't ask. "And guess what," he said. "I can talk to Mbaiso now, and to his friends. They taught me."

Ashley tilted her head. "You take off for a few hours and come back knowing how to talk to the animals. You're kind of an interesting guy, Bobby."

Bobby felt his face flush.

"Good God—talk about crazy dreams." It was Miranda. She sat up, wiped her eyes and adjusted her strips of clothing. She touched Mrs. Darnell's forehead. "Mrs. D, you okay?"

Mrs. Darnell moaned, like she was trying to say something.

"She really needs the medicine," Bobby said. "I'll go find Samuel and Mr. Darnell."

Ashley rose to her feet. "Not alone. Not again. I'm going with you. Miranda, you and Carlos stay here in case Mrs. D wakes up."

Bobby shook Carlos awake. "We're going to find Mr. Darnell. Will you be okay here?"

Carlos looked around. "Where's Addison?"

"Still gone," Ashley said.

Carlos closed his eyes again. "If he's down there, I'm fine here."

Ashley looked at Bobby. "Lead the way."

SAMUEL RELEASED the spider and it climbed back up to its web. He and Quentin made their way out of the flowering trees, and the steady thrum of insect wings faded away.

"So the trees here are in flower to attract the insects," Quentin said. "And the insects feed the spiders. All of that so the spiders can give you silk thread?"

"The spider silk allows the tribe to construct their dwellings high in the trees," Samuel replied. "In addition, the spiders frequently are eaten by the villagers. I have yet to acquire a taste for them, myself."

"Samuel, nothing like this has been done before. No one has been able to make plants and animals evolve in a desired direction so quickly. You have to share what you've learned."

Samuel stopped walking. "Do you not understand what is before your own eyes? Tell me, Quentin, why do you think the dwellings of this village are high in the trees?"

"To hide from everyone, I know. But surely you don't—"

"And tell me, why have the plants been made to grow over the trails? Why have the villagers learned to harden their spears and cook with fires that produce no smoke? And why, Quentin, do you suppose that intruders, as a matter of tribal custom, have hitherto been killed?"

"I get it. You're hiding this thing, the Lamotelokhai. But you said the villagers believe I am the one who will bring this to an end. Maybe it's time."

"Perhaps they do believe that, but I intend to convince them otherwise. In their primitive state, and in their isolation, they can scarcely comprehend the consequences." Samuel took a deep breath, which seemed to relax him a bit. "There are things, Quentin, you do not yet know. For whatever purpose you are here, be it God's will or a simple accident, it will be better served if you know more of the discoveries which I have made." With that, he resumed walking.

"You said God has forsaken this place."

Samuel nodded. "One day he may reclaim it for his own."

Quentin considered this. "If God is responsible for what has happened to my family and students, then I have a few things to say to him."

After a short silence, Samuel replied, "As do I."

Before long they stopped at the base of an enormous rainbow eucalyptus tree. Samuel extracted a rope ladder that had been concealed by a fat vine growing adjacent to the tree's bark. "I invite you now to my own dwelling." Without waiting for an answer, he started climbing.

Like the other tree houses, Samuel's was virtually invisible from below. Upon reaching the top of the ladder, Quentin entered a now-familiar leafy slit in the floor. But aside from that, Samuel's hut was nothing like the others. The hut was larger and was held up by at least four attachments to the supporting tree, resulting in four conical points in the hut's roof. In one corner hung a sleeping hammock that appeared to be made of spider silk. But it was the bewildering array of other objects that captured Quentin's attention. Nearly every inch of the floor and walls held items made entirely from natural materials such as skins and sticks and bones. Many of the devices Quentin could not identify, but others were clearly made to resemble household items—framed artwork, a table and two chairs, and drinking cups. There were hundreds of items hanging from the ceiling: small leather bags mostly, tied at the top, with several plant seedlings growing from holes in the sides of each bag.

Quentin puffed, winded from the climb. "This isn't what I expected."

"The villagers are a simple people. Civilized contrivances are not important to them. As for myself, however, such things prevent me from going mad."

Quentin looked around the hut. "I'm not so sure it has worked."

Samuel had been fingering one of the hanging plants, but he stopped and eyed him. Quentin tried to look back without smiling, but failed.

Samuel finally returned a half-smile. "Humor. I have all but forgotten it. To be honest, that is a possibility that frequently haunts me. I have tried to put a definition to madness and have concluded that it is a product of what a man values most. A man who holds no great regard for his own safety is truly a mad man, and will not be long for this world. A man who holds no regard for the society in which he lives—or once lived—is mad as well. Tell me, Quentin, do you care enough about the state of civilization from whence you came to do what you must to preserve its virtues? Perhaps it is I who should ask you of your own madness."

"It was only a joke." The conversation trailed off, but Samuel's words simmered in the back of Quentin's mind. Quentin was aware of his own obsessive disdain for imposing the modern world upon indigenous cultures. After what had happened with his dad, how could he be otherwise? Yet Samuel was accusing him of having little regard for his own society, as if modern civilization were an unknowing, vulnerable, indigenous culture. Quentin had never looked at his own bloated, high-tech, melting-pot culture in such a way.

Samuel proceeded to show him some of the items in the hut.

There was a flute made from the strange skull of a bird called a hornbill, an inventive water dispenser constructed with the skin of a crocodile, and spools wound with various thicknesses of corded spider silk. When prompted by Samuel, Quentin could not break even the thinnest of these. As he looked around him, he realized that at any given moment, several large and spectacular butterflies were flying about the hut. Samuel must have put something in the hut to attract them. Overall, the hut gave Quentin the impression of a comfortable existence.

Quentin finally said, "I appreciate you showing me all of this, but I'm worried about Lindsey and the kids. Lindsey seemed pretty sick this morning."

"You need not be concerned," Samuel said. "We will apply ointment from the Lamotelokhai and she will be well." He went to a darkened corner and lifted a covering of sago fronds. He returned holding a golden object in each hand. One was a sphere the size of a baseball. The other was a delicate-looking sculpture of a butterfly. He handed the sphere to Quentin, who nearly dropped it. It had to weigh at least fifteen pounds.

"Is this gold? I didn't think there was gold in Papua."

"To my knowledge it is not found here naturally," Samuel said. "That is of my own manufacture, from materials scraped from the ground."

"You made gold?"

"It is a simple task if one understands the Lamotelokhai. No more difficult than the transformation of your flying vessel into the soil of the Earth so that it may nourish new flora to replace the trees it destroyed. But alas, objects of gold have no value here, and I have long since grown weary of their artistic worth."

"This ability could make you the richest man in the world."

"Not true, Quentin. If the Lamotelokhai were introduced to civilized society, then these items would hold no more value there than they do here."

Quentin had to admit there was logic to this. If people could create whatever they wanted, there would be nothing to want. Buying and selling would be obsolete. But then so would hunger, and sickness, and death. Before he could make this argument, Samuel went on.

"I once made many such things, but I have long ago returned them to the earth from whence they came. Instead I turned to more considerable pursuits."

Quentin held the heavy sphere out to him, and Samuel exchanged it for the butterfly, which was also shockingly heavy. "Such as breeding new animals and plants," Quentin said.

"Directing the biological process is far more difficult—and rewarding—than working with the simple elements of the earth. Are you fond of butterflies, Quentin?"

Quentin paused. "I guess so."

"Well, I am fond of all the insects of the world, but I have particular passion for butterflies. That," Samuel pointed to a large blue and black butterfly circling the room, "is a species new to science, as are the others you see here."

Quentin responded at once. "Maybe they were new to science a hundred fifty years ago, but now most all large butterflies have been identified."

"These are quite new, I assure you. I have created them myself."

Again, Quentin's curiosity was piqued. It was one thing to breed a sago grub or a spider to grow larger. It was a very different matter to develop a new *species*. As he looked at the butterflies, his eyes were drawn to a particularly large white one on the ceiling. The butterfly was clinging to a glimmering green chrysalis attached to a living vine that seemed to be part of the hut, and was stretching its wings for the first time. And there were dozens of other chrysalises on the ceiling, of different sizes and colors.

Samuel gestured to the ceiling. "You see, I amuse myself by

creating new butterflies. They emerge from their cocoons and fly about my hut. Rather pleasing, is it not?"

Quentin admitted that it was.

Samuel seemed as if he were about to say more, but hesitated. He studied Quentin, creases forming over his eyes. "I have brought you here for a purpose, and I have delayed it enough. I have said to you before, have I not, that the Lamotelokhai has no limits?"

Quentin took one last look at the gold butterfly and handed it back to him. "I assumed you were exaggerating."

"During my years here, I have carried out hundreds of experiments in order to discover the true nature of the Lamotelokhai. I have learned much. But in recent months I fear I may have engaged questions that should remain unanswered." Again Samuel paused. "My most recent experiments, I believe, may concern you and your party."

"In what way?"

"The timing of your arrival gives me reason to think it was not a mere coincidence." Samuel placed the two gold objects back in the corner. He returned carrying something wrapped in leather and laid it gently on the table. He glanced up at a mat of woven fibers hanging on the wall and adjusted the table to line it up with the mat. He pulled a cord that bound the package shut, and the leather fell open. It contained nothing more than a dull lump of clay. Samuel pressed on the clay, forcing it into an elongated mound stretching across the tabletop. He then stopped moving, his hands resting on the mound, the angle of his body hiding his face.

Perhaps a full minute passed, and Quentin began to wonder. "Everything alright?"

Samuel finally straightened up and turned. "Quentin, have you an object in your possession that is familiar to you? Perhaps the mbolop talisman?"

Quentin pulled the figurine from his pocket.

Samuel pointed with his foot to a spot on the floor. "If you could position yourself here."

Quentin obliged. This put him in line with the table and the mat hanging beyond it.

"And now," Samuel said, "throw the talisman at the shield. And please indulge me by throwing it with all the force you may muster."

Whether Samuel was crazy or not, Quentin was curious enough to comply. He pulled back and hurled the talisman. It hit the mat—twice. Two solid thumps. The sounds were only a split second apart, but there were clearly two of them.

Quentin stared, confused. The light in the hut was too dim to see what had happened.

"Go and see for yourself," Samuel said.

Quentin sidestepped the table and knelt below the mat. The talisman appeared to have broken. He picked up the pieces. "What the hell?" he said.

It was not broken at all. There were two of them, fully formed and identical.

***

Mbaiso was there when Bobby and Ashley reached the forest floor. The two new tree kangaroos emerged from the brush and stopped just behind Mbaiso, forming a triangle.

"They are so cute!" Ashley said. "Pretty quiet, though, for animals that talk."

"They don't talk with their mouths. They use their hands." Bobby couldn't think of a greeting, so he just made the signs for each of their names. The tree kangaroos didn't respond. He glanced at Ashley. "I'll ask them where Mr. Darnell and Samuel are." He tried several gestures he thought might render this question, including the one he had learned for Samuel.

This time Mbaiso responded by signing. A scene appeared in Bobby's mind. He was moving through the forest with the tree kangaroos hopping along the ground ahead.

"They want us to follow them," Bobby said. "Did you see the picture?"

She eyed him. "No idea what you're talking about."

The three tree kangaroos hopped away. Mbaiso turned to them, waiting.

"Of course," Ashley muttered.

Without knowing their destination, they followed. As they walked the silence became awkward, so Bobby spoke up. "We have a name for Mbaiso. We should name the others."

"Just ask their names if you can talk to them."

"They told me already, but I don't know how to say them. Here's what they are." Bobby went through the hand motions he had learned. Then he turned quizzically to Ashley.

She scrunched her mouth to one side. "Just call them Mbaiso Two and Mbaiso Three."

Bobby considered this. "Let's call them Tupela and Tripela." He had learned some of the pidgin language used in Wamena using his smartphone tablet. These were the words for "two" and "three." He pointed out to Ashley that Tupela looked to him like a female and had more bronze on her face, and that Tripela's eyes were darker.

After walking some minutes in silence, Ashley said, "How do you keep all the memories out of your head?"

Bobby knew what she meant. With his now-perfect memory, he couldn't stop reliving the events of the last few days. "I can't. What stuff do you remember most?"

"Mostly Lori and Brent, and things we did together."

"Your parents." It still threw Bobby off when she called them by their first names.

"When I was little we did more together," she said. "I was just remembering when we went to Branson. It was the best time ever."

"Your parents are still together then."

Ashley let out a grunt. "Yeah, still together. I guess it's good they are."

"Mine aren't," Bobby said.

Ashley stared ahead. "I know." Then she turned to him. "Do you think these Papuans will help us get home?"

"They haven't killed us, so they must be planning to help us, right?"

"Maybe they just don't have refrigerators to keep us fresh."

It took a moment for Bobby to get it. "Jesus, Ashley."

The tree kangaroos led them to an area of gigantic trees. Some of the trunks were huge, like redwoods, and the forest floor was darker in the shade of these giants.

Finally, Ashley stopped and called out, "Mr. Darnell! Samuel!"

The tree kangaroos stopped. Bobby tried signing again, but they didn't respond.

"Bobby, we're being watched," Ashley said, her voice low.

Bobby followed her gaze. Two Papuan tribesmen watched them from behind a tree. He looked around and saw more. He whispered, "They're all around us."

"We're looking for Samuel," Ashley called out. "Is he here?"

The Papuans watched them for a moment more, and then they stepped into full view. Bobby counted seven in all. His pulse quickened as they approached. The men formed a circle around them. Bobby had seen three of them before, the same three they had first met at the plane, including Sinanie with his green feathers.

Sinanie pointed to the tree kangaroos. "*Mbakha-leké mbolop?*"[34]

Bobby and Ashley glanced at each other. Mbaiso hopped closer and began signing, talking to the Papuans. Bobby watched the signs and another vision appeared in his mind. Inside the tree house of his dreams, a tree kangaroo crouched in front of the Lamotelokhai. The creature was signing as if trying to talk to it. Then the kangaroo vaporized into a wisp. The wisp swirled and grew larger. It became solid again, and it was no longer a kangaroo—it was Bobby. He watched himself place both hands against the Lamotelokhai. And then the vision vanished.

The Papuans chattered to each other, apparently excited about Mbaiso's message. One of them pointed his finger at Bobby. "*Yu nggulun!*"[35]

Bobby shrugged. "I don't understand."

"What the hell's happening?" Ashley said.

"I'm not sure. Mbaiso said something about me touching the thing in the tree."

Sinanie pointed to Bobby and waved for him to walk. He spoke rapidly, and Bobby heard the words, *yu nggulun*, again.

"I guess we're going to the tree," Bobby said.

"No, we're not," Ashley said. "We came to get medicine for Mrs. D."

The Papuans and tree kangaroos all seemed to be waiting. Bobby turned to Mbaiso and signed what he could to explain what Ashley had said. Mbaiso signed back. In Bobby's mind a vision appeared of Ashley and a Papuan man walking, and then the two were in the tree house, and the Papuan was giving medicine to Mrs. Darnell. The meaning was clear.

It took some arguing, but Ashley agreed. Bobby would go on with the others, and Ashley would go back with a man named Ansi. Ansi seemed to smile at everything. He wore a penis gourd with black painted patterns, and like the others he had a leather medicine pouch hanging from his neck. He was the first one Bobby had seen who wore paint on his face. A band of black ran across his eyes from one ear to the other. There was a white stripe above it, across his forehead, and one below it, across his nose. He reminded Bobby of a raccoon.

When Ashley and Ansi left, the tree kangaroo Bobby had named Tripela followed them. Bobby watched as they moved away, two humans and a kangaroo. *Which of these three doesn't belong,* he thought, smiling to himself.

The remaining Papuans formed a single file line, with Bobby at the middle, and they made their way toward what Bobby assumed would be the Lamotelokhai tree. Eventually the tree canopy became so dense that only a few slivers of sunlight made it through. Bobby kept an eye on the nearly solid ceiling above them, and soon he saw it—a darker area with no light passing through. But this tree house was not rectangular like the others. Instead it kept going, like a long tunnel. Walking beneath it, Bobby kept glancing up to see if it would end, but it didn't. Finally there was a larger shadow, a hut attached to the tunnel. As Bobby gazed at it, he ran into the back of the tribesman in front of him.

"Oh, sorry," he said. He realized the entire group had stopped.

"*Khofé mbakha mo-mba-té?*" The Papuan said.[36]

Bobby shrugged and apologized again. They were at the base of a great tree. Mbaiso scrambled up the trunk, and soon a rope ladder appeared from above. Bobby watched it fall, uncoiling in the air, and he thought of the wisp of smoke from his last vision. As the first Papuan climbed, Bobby inspected the huge trunk. In his dream, after the stars and running into the earth, Mbaiso had led him here to this very tree. The back of his neck began to tingle.

The Papuans motioned for him to climb next, and soon he stood in the tree house with Sinanie and the other tribesmen. Next to them was an opening in the wall where the hanging tunnel joined the hut. And it was not the only tunnel. Bobby counted five others. They all branched out from this room, like spokes from the hub of a wheel.

The men pointed to the tree growing through the hut's floor. Bobby scrutinized the bulge where the tree split at chest level. It was just as it had been in his dream—smooth and gray, like a lump of clay pressed around the tree.

The Papuans talked excitedly as Bobby stepped closer, but when he reached out for it they fell silent. His hand shook as he held it just above the surface. He didn't know why he should be afraid of it now, but he couldn't stop shaking, so he pressed his hand against it. It felt warm, and he could push his fingertips into it like mud. A tingly feeling started in his hand and moved up his arm, the same feeling he'd had upon swallowing the stuff from Mbaiso's gut. The sensation spread into his neck and face, up to his scalp. He closed his eyes to fight off the panic that had nearly overwhelmed him before.

And then something happened. Symbols appeared in his mind. They were symbols he recognized. He'd seen them artfully etched into the shafts of the Papuans' spears. But now, displayed the way they were, he recognized them from before that. He knew these symbols because he had worked with them for two years. His eyes sprang open, and the symbols were still there, plain as day.

Bobby now knew what the Lamotelokhai was.

CHAPTER FIFTEEN

QUENTIN EXAMINED THE TWO FIGURINES. They were identical in every way, even the smudges and flaws.

Samuel waited patiently for him to study the objects before speaking. "It would be difficult to provide an account of all events leading to my discovery of such a phenomenon. However, some explanation is needed." He grabbed one of the chairs and offered it to Quentin, and then sat in the other. "Imagine living in this place for all of the years that I have. It is true I have enjoyed more than a lifetime's worth of scientific pursuits. But there are times when I feel a great yearning to return to the life I once lived. I have told you of the murder of my fellow travelers, which was when I fell into the midst of my Papuan hosts. I remember the day as if it were only moments ago. But many days have passed since. Fifty-two thousand and five-hundred twenty-four, if you care to know."

Quentin tried to do the math in his head, but Samuel continued.

"That is all the days of your lifetime and threefold more, Quentin. Imagine it."

Quentin did, and it made him feel hollow.

"I once had a family. A mother and a father, and there was a dear woman, for whom I cared very much." Samuel's eyes flicked toward Quentin. "Her name was Lindsey, if you can imagine such a coincidence. Lindsey Ennis." He pronounced the name in a whisper, like he wasn't sure it would come out right. "We were to be married upon my return."

"I didn't know that," Quentin said quietly.

"I see her face every day, as if we had only just parted." Samuel shook his head. "She and my parents are all long since passed away, I imagine." He paused for a moment. "As I have studied the Lamotelokhai, I have uncovered surprising qualities. In fact, one might reasonably infer that it can be made to perform any task, no matter how improbable."

Quentin eyed the two statuettes. "I'm starting to see how you might think that."

"Recently I found myself in a particularly dreadful state of regret. In my troubled condition, I attempted a most irrational action."

"What action was that?"

"To employ the assistance of the Lamotelokhai in returning to my previous life."

Quentin waited for more explanation, but none came. "You mean to help you escape from here? To get back to your home in England?"

Samuel leveled his gaze at him. "Perhaps. But more precisely, to my *time.*"

Was Samuel trying to make a joke? He wasn't smiling, so Quentin said, "You're still here, so I guess it didn't work."

"Indeed. There are some pursuits that are not for men to follow. In my despair I strayed into such a pursuit. My actions have caused suffering."

"So you tried to go back in time—back to what, 1850?"

"I departed from England in the year of 1865."

"And it didn't work. What does that have to do with me, and with people suffering?"

Samuel rose from his chair and paced. "It is possible that the Lamotelokhai's only limits are those of the man seeking its truths. My challenge lies in my own capacity for conveying to the Lamotelokhai what it is that I seek."

Quentin thought of Samuel resting his hands on the substance before telling him to throw the talisman.

Samuel continued. "In my condition, I acted hastily, and the results were disastrous."

"What results?"

"That is exactly what I have been trying to find out. From my observations, I can conclude that upon my request, the Lamotelokhai influenced the passage of time."

Quentin began to speak, but Samuel held up his hand.

"I managed to duplicate the event under more controlled conditions, such as you have witnessed on the table here. Quentin, I have concluded that the second talisman could appear only if the passage of time were altered as the first flies over the table. That, in fact, is what I instructed the substance to do. But something unexpected happened. Rather than simply transporting objects in time as I'd hoped it would do for me, the substance appears to alter the progression of time in the space near it, in this case directly above the table. It is my opinion that when an object passes through such a space at sufficient speed, this *fuses* two moments in time into a single location of space. This would explain the duplication of a physical object."

Quentin stared in disbelief. He ran through the events in his mind. If a moving object, say a stone talisman, experienced a brief shift back in time, it would appear just behind the other version of itself. But if the present and past both existed over the table, was a chunk of space missing from the past? Or were both moments present there as well? If so, perhaps the two objects would continue to exist after passing over the table, and both would then hit the mat and drop to the floor, which is exactly what he had witnessed. Mystified, Quentin shook his head.

Samuel proceeded to demonstrate further. He produced a hunting arrow and broke it into two half-meter pieces. Like a small spear, he hurled one of the pieces over the table. It hit the mat, and two identical pieces fell to the floor. After Quentin inspected them, Samuel repeated this with the other half, only this time he gently lobbed it. Quentin watched the object's slow arch. As it passed over the table, a second piece appeared. But one of them fell short of the mat. Quentin picked them up. They were not identical. One was damaged at the tip. Not just splintered, but misshapen—boiled outward like a cauliflower.

Samuel explained, "When moving slowly, the copy of the object bringing up the rear is invariably damaged, whereas the one before is not. Very curious, would you not agree?"

"Yes, curious," Quentin whispered. He stared at the arrow's deformed tip. He had seen this before. The remains of the Twin Otter's nose and cockpit had been deformed in such a way. He had assumed it was caused by the crash. And then he remembered the pilot. As the poor man had struggled and died before Quentin's eyes, his feet appeared to have exploded from the inside. Quentin's hands suddenly felt clammy, and he had to steady himself.

He turned to Samuel. "You said when you first did this it caused suffering. When exactly was that?"

"I believe you know the answer, Quentin. Four days and nights have passed. It was the very day your flying vessel ran aground."

AFTER DESCENDING THE ROPE LADDER, Samuel led Quentin to an area where massive eucalyptus and strangler figs created an impenetrable canopy. Samuel located a rope ladder and climbed into the tangle above. Quentin followed and was soon standing in a room that appeared to be a bulge in a long, narrow tunnel. The hut was small, but there was a fire pit in the center as if it were a gathering place. No villagers were in sight.

Samuel led him out of the room, and they made their way along a hanging corridor. The tunnel was tall enough for them to walk upright, but Quentin had to stoop occasionally where the ceiling hung lower. It was difficult to see far ahead because the corridor twisted left and right before them, undoubtedly to line up with the varying tree limbs from which it hung. The floor of the tunnel bounced beneath their feet as they walked—a distasteful sensation considering the height. But the tunnel was an engineering triumph, and Quentin wondered how the villagers could have constructed it with their bare hands.

After they'd walked some distance, they came upon another room. Samuel signaled for Quentin to wait and then leaned into the room. He spoke gently, perhaps alerting the occupants that he was not alone. When Quentin stepped through the opening, three Papuans stood at the far end of the hut, but one of them quickly slipped out another opening there. It was hard to tell in the dim light, but the figure appeared to be female. If so, this was the first woman he had seen among these people. The two remaining men were strangers to Quentin. One of them, a small man with caked mud on his head resembling a solid bowl, pointed to the floor at their side.

"*Walukh, Joamba,*" the man said.[37]

Quentin turned to look. Sprawled there on a sleeping mat was a dark figure. The figure was alive; Quentin could hear it snoring. But something about it wasn't right. Quentin looked to Samuel for an explanation.

"That is Joamba," Samuel said. "Examine him closely, if you would."

Something about the situation told Quentin he would regret it, but he approached the still form. Wooden bowls of water and food were arranged around the mat. Joamba appeared to be lying on his side, facing the wall, but it was hard to tell. Quentin knelt where the man's head appeared to be. What he saw there confused him. The head and shoulders were disfigured, not even recognizable. Quentin wasn't sure what he was looking at. The thing then let out an agonized moan, but it came from the other end. Quentin turned to the sound. Suddenly his confusion turned to panic. The man was not facing the wall at all. Two eyes stared directly at him. But the eyes were not set in a face. Instead they bulged, lidless, from a mass of shapeless flesh. Quentin toppled backwards, involuntarily pushing himself directly into Samuel's legs.

"Joamba is no threat to you," Samuel said. "Surely you can see that."

Samuel was right. The poor thing could not possibly harm him. In fact, it barely had any arms. A few puffy fingers protruded from a mangled bulge, and one of them even twitched a few times. Quentin stared, unable to fathom how or why such a thing could be kept alive.

Samuel knelt next to Quentin and spoke softly. "Joamba was a skilled hunter. Like his fellow tribesmen, he insisted on hunting in the old ways, even though it is no longer needed."

Quentin turned to him. "A hunter? How is that possible?"

"He was as healthy and robust as any of us, until the event in question."

"The event."

"Recall the arrows thrown in my hut. One thrown hard, with no ill results but that there are now two. One thrown softly, with dreadful results to one of the arrows."

Quentin failed to see a connection. "But that was in your hut, over a table."

"That was but a demonstration within controlled conditions. There were no such controls for the initial event of four days past. I believe the effects of the event extended for miles. Any object, or beast, or human soul that was at rest at the time was not affected. But those that were moving about, such as birds and insects flying—"

"And airplanes," Quentin said.

"Indeed. Joamba and two of his companions were hunting at the time. In pursuit of a cassowary, his surviving companion told me. Making hasty chase at precisely the fateful moment."

Quentin considered Samuel's demonstration. "The talisman I threw—there were two of them after it passed over the table. Is that what happened to Joamba?"

"That possibility seems to be subject to the object's quickness. Recall the arrow you tossed lightly. I have concluded that a man could not run quickly enough to result in an undamaged duplicate. Instead, Joamba's duplicate is wretchedly merged with his own body. Joamba's other companion, Ahea, was not so lucky as this." Samuel's voice became a whisper. "There are conditions beyond even the power of the Lamotelokhai to heal. It is a rare thing indeed to have to dispose of a member of this tribe. It makes the tribesmen nervous."

Quentin looked at the horrifying form before him. How could Samuel call Joamba lucky? Surely death would be better than this.

As if to answer his thoughts, Samuel continued. "The medicinal effects of the Lamotelokhai have taken hold. We have but to wait for Joamba's complete recovery."

Quentin was skeptical. "You believe he's going to be normal again?"

"It is but a matter of time."

After a final look, Quentin rose and turned away from Joamba. He wrapped his arms around himself and tried to control his breathing. "Why did you bring me to see this?"

"I wish you to understand, Quentin, that the Lamotelokhai is as dangerous as it is miraculous. I am but one man, compassionate and educated in comparison to many others, even in civilized society. And yet in a moment of despair I have abused the powers I have discovered here, resulting in great suffering. Imagine what might happen if the Lamotelokhai were to be taken from this place and put in the hands of less reasonable men."

Samuel gripped Quentin's shoulders. "Whether or not you hold faith in God, you must surely see that men are better served by dreaming of an invisible God than to have the power of God placed into their own hands." Samuel seemed to realize he was touching Quentin, and he pulled away. "For many years it has been upon my shoulders to assist my indigene hosts in keeping their secret. But I fear that my recent actions have set into motion events that cannot now be undone, and the burden of this secret may no longer be my own."

Quentin studied him for a moment. "I don't think I can handle any more burdens."

"It is upon you, nevertheless." Samuel pointed to the tunnel opposite of where they had entered the room. "We are now very near to the Lamotelokhai itself. Perhaps if you were to confront the source of your consternation—to touch it with your own hands."

"I need to get back to Lindsey."

"Indeed. She will need healing ointments. I will show you how to gather them from the Lamotelokhai yourself, and you may take them to her." Samuel moved to the opening.

Quentin looked once more at the disfigured man lying at his feet. Guttural breathing pervaded the silence of the hut, but Quentin could not tell where the respiratory opening was. In fact, for a moment he was sure that the sounds came from both ends of the figure, as if it had two heads. Oddly, he was reluctant to leave, feeling that he should somehow offer comfort to this mass of flesh that was once Joamba, the skilled hunter.

But then Quentin heard another sound. Was it shouting? He turned to Samuel as the two villagers slipped into the tunnel and disappeared. They must have heard it, too. The sound came again. It was definitely shouting—angry shouting. "Samuel, what's going on?"

Samuel's seemed to be straining to hear, and he did not answer.

One of the distant voices screeched in anger or pain, and Quentin suppressed a cry. It was Addison.

QUENTIN PLUNGED INTO THE TUNNEL, Addison's distress calls pulling him forward with savage force. He was only vaguely aware of Samuel following him. Before long the tunnel gave way to another room, and Quentin entered. Addison stood in the center of the hut with his back against the Lamotelokhai, which was molded to a branching tree just as it had been in Quentin's dream. Papuan tribesmen wielding spears and clubs surrounded Addison. He was now naked, and fresh wounds covered his body. Nevertheless, he stood straight and defiant, and his previously stick-like limbs now looked more formidable. He stared down his attackers, his eyes dark with anger so palpable that it seemed to hold them back like a force field.

"Mr. Darnell, they're going to kill him!" It was Bobby. He stood across the room at the entrance to another tunnel.

"Bobby, what are you two doing here?" Without waiting for an answer, Quentin stepped forward and bellowed, "Hey! Leave him alone!" It was a standard teacher ploy, designed to break up fights. The Papuans hesitated.

Samuel entered the room, took in the scene, and stopped short.

"Samuel, help us," Quentin said.

One of the tribesmen pointed a club at Addison. *"Gu laléo-lu!"* Quentin recognized the white feathers in the man's hair. It was Matiinuo, the elder tribesman who had questioned him.[24]

Addison stood taller, his face such a frightening visage of hatred that Quentin barely recognized him. "*Nu be-khomilo-n-din-da,*" he said, his voice seething. "*Nu khén-telo!*"[38]

But there were six tribesmen closing in on Addison.

"For God's sake, Samuel, stop them," Quentin said. "He's my son."

Samuel shook his head. "On this point, you are wrong. Your son has already been taken from you. The indigenes know this to be true."

Quentin stared in disbelief. "Samuel, please!"

Samuel watched the tribesmen, avoiding Quentin's eyes. "I am but a guest here. I have little influence over Matiinuo."

The Papuans attacked. Their weapons blurred as they pummeled and punctured Addison's body and face. All that could be heard were grunts of effort and the sickening sounds of weapons striking flesh. Quentin moved in to stop the assault, but it felt as if he were moving in slow motion.

Suddenly Addison ripped Matiinuo's club from his grasp. With shocking speed he leapt upon the elder tribesman and drove him to the floor, his knee against the Papuan's chest. Addison's bloody, sinewy arms shoved the club into Matiinuo's neck, forcing a wet gurgle from his throat and rendering him helpless. The other tribesmen halted their onslaught and stood frozen in place. In the seconds that followed, the only sounds were Matiinuo's attempts to breathe. Quentin's eyes were drawn to Addison's ravaged face. A spear point had torn his forehead, leaving a strip of scalp dangling in front of one eye. His visible eye bored into the tribal elder.

"*Gekhené khup lefu. Gekhené wola-maman-é,*" Addison growled. "You don't know what it is." He leaned forward, putting all his weight onto the club. Matiinuo's eyes bulged.[39]

The others raised their weapons again, but Addison sprang from the elder's chest and darted into one of the tunnels. Matiinuo writhed on the floor, clutching his crushed throat. The Papuans gathered around to help him.

"Bobby, follow me!" Quentin skirted the tribesmen and entered the corridor where Addison had disappeared. With Bobby on his heels he charged ahead. After rounding two bends, Quentin called out, "Addison!" There was no answer. They rounded another bend and stopped. The tunnel ahead was straight for some fifty meters, but there was no sign of Addison.

A dark figure suddenly dropped from above and landed like an ape just in front of them. Addison then stood upright.

Quentin reached for him. "Son, you're hurt. We'll get you out of here now, and—"

"It doesn't matter," Addison said. With one hand he lifted the strip of scalp dangling before his eye and pressed it against his forehead. It stayed in place. Both eyes were now visible, and they turned to Bobby. "He knows what it is. He can talk to it, too." Addison pointed down the tunnel, toward his attackers. "It's not for them anymore."

"Addison, it's time to go," Quentin said. "We'll get the others and leave this village."

Addison moved toward them. "It doesn't matter!"

Quentin instinctively stepped back. The look in Addison's eyes —the same anger he had shown Matiinuo—was fearsome.

Addison said, "You know what it is, Bobby. They can't use it. It's a computer."

Quentin blinked at him. "What? A computer?"

"He's right," Bobby said. "We can talk to it, because it uses Kembalimo."

"Kembalimo? The game?"

Bobby shook his head. "It's not a game."

Quentin turned from one boy to the other, bewildered. The tribesmen were coming; their bird-like voices grew louder, and the hanging tunnel shuddered with their footsteps. They would surely kill Addison—perhaps kill them all.

"Let's go, now!" Quentin ordered. He started forward but Addison blocked the way.

"It is not for them," Addison said. "Their time is over." Then he leapt up, straight through a hole in the tunnel's roof.

Through the hole, Quentin saw Addison crouched on the tree limb that supported the tunnel. The tunnel shook as Addison launched himself into the air, out of view. Quentin moved to the side to see, and then gasped. Addison now hung from a limb at least six meters above them. With astonishing grace he swung to his feet and leapt out of sight.

Quentin stared, trying to comprehend what he had seen. Finally he turned back to Bobby, but it was too late to flee. Four tribesmen were upon them, their spears ready.

Samuel came up behind them. "It appears, Quentin, that the indigenes are correct in their notions of the being who was once your son."

As the tribesmen led them through the hanging passageway, Bobby's fear began to subside. After all, the Papuans hadn't killed them on the spot. They reentered the Lamotelokhai hut, and Matiinuo was still on the floor. Another tribesmen held his hands against the injured man's throat. Mr. Darnell asked if Matiinuo would be okay, and Samuel said that the Lamotelokhai would repair him.

Mr. Darnell grabbed Samuel by the shoulders. "What has happened to my son?"

"Sinanie has told me your son had been badly wounded when he found him," Samuel said. "As Sinanie put it, Addison's body did not yet know it, but his spirit had returned already to the land of your ancestors. Your son's body still lived, but his mind was beyond healing."

"But what about the man you showed me, Joamba? He was hurt far worse than Addison. Yet you seem to think the stuff will cure him."

"With one critical difference, Quentin. Joamba has been exposed to the Lamotelokhai before."

"What difference does that make?"

"Joamba is known to the Lamotelokhai, both his mind and his body. That which is known can be rebuilt. To a limited extent, I should say. Joamba's companion, Ahea, was beyond rebuilding."

Bobby spoke up. "Did you say Ahea? Addison said that name to me today. He said he had Ahea's memories, like he was two people."

Samuel frowned. "Ahea's memories?" He rubbed his chin, apparently puzzled.

As Samuel and Mr. Darnell continued discussing this, a tribesman nudged Bobby toward the Lamotelokhai. This time Bobby's hands were steady. He pressed against it, digging in with his fingers. Again the symbols appeared in his mind as if they were floating before his eyes. More than a hundred of them: rectangles and triangles, a three-dimensional tetrahedron, a hexagon, quadrilaterals. And there were irregular shapes: spirals, zigzags, loops. Bobby knew them all. Most recently, he realized, he had seen them painted on the Papuans' spears. But more importantly, they were the symbols of Kembalimo. He didn't count them, but he knew there would be a hundred and twenty-eight. That's how Kembalimo worked.

The symbols floated before Bobby, waiting. In his two years of playing Kembalimo, he had worked on only one lingo, and he was far beyond the initial sorting tasks. But now he remembered all of it, even the very first level. First you sort all hundred and twenty-eight symbols into piles based on how you think they are alike. The first level starts with sorting groups of four. Then you sort groups of eight, and then sixteen, and so on.

If he were starting a new Kembalimo lingo on his smartphone, Bobby would clear the screen and begin sorting. But here he wasn't sure how to do that. He put a hand out toward the symbols—nothing but air. On a gut feeling, he pretended to swipe them to the side. The symbols disappeared—all but four, hanging there, waiting to be sorted. He swept two of them into a pile. The two had round edges. The other two had corners, and he swept them to their own pile. The symbols disappeared, replaced by four more to be sorted.

Now there was no doubt. The Lamotelokhai was a computer, and it wanted him to start creating a Kembalimo lingo. Kembalimo was all about creating your own lingo to communicate with people who don't speak your language. The Lamotelokhai wanted him to learn to talk to it.

QUENTIN RETURNED ALONE to their tree house, easily remembering the way. Bobby's excitement over the Lamotelokhai had prompted the villagers to insist that Quentin leave him there to continue his work with it. Samuel assured him that Bobby was perfectly safe if Quentin wished to return to Lindsey. Although doubtful of this, Quentin felt that he had little choice.

Bobby apparently had discovered how to *talk* to the Lamotelokhai. Quentin had placed his own hands on the stuff, and was shocked to see a hallucination of objects appear before him. The objects did indeed resemble the symbols he had seen in Kembalimo, but he didn't play the game, so it made no sense to him. It seemed Samuel was wrong—it was not Quentin's capacity to communicate with the Lamotelokhai that the Papuans had been waiting for. It was Bobby's.

As he made his way back to the tree house Quentin called out for Addison but saw no sign of him. The rope ladder still dangled from the tree. He removed his boots and his hands and feet gripped the ladder as if he had been climbing it all his life. When he entered the hut, a Papuan tribesman with paint across his eyes stood between him and the others. The man smiled.

"We were starting to worry about you, Mr. D," Ashley said. "That's Ansi. He brought medicine. Addison got mad and left, and Bobby went with the Papuans. They're still gone."

"I've seen them both," Quentin said. He warily circled the villager to where Lindsey lay. Ashley, Miranda, and Carlos were at her side.

"She's been sleeping, but she looks better now," Miranda said.

Lindsey stirred as Quentin touched her face. Her skin was dry and cool. No fever. And she *did* look better. The insect bites and scrapes were all but gone. Even her hair seemed less tangled and matted. He spoke softly to her, but her eyes remained closed.

Quentin ate some khosül and drank from the water supply in the corner of the hut. He paced back and forth. He left the tree house again and made his way back to the Lamotelokhai tree, but he saw no sign of Addison. It was growing dark and starting to rain, so he returned to the tree house.

As the remaining light faded to emerald shadows, Quentin sat by the opening in the floor with his back to the others. He watched the rope ladder, hoping it would go tight. The weight of the entire day was upon him, and a sob rose to his throat, but he forced it back. The students were watching, and he could not break down now.

Quentin was pulled from his thoughts by a warm hand on his shoulder. He glanced up and saw that it was Lindsey. They gazed at each other, silent. The slightest smile appeared at the corners of her mouth.

She sat on the floor at his side. "I told you I didn't want their medicine."

"Yeah, well, it seems we don't have much say in what happens here."

Lindsey looked around the hut at each of the kids, at the tribesman called Ansi, and then at Quentin. Her smile faded. "Where's Addison? And Bobby?"

Quentin gazed through the entryway. "Bobby is safe. He's with Samuel and some of the villagers. It's a long story, but he's learning to talk to a lump of clay by playing Kembalimo."

"The thing from space," she said.

Quentin glanced at her. "You had the dream?"

"It was more than a dream."

Quentin was silent.

She put her hand on his. "Quentin, where is Addison?"

His eyes filled with tears. "I don't know. He was with me, and then he was gone."

She slid closer and laid her head against him. Her presence allowed him to finally let go, and his tears ran down his face to his chin and dropped through the hole in the floor.

CHAPTER SIXTEEN

Bobby made remarkable progress with the Lamotelokhai, partly because he recalled the choices he had previously made with Kembalimo on his smartphone. In almost no time he had sorted the symbols into groups, and then into a specific order. Once he had decided on the symbols' order, they were like numbers, and the next level was to solve hundreds of puzzles using the symbols. This way the rules of logic for his lingo were established. The next level beyond that was the hardest part—coming up with combinations of the 128 symbols to represent meanings. It was like creating a language using 128 numbers, and the logic of grouping them was completely different from a typical language. Once you got used to the process it was easier than learning any other language because it was based on rules you created yourself in the earlier stages. On his smartphone, Kembalimo would show him pictures, and he would group symbols together to have those meanings. But with the Lamotelokhai, instead of pictures on a screen, there were visions in his head, and sounds—even feelings. It was easy.

Samuel and the Papuans had silently watched him until after dark. Finally, Samuel approached Bobby.

"I must say I am mystified by your apparent knack for utilizing the same symbols that I have floundered with for many years."

"It's just Kembalimo," Bobby said. "I was already pretty good at it." He glanced at Samuel's perplexed expression. "It's a language program. It's made to be like a game, so lots of people like it."

Samuel looked no less confused. "How could it be that this Kembalimo involves the same symbols?"

Bobby shrugged. "You'd have to ask Peter Wooley that."

Samuel suddenly stiffened. "Did you say the name Peter Wooley, sir?"

"He's the guy that invented Kembalimo. He's famous."

Samuel's face went pale, and Bobby was tempted to take a step back.

"It cannot be," Samuel half-whispered. "Peter was killed before my eyes. He was beaten beyond hope of repair."

"Maybe that was a different Peter Wooley," Bobby offered. "The guy I'm talking about is alive and well. He's really rich and he lives in Australia."

Samuel looked at the floor and shook his head, like he was dismissing this. "But the symbols," he said. He furrowed his brows and fingered his vest. Slowly his face regained its color, and he seemed to relax. One edge of his mouth turned up slightly, as if he were pleased with something very personal. "How extraordinary," he said.

Bobby shifted back and forth and nodded toward the peculiar mass beside him. "Do you mind if I..."

"Yes, do continue," Samuel said. He then turned away, apparently still deep in thought.

Several hours later they walked Bobby back to the tree house. A man named Tengorros was staying there, along with Ansi. Samuel said this was for their protection, but Bobby suspected it was to stop them from leaving.

Mr. and Mrs. Darnell wanted to know what he had learned.

He tried to explain but found this to be more frustrating than actually working with the Lamotelokhai. So he told them he had a headache, which wasn't true. In the darkness of the tree house, he watched the two villagers' silhouettes as they whispered to each other. Eventually they stopped talking, and Bobby was the last one awake, feeling very alone with his thoughts. The rain had stopped, and the only sounds were trilling insects and tree frogs.

THE STARS WERE the only constant in an otherwise fluid setting. Everything around the tree kangaroo had always been and was still flowing, changing, evolving. But even the positions of the stars themselves were gradually shifting, revealing movement across the planet of the landmass upon which the mbolop lived. And according to archived data, the land mass had been moving long before Mbaiso had been around to measure it.

Clutching the highest limb it could find, the creature extended its legs, pushing itself high enough to see the horizon. This allowed it to triangulate the positions of key stars. It filed the information away and then settled back to a more comfortable perch, completing a routine it had carried out many times before.

Before descending the tree, Mbaiso sat motionless, listening. Although it could not know what sounds to expect, significant events would likely occur soon. Mbaiso and the other tree kangaroos were given little leeway for interfering, but they could observe and document. And Mbaiso was acutely interested in the outcome. The unusual new humans would probably take actions harmful to themselves or to their species. That was expected, but it would mean more waiting—possibly *much* more waiting. Perhaps the Creator, the Lamotelokhai, was unconcerned with waiting indefinitely, but Mbaiso had been given traits of a living biological entity. Including some sense of mortality, spawning impatience.

The mbolop was ready to move on to what events may unfold next, even if this meant testing the boundaries of its permissions.

Mbaiso continued to listen, but so far the night revealed nothing beyond the chorus of night creatures.

———

THE HUT SHOOK SLIGHTLY and Bobby was alert again. Something rose up through the entrance in the floor where the Papuans slept.

Bobby whispered, "Addison, is that you?"

There was no answer. The figure took a silent step toward the sleeping men and touched their faces one at a time. It then dropped through the hole and was gone.

Both men sat up. They wiped at their faces and mumbled to each other, and then they were quiet again. They didn't seem to have seen the mysterious figure. And now Bobby wasn't sure he had seen it himself. He closed his eyes.

He was nearly asleep when he heard a cry in the distance. It rose and then trailed off like the call of a wolf. But it was human, and it was filled with sorrow or pain. Then another cry rose from a different direction. Soon there was a third. One of the Papuans lifted his head. He listened for a moment, then sank back to the floor and didn't move again.

The cries went on for some time. Bobby stared into the dark, listening to them, haunted by their misery, until sleep finally came.

———

QUENTIN WAS the first to wake in the morning. For some minutes he lay still as the chatter of birds filled the air. He wished he could go back to sleep. He had dreamt of a life without the plane crash, where his only burdens were those any man could bear. The stresses of his life before the crash seemed so trivial now. Quentin thought of Samuel's desire to return to his past and understood how desperate the feeling could be.

But sleep would not return. Addison was still out there, and Quentin had to find him. Then he would convince the villagers to let them leave. If that didn't work, they would escape and find their way to civilization on their own.

Having made this decision, Quentin felt better. He forced himself up, intent on waking the others and getting started. He glanced at the two Papuans who had stayed with them through the night, and then his confidence dissolved in a single wave of shock.

The villagers were gone. In their places were two piles of reddish dirt. Much of the dirt had fallen between the sticks and vines of the floor, but the remaining piles still resembled two sleeping bodies.

———

Minutes later, Quentin paced the length of the small hut. Everyone else stared at the remains of the two men. Quentin wanted to find Samuel and get some answers. But he didn't want to separate the group again.

"We're all going," he said. "We'll find Addison and then we're getting out of here."

"I think Addison was here," Bobby said.

Quentin stopped pacing. "What do you mean?"

"Last night. I saw someone come in. He did something to Ansi and Tengorros. He touched their faces. I think it might have been Addison."

"Why didn't you wake us up?"

Bobby looked at his bare feet. "I don't know. I guess I wasn't sure."

Quentin closed his eyes and tried to control his breathing.

Addison would not have killed two men. He opened his eyes. "We're all going now."

They drank from the container of water until it was empty. Lindsey and Ashley both insisted that they now felt strong enough to climb down the ladder without being lowered down. So one at a time they all descended to the forest floor.

Quentin led them to Samuel's tree house. It was some distance away, perhaps a half-mile, but he remembered the route, and before long they stood beneath it. He called to Samuel but there was no response, so they headed for the Lamotelokhai tree. As they approached it, the shuffling of their feet echoed among the massive tree trunks. Quentin spotted the dark outline of a hanging corridor above, and he pointed at it without stopping. He followed the shadow of the hanging tunnel until they finally stood at the base of the Lamotelokhai tree. Quentin cupped his hands to his face to call out, but then he stopped. There was movement in some foliage perhaps fifteen meters above them. At first he saw only leaves and shadows. But then something twitched—something with a face and dark eyes.

"Addison?" Quentin called out. "Is that you?"

The foliage exploded as the form flung itself into the air. Quentin stumbled backward in shock as the thing dropped the entire distance to the ground. It was a fall that would kill—or at least break the legs—of any human being. It hit the ground with a loud thud, bounced a few inches into the air, and landed in a controlled crouch. It then lifted itself fully erect.

There was stunned silence as they all stared at Addison.

"Oh, my God," Lindsey whispered.

Addison's body was changed. His arms were longer, like those of a chimpanzee, with sinewy fingers. There was no sign of Addison's boyish body fat. Instead, his arms, legs, and torso were braided with ropes of muscle. A cord was tied around his waist, and from it hung a pouch that only partially hid his genitals. If it weren't for

Addison's face, Quentin would not have known who—or what—it was. But even his face was changed, no longer that of a boy. It was now hard, with sharp angles. The wounds from the previous day were all but gone except for a jagged valley in the skin running from his left eye up past his hairline. Addison's eyes darted back and forth as if he were a cornered animal. Quentin felt a mix of loathing and affection as Addison stepped toward them. He fought the urge to back away.

"*Yanop khomile-lé-dakhu*," Addison said.[25]

Quentin found his voice. "Addison, we're leaving. You're coming with us."

"No. You will help me now."

"Help you with what?"

"Kill them." He pointed a long finger upward. "The rest are there."

Before Quentin could speak, Bobby stepped forward. "Addison, what did you do? That was you last night, wasn't it? And I heard yelling. What did you do?"

Addison leaned forward, placed one hand on the ground, and shoved his face up toward Bobby. The movement was chillingly nonhuman. "*Nu khén-telo*! You can talk to it."[33]

Bobby nodded. "Yes I can."

"So you know." His finger stabbed upward again. "Help me kill the rest."

Quentin wrestled with the weight of Addison's words. "What do you mean *kill*, Addison? You didn't kill someone, did you?"

Addison stood erect again. "Yes. I am almost finished. Help me kill the rest."

Quentin didn't move or speak, afraid to trust his own judgment.

Addison shifted from one muscled leg to the other, glancing at the canopy and back to Quentin. "Help me now!" he cried.

Quentin knew they had to reason with him, convince him to leave with them. They could find their way to civilization and then get help for him. "Addison, whatever you've done, we can work it out. It's time to go home."

"You don't listen. You can't go there. Help me kill them."

"No, Addison!" Lindsey said. "We don't kill people. What's wrong with you?"

Addison stooped forward until both his hands were on the ground. "Then I'll kill you, too."

Following those words, everything seemed to go silent.

Quentin opened his arms to the creature that still might be his son. "Please talk to us. Help me to understand."

Addison held out a balled fist. "Look at me. I can do anything now." Then he leapt into the air. He grasped a limb, swung over it and landed on his feet on top of it. He gazed down at them for a moment before dropping back to the ground. "I'm better now. You can be too." He eyed them, expectant, but no one spoke. "The Lamotelokhai knows you now. It has your *keliokhmo*. It can make you better." Addison looked at each of them. When his eyes fell upon Ashley, he pointed. "You did not like the *khofémanop*, Addison. You wrote things about him."[40]

Ashley's face darkened with anger. She left Lindsey's side. "How do you know what I wrote, Addison? Did you read my journal?"

"The Lamotelokhai knows your *keliokhmo*. And now I know, too. You wrote things about him—about me. Bad things."

Ashley's hands clenched. "You bastard."

Addison continued, "You didn't like him. But his father," he jabbed a finger toward Quentin, "you wrote different things about his father, didn't you?"

Ashley shrieked, "Shut up, you twisted freak!"

Addison lunged at Ashley, closing the gap with alarming speed. Quentin tried to get between them, but Miranda beat him to it. She blocked Addison with a hand against his chest. "Leave her alone!"

Addison sneered. "You didn't like him either." Without shifting his eyes from hers, he dipped his hand into the pouch at his waist.

Bobby lunged. "Addison, don't!"

But Addison had already grasped Miranda's face. His long fingers wiped at her eyes, forcing the stuff from his pouch between her lids. Then he pulled back and glared at her.

Miranda fell to her knees, her hands pressed to her face.

Quentin shoved Addison away from her. "What have you done?"

For a moment Addison's brows furrowed in confusion. But then his features hardened again. "You want to take it!"

"We don't want to take anything," Quentin said.

Again Addison's face softened. He gazed at his own hands for a moment. Suddenly he turned and sprinted away.

———

MIRANDA SEEMED SHAKEN from the attack but physically unhurt. Quentin examined her eyes. They were red and watering.

She began crying. "What's happening to me?"

"Nothing is going to happen to you," Ashley said. But her voice betrayed her fear.

"I'm going to die, aren't I?"

Everyone assured her she'd be fine. But Quentin sensed they were wrong. Addison had clearly meant Miranda harm. Samuel had to be right—Addison's brain had been damaged in the plane crash.

Miranda sobbed. "Nothing can hurt me now, right? They fixed me after a plane crash and a broken leg." Her words were beginning to slur. "Ashley! I can't see." Miranda held out a hand and Ashley took it.

"I'm here, Miranda," Ashley said. "You'll be okay."

"I'm afraid, Ash. I see stars. Why do I see the stars, Ash?"

Quentin's eyes were drawn to Miranda's hand, gripping Ashley's. The tips of her fingers were turning brown, and they stood out against Ashley's pale skin. Quentin ran in the direction that his son had disappeared. "Addison, come back! You can stop this!"

He paused and listened. The forest was silent except for the stricken sobs of his wife and students as they watched Miranda die.

MIRANDA'S BODY turned to soil before Bobby's eyes. It started with her fingers and toes. They turned brown, and the tips began to fall away. And then her eyes became dirt and crumbled into her skull. The dark sockets seemed to stare at Bobby, and he had to turn away. He leaned against the Lamotelokhai tree, trying to flush the image from his mind. But even without his flawless memory, Miranda's decomposing face would have haunted him for the rest of his life. As the others were gathered around Miranda's remains, Bobby sat to the side, watching the trees for signs of Addison's return.

Before long Samuel appeared. His face was pale, and he appeared old and tired. Standing over Miranda's body, he spoke to Mr. Darnell.

"The loss of another of your pupils is regrettable. But the creature has also murdered many of the indigenes. You are aware that I have lived among these people for the majority of my days. Their murder is a devastation beyond reckoning—a loss not only to me but quite possibly to the welfare of all beings of this earth."

Mr. Darnell stayed quiet and stared at Miranda's remains.

Samuel continued. "You must not encumber your need to do what must be done by reasoning that the creature is your son. He no longer is, and he must not continue this amok."

"What are you saying?" Mrs. Darnell said.

Mr. Darnell held up his hand. "He's right. Addison couldn't have done this. We've already lost him." His voice was low and uneven, like he had snapped from too much grief.

Samuel went on. "Addison has employed the powers of the Lamotelokhai to take the lives of my indigene hosts, and of your pupil." Samuel then pointed at Bobby. "The boy possesses an aptitude for relating with the Lamotelokhai, as if he were born to accomplish that very task. He has progressed beyond my own achievements. If we are to employ the substance to overcome Addison, then Bobby may be the only practicable hope."

"*Overcome* him?" Mrs. Darnell said.

Mr. Darnell's face showed that he already knew what Samuel meant. "Bobby's only fourteen. I can't ask him to do that. If it's anyone's responsibility, it's mine."

Bobby recalled the vision Mbaiso had shown him, the brutal killing of Addison, and then him holding the bloody club. Mbaiso had tried to tell him something important. But now it would take more than clubs to kill Addison. Bobby thought of Miranda's eyes, crumbling into her skull as she died. "I'll do it," he said.

The others turned to him.

Bobby swallowed hard. "I understand what has to be done, and I'll do it."

CHAPTER SEVENTEEN

Bobby counted only eight Papuan villagers in the tree house. Samuel had said the Lamotelokhai hut was where they would all come when something bad happened. How many others had Addison killed?

Sinanie was one of the eight remaining villagers. Also among them were three women, the first ones Bobby had seen. Their faces looked similar to the men's, but they had breasts that weren't covered up. Down below they each wore a clump of dried grass over their privates, hanging from a cord around the waist. There were no children present.

The villagers should have been enraged. Instead they were quiet, staying together on one side of the hut, watching the Americans. Bobby had asked Samuel about this, and was told that the villagers knew Bobby could talk to the Lamotelokhai, and because of that they believed their world was going to end anyway. They now wanted to stay with Bobby to protect him in case Addison should return. It seemed as if everything was suddenly about Bobby.

It was hard concentrating with so many people in the hut, but still Bobby made progress. For whatever reason, the Lamotelokhai was programmed with the ultimate version of Kembalimo. Bobby had passed all the early levels and was now arranging symbols into groups representing ideas and simple sentences. Samuel hovered over him for a while, asking questions. But then he must have realized this was only slowing things down because he backed off.

As the morning stretched into afternoon, Samuel and a guy named Vututu left to get food and water. Vututu was taller than the others, even taller than Samuel, and he looked like he'd be a fierce fighter. The women seemed unwilling to let him leave the safety of the hut, and Bobby figured he must be married to one or more of them. Vututu took two spears, but Samuel took no weapons. As they left through one of the connected tunnels, the four women cried out—"Yeeee..." It was the same cry Bobby had heard in the middle of the night.

Eventually Carlos came over and asked questions about the Lamotelokhai. Did it really come from another planet? Why did it come here? Was it alive? Bobby didn't have answers, so he tried telling Carlos about his progress with it.

Carlos twisted his face. "I don't play Kembalimo, so I don't get it." He nodded toward the Papuans. "Why not just ask them to kill Addison? Instead of going to all this trouble?"

Bobby rubbed the scar on his chest and looked at the Papuans. Sinanie's eyes met his and stared with no expression. Sinanie seemed smaller now, and older. Bobby stepped closer to the villagers and tried speaking to them. *"Gu mbakha-to-fosu le-bo? Mba-mbam?"* He wasn't sure what the words meant; he just pulled them from his memory. He repeated the same words, and then added more: *"Anggufa diabo?"*

At first they just stared at him, but then Sinanie spoke. *"Khofé mbakha mo-mba-té?"*[36]

Bobby waited to see if a vision appeared in his mind but nothing happened. He shook his head. And then an idea came to him. These people could talk to Mbaiso, and now he could too. "Sinanie," Bobby said. The Papuan looked at him. Bobby made the sign for Mbaiso's name.

Sinanie's eyes widened. "*Mbakha-leké mbolop?*"[34]

Bobby nodded. "Mbolop." He then signed the names of the other two tree kangaroos.

Sinanie signed quickly and then waited. A vision appeared in Bobby's mind of a tree kangaroo signing to a person. He realized the person was himself. "Yes, I talk to the mbolop." Bobby sensed someone behind him, and he turned to see Mr. and Mrs. Darnell there. "I can speak tree kangaroo." They seemed confused, so he said, "I'll tell you about it later."

Bobby turned back to the Papuans. Mbaiso had shown him a sign for Addison, so he used it. Then he used Mbaiso's signs to describe Addison getting pulverized by men with clubs, and then himself holding a club. The villagers were now watching him closely. Bobby motioned once more: the sign for *no*. He shook his head. "I don't want to kill anyone."

Sinanie eyed him for a moment and then started signing.

In his mind, Bobby saw villagers. They talked and walked together. Some of them carried things, like water and animals they had killed. And there were women there, talking and smiling. The villagers looked up. Something fell from the sky into the trees. Bobby sensed that it was supposed to be an airplane, although it didn't look much like one. A person walked from where the object fell. And there were others. They looked different from the villagers. Their movements were stiff and clumsy, and they had big heads. Bobby realized this must be how Sinanie saw them. As the people from the plane became clear, one of them stood out. It was Addison, but not Addison his friend. It was the dead, scary Addison —Addison the killer.

Suddenly the vision changed. The sky came crashing to earth, like ropes that held it up had finally broken. Villagers, trees, and chunks of earth began drifting upward as if gravity no longer existed, until the last remaining bits fell away into nothing. The blue sky below evaporated. And then there was only darkness and stars.

The vision dissolved. Sinanie's hands now hung at his sides, and he said, *"Ya nokhu wola-maman-é. Nokhu solditai imoné khomilo."*[41]

"So, what did he say?" Carlos asked.

Bobby turned to the others around him. "The world turned upside down, I think. Because we came here." It was the best description he could come up with.

"That's what Samuel told me," Mr. Darnell said. "They're convinced their world is eventually going to end, and that they should allow it to happen."

"So they're just going to let Addison kill them?" Carlos said.

"I don't know," Mr. Darnell said. "But *we're* not letting that happen."

Bobby turned back to the Papuans. He started to sign that he needed Sinanie's help, but then he stopped. He sensed a change. The air became still, as if all breathing had stopped. He spun around. A dark figure entered from one of the tunnels. It was Addison, his muscled figure looming menacingly in the hut.

They all stared, speechless. Addison had changed even more. The leather pouch that had covered his privates was gone, and he wore a crudely fashioned penis gourd. His skin was darker, or maybe dirtier. His arms seemed even longer, and his hands grabbed the floor as he bent over like an animal and went straight for the Lamotelokhai. Bobby felt an urge to turn and run. Addison put a hand on the Lamotelokhai. With his other hand he shifted invisible objects in the air.

Addison was talking to the Lamotelokhai, learning, gaining strength, maybe even instructing it to kill them. Someone had to stop him. Bobby stepped forward. "Addison, we need to talk."

QUENTIN STARED AT THE CREATURE. It was not Addison, yet it was. His son had become a horrifying, murdering monster. And now the only way to stop him was to kill him. How could a father do such a thing? Quentin shut his eyes and remembered Addison as he had been: pointing wide-eyed at a birthday cake in the shape of a bear; screaming with delight at catching his first fish. That was the real Addison. But when Quentin opened his eyes, the boy was replaced by something dreadful. The face was still mostly Addison's, but it held no innocence. Instead it seethed with hatred, or perhaps insanity. Insanity was easier to accept.

Addison was dead. Quentin would do what he had to do. This thing had murdered innocent villagers, and then Miranda. It intended to kill them all. *Addison was dead.*

Bobby was the first to act. "Addison, we need to talk."

Addison took no notice as Bobby approached him. One of his hands rested on the substance and the other seemed to be moving invisible objects in the air.

"Addison," Bobby said.

Addison shot a glance at Bobby and curled his lip, like a dog defending its food.

Quentin started to speak, but Bobby held up a hand to stop him.

"I can help you, Addison. I've played Kembalimo, too, for even longer than you have. It'll be better if we do it together."

Addison seemed to consider this. Then he turned back to the substance. "Too late. I don't need help." His hand continued its peculiar movements.

The hut became unnervingly silent. The Papuan women slipped into one of the tunnels, leaving only four men standing with their spears held ready.

"There's a better way to do that," Bobby said. "A faster way."

Addison stopped. He glared at Bobby. Whatever Bobby was trying to accomplish, Quentin thought it was too dangerous. Addison could turn on him as quickly as he had on Miranda. Quentin moved to intervene, but Bobby motioned him away again.

"There's a better way," Bobby said. "I'm surprised you haven't figured it out."

"What way?" Addison demanded.

Bobby stepped even closer, now within Addison's reach. "The tree kangaroos. They can help us talk to it."

Addison's hand dropped to his side, hanging to his knee. "Mbolop?"

"Yes. The mbolop taught me their language. And they're connected to the Lamotelokhai somehow." Bobby touched the Lamotelokhai, and Addison struck his hand away. Bobby clutched his hand but didn't back off. "It's true! Mbaiso is made out of this same stuff." He pointed, this time without touching. "You can see for yourself. Just go find one of the tree kangaroos. They can show you."

Addison flung himself onto Bobby in an explosive blur, striking his face and knocking him to the floor. Again the violence caught Quentin off guard. He should have seen it coming, but he couldn't let go of the boy Addison once was.

"*Yu khokhukh-telo-dakhu dialun,*" Addison growled as he pressed Bobby against the floor. "Where is the mbolop?"[42]

Bobby struggled to free himself. "I don't know! You have to go find them."

Quentin rushed forward and shoved Addison off of Bobby. Addison attempted to rise, but suddenly the Papuan men were upon him, forcing him back with the ends of their spears. Addison thrashed at the spear shafts, but the tips penetrated his flesh and pinned him to the wall.

BOBBY CRAWLED to a corner of the hut. His face throbbed and his mouth was bleeding. The Papuans held Addison against the wall while Mr. Darnell tried to calm him down, but it wasn't working. Addison thrashed and growled.

Bobby made his way back to the tree trunk at the center of the hut. This might be his only chance to do what he knew must be done. He laid his hands on the substance, and the symbols appeared in his mind. But where to begin? He thought of the questions Carlos had asked him. 'Where did it come from?' 'Was it alive?' Bobby had been so busy making the rules of his lingo that he hadn't considered that he might be ready to actually talk to it. He shoved the symbols to move them into piles. He stopped. *No. Talk to it. Tell it what you need.*

He moved the symbols, forming a simple sentence: "I am Bobby." And then a question: "Do you understand me?" Bobby stopped and waited. The struggle with Addison behind him was making it hard to think. And then the symbols moved without his help. They formed a group before his eyes. Bobby stared at the message.

It said, "Yes."

QUENTIN AND LINDSEY tried reasoning with Addison. They told him they loved him in spite of everything he had done. Addison didn't seem to hear any of it. The four spears dug into his body.

If the villagers ran Addison through now, perhaps they could kill him and be done with it. When Quentin looked at them, the one called Sinanie nodded toward Bobby, who was now standing with his hand on the Lamotelokhai. They were waiting for Bobby to do something.

Quentin turned back to his son. "Addison, do you understand

that they are going to kill you? Listen to me. There has to be another way!"

Addison's eyes showed no recognition, or sorrow—only anger. "It's mine," he hissed. Still staring at Quentin, he grasped one of the spear shafts and pulled hard, forcing it through his own body and the wall of the hut, and pulling the villager who held it closer to him. There was a moment of stunned silence. The Papuan holding the spear was now within Addison's reach. With astonishing speed, Addison grabbed the man and pulled him closer, biting him viciously on the face. The other Papuans loosened their grips to help the man.

That was all it took. With an explosion of ferocity and swinging fists, Addison was free and the men were pushed back with their own spears. One of the spears still hung from Addison's body and he yanked it out with one hand. Blood flowed from his abdomen and ran down his legs. His chest heaved with the effort of breathing, and for a moment the gurgling sound of this was all Quentin heard. Addison's shoulders then slumped and he coughed, spurting blood onto the Papuans' faces as they watched. He let the spear fall to the floor.

The hatred was gone from Addison's eyes and he looked almost human again. He approached Bobby, shoved him out of the way, and plunged his hands into the Lamotelokhai. He tried pulling loose a large mass, but the stuff seemed to hold tight. As he pulled at it the Papuans grabbed their spears and moved in to attack. But the stuff came loose and Addison turned to face them. They stopped.

"I'll kill all of you," he said. He then backed away and stumbled into one of the adjoining tunnels.

BOBBY WATCHED Addison leave the hut. Addison's wounds would

not be fatal, and he would come back. Bobby was sure of that. Bobby would have to be ready for him, so he returned to the Lamotelokhai. The stuff had smoothed itself out where Addison had removed the chunk, and it looked the same as before.

The Lamotelokhai had said, "*Yes.*" A lump of clay stuck to a tree in the middle of nowhere actually understood him. Bobby arranged symbols to ask another question: "Did you come from space?" He had a hard time with *space*. It was more like, *away from the earth.*

Again the symbols responded: "Yes."

"I knew it!" Bobby said to himself. He asked another question: "Are you a computer?"

"Yes."

Bobby had been right about this, too. Then another of Carlos's questions came to mind: "Are you alive?"

"Yes."

Bobby frowned. Maybe the stuff didn't really think after all. Maybe it just agreed with everything. Bobby thought hard. He asked: "Am I a computer like you?"

"No."

Bobby's excitement returned. "My friend has changed. He kills people. Did you know that?"

"Yes."

"My friend is Addison." Bobby made a name for him. "Did you do something to Addison to make him change?"

"Yes."

"Did you give him part of yourself to help him kill people?"

"Yes."

Bobby stared for a moment. "Why?"

The answer came instantly. "Addison asked."

Bobby frowned again. This didn't seem right. He arranged symbols. "It is bad to kill people."

There was no response, so Bobby tried again. "Did you know it is bad to kill people?"

"I cannot know what is bad."

"Why?"

"A thing that is bad now is not bad after time. A thing that is bad for you is not bad for another."

Bobby considered this. The Lamotelokhai was right. He was, after all, going to ask for its help to kill Addison. But that was to stop Addison from killing more people. Bobby suddenly felt uncertain. He shuffled the symbols. "Can I ask you to help me?"

"Yes."

"Addison is going to kill me. Addison is going to kill the people who take care of you. Addison is bad." Bobby waited but nothing happened. It had been hard to make these thoughts and he wanted to be sure he was understood. "Did you know that Addison wants to kill people?"

"Yes."

"Did you know that is a bad thing?"

"I cannot know what is bad."

"Can you change Addison to the way he was before he was hurt?"

"No."

"Why?"

"I cannot make something I do not know of."

Bobby felt a hand on his shoulder and he turned to face Mr. Darnell.

"How's it coming?"

Bobby had been concentrating so hard he had almost forgotten where he was. He looked around the hut. The four women had returned. They sat on the floor behind the men, silently watching. "It talks to me," Bobby said. "I can ask questions and it talks to me."

Mr. Darnell lifted his brows. "Did you ask it about Addison?"

"It says it can't fix him. It doesn't know him from before the crash."

Mr. Darnell looked down at the floor. "Bobby, I think Addison is going to keep coming back. We can't let him do what he's trying to do." He squeezed Bobby's shoulder and looked him in the eye. "All your other questions can wait. We need something that will stop Addison. Can you ask it for that?"

"I think so."

"Then please try. If it gives you what we need, give it to me. I'll use it." Mr. Darnell squeezed his shoulder and then walked away.

SAMUEL AND VUTUTU returned with a skin bag filled with water and another ball of khosül. They unwrapped the leaves from the khosül and passed it around, but no one seemed to be hungry. After Mr. Darnell had explained the confrontation with Addison, Samuel came over to watch Bobby work with the Lamotelokhai.

"Couldn't you do this faster than me?" Bobby asked. "Or couldn't they?" He nodded toward the Papuans.

Samuel said, "As a general rule, they do not communicate directly with with the Lamotelokhai. As for me, I have spent many years learning to use it primarily for tasks involving production of food." He paused. "On occasions where I have attempted more remarkable efforts, the results have been rather grievous. But you, Bobby, possess a faculty for comprehending the Lamotelokhai that bewilders me. The indigenes believe you are a departed ancestor, returned to the living earth for this very purpose."

"I'm just a regular kid," Bobby said.

"Still, it seems that something in your schooling or your inherent nature has prepared you for the task. And I fear that the indigenes' weapons are not sufficient to stop Addison's murderous amok. There is urgent need for a poultice tailored for encumbering him." He stopped and eyed Bobby like he was waiting for an answer.

"I'll try," Bobby said.

Samuel nodded slightly. "Very well. And now I must call upon one service of the Lamotelokhai that I hoped I would never again employ." He moved to the wall of the hut and pulled a lump of the stuff from his pouch. After sitting on the floor he began shaping it with his hands, stretching it out like a long rope.

Reluctantly Bobby turned back to the tree. Everyone expected him to do this, whether he wanted to or not. He concentrated, trying to think of another way.

Mrs. Darnell interrupted his thoughts. "Did you hear that?"

Everyone became quiet. There was a voice, very faint. "Help me! Father, help me!"

"Quentin..." Mrs. Darnell whispered.

The cry came again. "Help me! Father, help me!"

Mr. Darnell's face went pale. "It's Addison." He headed for one of the tunnels.

"I'm going, too," Mrs. Darnell said.

"This is ill-advised." Samuel rose from the floor.

"We can't just ignore him," Mr. Darnell said.

Samuel stepped in front of him. "Hear me now. If indeed the creature is injured, you must appreciate this as an opportunity. We may prevent further murder by killing it." Samuel held up a finger for Mr. Darnell to wait, and he went over and talked quietly to the Papuan men.

The cry came again. "Help me! Father, help me!"

Something about the situation felt wrong to Bobby. If Addison were really hurt, wouldn't he use the medicine to heal his body?

Samuel returned. "Vututu and Aguisa will accompany you and will help with the difficult task you face. If the creature is injured, it will be helpless for only a short time."

The two Papuan men dropped their spears and grabbed short,

thick clubs. Then Vututu and Aguisa left the hut, followed by the Darnells.

Samuel spoke softly to Bobby. "I am doubtful of their success. I beg you to persist in your efforts. Better to prepare for the worst, I should think."

VUTUTU AND AGUISA descended the rope ladder first, forcing Quentin and Lindsey to cope with their conflicting thoughts while waiting. Addison's voice continued calling from below, the same words over and over: "Help! Father, Help me!"

Quentin's nerves were torn. The cries were desperate. Could there be something left of Addison's consciousness, some remnant of their son? But their task would be easier if there weren't. Against his every instinct, Quentin silently hoped that Addison would simply die from the wounds he had suffered. For the first time since the crash, Quentin felt like his sanity was truly slipping away, like he might snap from the pressure.

When all four of them were on the ground, the Papuans headed in the direction of Addison's cries without speaking.

"Help! Father, help me!"

The cries were closer, but Quentin saw only understory foliage and tree trunks. His anxiety grew with every step, and he pushed harder, leaving Lindsey and the Papuans behind.

"Help! Father, help me!" Addison was just ahead.

"I'm here, Addison!" Quentin pushed his way to a small clearing. "It's okay, I'm—" He stopped. "Oh Jesus," he heard himself say. He couldn't move. He could only stare.

Lindsey and the tribesmen broke through the tangle and stood by his side. No one spoke.

"Help! Father, help me!" It was Addison's voice, but it wasn't Addison. The voice came from a horrifying mass of tissue lying on the ground against a buttress root. No, Quentin realized. Not next to the root, joined to it—fused to the root with sinewy tendons. The figure had a head and chest, but the arms quickly diminished into tendons that extended to the ground and the tree, holding the entire mass in place. Below the chest it was the same: strands of flesh fused with the surroundings. There was nothing else—no pelvis, and no legs.

"Help! Father, help me!"

Quentin stared at the thing's face. Addison's details were missing, as if God had decided to start over with it, erasing the features down to generic blank stock. There were no eyes, only slight depressions where eyes should be. And the nose was flattened, no more than a slight bulge with two holes in it. Only the mouth appeared fully developed, as if the entire nightmarish visage existed for one purpose: to call out to Quentin.

"Help! Father, help me!"

"That's not Addison," Lindsey said, her voice hollow.

They had made a mistake coming here. Quentin took her hand. She resisted, as if afraid to take her eyes off of it. But then she allowed him to lead her away.

The Papuans did not follow. Quentin glanced back at them. Vututu caught his gaze and lifted his club to where Quentin could see it. Quentin nodded. As they made their way back to the rope ladder he heard the two clubs striking flesh, and then there was silence.

―――――

Bobby put one hand on the Lamotelokhai and began shifting symbols with the other. He wrestled with an idea that was forming in his mind. The thing had said it could not make Addison the person he was before the crash. But that didn't mean they had to kill him. Maybe they could give Addison something to make him love Mr. and Mrs. Darnell again. He tried explaining this to the Lamotelokhai.

"Addison is going to kill the villagers. Addison is going to kill me. Do you know how to stop Addison?"

"Yes."

Bobby waited, but there was no more. "How can I stop Addison?"

"Kill Addison."

"No. I don't want to kill Addison. I want to change Addison. Do you know how to change Addison so he won't kill?"

"Yes."

"How do I change Addison so he won't kill?"

"Kill Addison."

This wasn't working. Bobby had to explain what he wanted, but it seemed impossible. He had no words for feelings like love. It would take hours, maybe days, to make that kind of progress.

Again Bobby heard Addison's cry from far below. "Help! Father, help me!" Mr. Darnell and the others were probably almost there by now. If Addison were really hurt, why wasn't the Lamotelokhai healing him? Panic started to grip Bobby, making it hard to focus his thoughts. He moved the symbols again.

"Addison is shouting. Does Addison need help?" Bobby waited, but no answer came. He tried again. "Do you know where Addison is?"

"Yes."

"Is Addison hurt?"

"No."

Bobby stared. Maybe he didn't ask the question right. "Where is Addison?"

"Addison is above you."

Bobby heard vines and sticks breaking. Long fingers forced their way through the living roof of the hut and ripped open a hole. A figure dropped through headfirst, flipped over, and landed on its feet next to Bobby. Before Bobby could back away, Addison grabbed him by the hair, and his other hand smashed into Bobby's face, rubbing damp, gritty death into his eyes and mouth.

Bobby couldn't see. He fell to the floor and crawled to a corner. Cries filled the hut as Addison attacked the others. Bobby wiped his eyes, trying to get the stuff out. But it was too late. It was in his body, and it would eat him from the inside. Again he saw Miranda's empty face, her eyes collapsing into her head.

Bobby heard himself crying over the din of the struggle. He suppressed it and tried to think. How much time did he have? Would he feel his heart and his bones turning to dirt? He rose to his feet and stumbled forward with his hands out until he bumped into something soft—the Lamotelokhai. Bobby put both hands on the substance. The symbols appeared in his mind, even though he could see nothing else. He shifted them into a message.

"Addison put something from you in me. Will it kill me?"

"Yes."

Bobby choked. He was sure he could feel it now, a tingle in his stomach, the stuff starting to eat him alive. He pushed the symbols as fast as he could.

"Can you help—"

Bobby was knocked off his feet. He landed hard under the weight of a writhing body. The body rolled to the side. Bobby forced his eyes open and saw green feathers. Sinanie lay next to him, rubbing desperately at brown smears on his face. Another Papuan—one of the women—lay on the floor nearby, moaning. There were more screams as the last Papuan man and another of the women fought with Addison, trying to hold him back with spears. But Bobby's eyes were drawn to the corner. Ashley, Carlos, and two Papuan women huddled against the wall behind Samuel, who was crouched with one hand on the roll of substance he had stretched out on the floor. Samuel held his other hand out to the fighting Papuans.

"*I le-ba-lé ye-mén!*" he yelled.[43]

Addison attacked the man and woman. Their spears pierced him, but he managed to grab the man and throw him to the floor.

Samuel yelled again, "*I le-ba-lé ye-mén!*"

The woman retreated from the fight and Samuel pulled her behind him.

The man beneath Addison grunted and tried to roll away. There was blood on his face, mixed with some of the Lamotelokhai from Addison's palm.

Samuel cried out to Addison, "*Gu nu u-ngga-lekhén-ma-té.* I am here!"[44]

Addison jumped up and lunged at Samuel, screaming and grabbing for Samuel's face. But then something happened. As Addison passed over the substance there was a crunching sound. He collapsed onto the floor, and his screams became a choking gush.

Addison's body shook, splattering wetness on the floor. Bobby moved closer to see. It was no longer Addison's body. Instead it was a sickening heap of skin and flesh. Bulges of bloody tissue stuck out everywhere, like it had exploded from the inside. The legs had not crossed over the strip of Lamotelokhai, and they still looked almost normal. But above the waist it was impossible to recognize anything, other than one arm protruding at an unnatural angle. As Bobby stared, the arm thrashed like it was still trying to fight.

Ashley was the first to speak, her voice barely a whisper. "What happened?"

Samuel kicked at the body with his foot. "There is no time to explain." He then wiped his eye and held out his hand for Bobby to see. The brown substance was smeared on his fingers. "Death is upon us, Bobby. But if there is one who might prevent it, it is you. Perhaps my death is past due, but I beg you to save your life, and those of the remaining indigenes."

The tingling was growing inside Bobby's body. "I don't want to die."

"Then you must hurry."

Tears streaming from his eyes, Bobby put his hands on the Lamotelokhai. He tried to concentrate on the symbols but it was getting hard to think.

"Oh shit, it's changing!" It was Ashley.

Addison's body had rolled over, and now there was a second arm protruding from the mess. This arm was bigger than the other, and it seemed to grow before their eyes. With a moist grunt, the body pushed itself to a sitting position. At the top of the body, where Addison's head should have been, an eye looked directly at Bobby. Muscle and skin around the eye began to change into a lump, and then the lump grew upward. It slowly took the shape of a head.

Suddenly Ashley snatched up one of the clubs, raised it high, and brought it down on Addison with a wet thud. Addison screeched. Ashley swung the club again, but this time the larger arm snapped out and ripped it from her hands. Addison flopped over and then somehow rose to his feet. His upper body was transforming, getting taller.

Addison turned to face Bobby. There were now two eyes on his face. "It is mine!"

Addison stepped toward Bobby, but then Samuel and Ashley attacked from behind. Between blows, Samuel shouted, "Bobby, make haste!"

Bobby moved the symbols. "Addison kills. Can you help stop Addison?"

"Yes."

"Tell me what to do."

"Take some." A bulge formed on the Lamotelokhai.

But Bobby hesitated. "Will this kill Addison?"

"Yes."

There were grunts and sickening blows and cries of pain. Bobby tried to focus. "I want to stop Addison, but not kill Addison."

No response.

"I want Addison..." Bobby struggled to form words. "...to want to not kill. Can you help?"

"Yes. Take some." The bulge grew larger.

Carlos's voice rose above the clamor. "Ow! Goddammit!"

Bobby turned to see Carlos fall to the floor, holding his shoulder. Addison was bloodied, but he fought viciously. There was no more time.

"Will this kill Addison?"

"Yes."

Bobby realized it was no use. He had no other choice.

QUENTIN HEARD the shouts as he reached the rope ladder. Instead of waiting, Lindsey started up the ladder just behind him. Quentin started to protest, but decided against it. If the rope broke, it might be an easier death than what awaited them above.

The ladder held. Quentin helped Lindsey into the hanging tunnel and they made their way toward the shouts. At last they entered the central hut. Addison was in a savage fight with Samuel, Ashley, and a small Papuan woman. Bodies were strewn on the floor around them—some of them writhing in pain, others still. And at the center of the hut stood Bobby. He held one arm up, ready to throw something cupped in his hand. Without faltering, Quentin rushed in and grabbed Bobby's arm.

Bobby blinked at him, tears flowing from his eyes. "Mr. Darnell! I have to get this into him."

It was not Bobby's burden to do this. Quentin scooped the stuff from Bobby's hand and pushed him out of the way. As Quentin turned to the fight, Ashley caught a vicious blow to the face from Addison, and she crumpled to the floor. Addison snatched her club and flung himself at Samuel and the woman.

They tried blocking his blows, but their movements were slower than his.

Quentin screamed, "Addison! Look at me!"

Addison stopped his attack and spun around. Quentin caught a full view of his face. It was torn and blood-soaked. But there was something more. The shape of Addison's face seemed to shift before Quentin's eyes, as if it were made of clay.

Suddenly, from behind, the Papuan woman smashed her club into Addison's head. It was a crushing blow, but Addison ignored it. In fact, he seemed to smile at Quentin as the depression in his skull smoothed itself out. The woman moved to strike again.

"*Manda-é,*" Samuel said. "*Yu lé khomilo-mbo iMoné.*" He motioned for her to wait.[45]

Addison's body tottered peculiarly as he edged closer to Quentin.

"You came back," Addison said. "But you can't hurt me now. You can try. Do you want to hurt me?" Addison held his arms out as if inviting Quentin to strike him.

"No, I don't want to hurt you," Quentin said. "I just want my son back."

"Your son..." Addison looked uncertain for just an instant, but then the smirk returned. "Not here." Addison stepped closer, holding out a hand smeared with brown clay.

Quentin backed away. *Now,* his mind screamed. He flicked his wrist, throwing the substance directly at Addison's face.

Addison's hand was a blur and he struck the stuff in mid air. The lump of Lamotelokhai splattered and fell aside. But smaller pieces struck Addison's face. His smile faded, and then he charged, shoving the material in his own hand toward Quentin.

Quentin managed to grab Addison's wrist with both hands, but he tumbled back under the weight. He struck the floor hard but focused all his effort on holding the hand away from his face. But then the struggle abruptly stopped. Addison simply relaxed, allowing Quentin to push him over on the floor. The hatred in his eyes melted away and his face went slack. Quentin rose to his feet. Addison's eyes darted from one of them to another but showed no expression.

Bobby stepped to Quentin's side. "It worked, Mr. Darnell. You got some in him." Without another word, Bobby moved to the Lamotelokhai and began working with it.

Quentin looked to Lindsey. She stood with her hands over her mouth, staring at Addison. Bodies were scattered on the floor. They all appeared to be conscious, but they just lay there, making no attempt to get up. Bobby stood in the center of the hut shuffling one hand rapidly in the air, moving objects that no one else could see. And at Quentin's feet, dying, lay a creature that was his son. He had killed Addison himself, an appalling duty no parent should ever have to perform. But he had done it.

Quentin knelt down and cautiously rested his hand on Addison's shoulder. "I'm sorry, Addison. I'm so sorry."

Addison suddenly sat up. He looked at Quentin with confusion. His eyes drifted around the hut and then locked onto a spot on the roof. There was a hole there, as if someone had torn through it. Without a word, Addison bounded across the hut and leapt for the hole in the roof. He pulled himself through and was gone.

The hut was completely still.

"Remarkable," Samuel finally said. He turned from the hole in the roof to face Bobby. "Please make haste, Bobby. Our remaining moments are few." Samuel then sat on the floor, holding his stomach as if he were sick.

Bobby scraped a handful of the substance from the Lamotelokhai. "I've got it!" He stepped away from the tree. "At least I think so." He then smeared some onto his tongue.

Bobby handed Samuel a portion, and then he went to Ashley and Carlos and placed some in their mouths. They accepted it without argument. Bobby moved to the Papuans, and they each accepted a portion. He then turned to Quentin and Lindsey. "Did Addison get any on you?"

"I don't think so," Quentin said. He then looked at the hole in the roof. "Maybe we can find him. We can give him some, too."

"Addison doesn't need this stuff," Bobby said. "He's not dying."

Lindsey finally took her hands from her mouth. "He's not?"

"I didn't want it to kill him," Bobby said. "I couldn't figure out how to make him the way he was before. So I made him forget."

"Forget what?" Quentin said.

"Everything," Bobby said. Then he looked at the floor. "It was all I could think of."

Following the boy known as Addison was demanding. The tree kangaroo, Mbaiso, moved nimbly from tree to tree, but the much larger human boy changed directions frequently, apparently without a destination, and the boy sometimes walked on the ground but then would take to the trees as skillfully as any mbolop.

Mbaiso made no effort to be stealthy, but the boy showed no recognition or interest.

Mbaiso finally paused, claws piercing the spongy bark of a breadfruit tree and holding him steady as his body heaved from the efforts of his lungs to meet the demand for air. He turned and waited for Tupela and Tripela. The other tree kangaroos were several trees behind, and he watched as they bounded between branches, their weight counterbalanced by long tails of mottled brown.

When the three creatures were side-by-side, they watched the human boy recede into the tangle of the forest. It appeared that this human was no longer relevant, so there was little purpose in continuing to follow him. And the tree kangaroos would surely be needed for what was to come next. They descended to the forest floor.

After looking one last time in the direction of the boy, they hopped off, making their way back home.

Before long, Mbaiso stopped. With a quick motion of his forelimbs he instructed the others to go on. He then began climbing and didn't stop until he was high in the canopy, in a position where he could see for some distance. It was a suitable place to process information—to think. And there was much to consider.

Mbaiso was aware of his own origins and purpose. Many centuries ago, following a fierce incident such as Mbaiso had witnessed today, the villagers had determined that it was not their place to communicate directly with the Creator, the Lamotelokhai. The stricken villagers had made one last direct request, for the Lamotelokhai to produce an entity that could serve as a mediator. The Lamotelokhai had complied, as it always did, and had created a creature the villagers would be familiar with but possessing cognitive and data processing proficiencies allowing it to serve a multitude of functions. In short, Mbaiso had been important, to the Creator as well as the villagers.

Although unique, Mbaiso's structure was biological. As a living creature, he was self-aware. And whether the Creator had intended it or not, Mbaiso was capable of making independent conclusions. Long ago he had determined that more could be accomplished if he were not the only mbolop, and from his own tissue and elements from the forest he had created the creatures now known to Bobby as Tupela and Tripela. This was one of many autonomous decisions Mbaiso had made over the years.

But now change was imminent, and Mbaiso's role in the events that would come next was unspecified. He found this to be unsettling.

Perhaps the new humans' arrival was to be expected, but their behaviors and capabilities were unpredictable. Mbaiso could not know what might happen next. The humans would have to determine that.

There was so much to consider.

Mbaiso settled into a suitable spot and stared out at the expanse of trees and sky. Solar waves warmed his body and baked the forest canopy, throwing into high gear the molecular food-making machinery in the leaves of trees tall enough to emerge into direct sunlight. Countless insects in a thousand varieties buzzed over the canopy, swirling in the air like tempestuous thermals. Occasional birdcalls broke the insects' monotonous drone: The piping of a fruit dove, the trill of a honeyeater, the shriek of a tiger-parrot—all names that Samuel had given to these birds. It was a calming, familiar scene, having changed little in the nearly ten thousand years of Mbaiso's existence. But like most days in the Méanmaél River basin, drenching clouds would soon veil the searing afternoon sun, driven inland from the Great Ocean until they condensed against the *Maoke* Mountains to the South.

CHAPTER EIGHTEEN

THE SUBSTANCE BOBBY had given those who were injured in the fight seemed to stop the murderous effects of what Addison had forced upon them. Before long, three more villagers showed up: two women and a man. They had run off in the night when Addison had started killing. The man had white feathers in his hair, and his name was Matiinuo. Samuel said he was the oldest of all of the villagers, something like ten thousand years old. Bobby laughed at this, but then felt embarrassed when he realized Samuel was serious. There were now eleven villagers, possibly all that were left of the tribe. Bobby realized the Lamotelokhai might help with this, so he spoke to it in symbols yet again.

"Do you know if more villagers are alive?"

"Only those near you live."

"How do you know?"

"No others live."

"How do you know no others live?"

"I do not know of others alive."

This might be the best answer he would get. Then Bobby had another idea. "Is Addison alive?"

"Yes."

Bobby was suddenly alert. He hadn't known for sure if the stuff he'd created would work, or if it would kill Addison. "Where is Addison?"

"I cannot know where Addison is. I know the distance of Addison."

"What is the distance of Addison?"

"Distance unit is needed."

Bobby pressed two fingers onto the Lamotelokhai about a foot apart. "This is a foot." He had to create a symbol for *foot*.

The substance answered immediately. "The distance of Addison is 6,404 feet."

Bobby thought about the answer. Over 6,000 feet—that was more than a mile. Why had Addison gone so far away? "What is the distance of Addison now?"

"The distance of Addison is 6,426 feet."

He was still moving away from them. Mr. and Mrs. Darnell would want to know this. They were in a nearby hut, resting with Ashley and Carlos. So Bobby left the Lamotelokhai and went to find them.

As Bobby walked, the floor of the hanging tunnel bounced under his feet, making the distance seem longer. He considered the news he carried. It was his fault Addison was gone. Maybe it would have been easier for the Darnells if he had just killed Addison. That might be better than knowing he was wandering around in the jungle with no memory.

In a smaller hut, Ashley, Carlos, and the Darnells sat on the floor picking at a lump of khosül paste. They glanced at him as he entered, but said nothing. Bobby sat down, pulled off a handful of khosül, and squished it between his fingers to make sure there were no beetle heads. Then he told them Addison was alive, but far away, and how he had come to know this.

They sat in silence, eating.

At last Mr. Darnell spoke up. "We're leaving. Tomorrow."

Mrs. Darnell nodded. "Tomorrow morning. We've decided."

"What about Addison?" Bobby asked.

Mr. Darnell looked up. "Addison died when the plane crashed. The Lamotelokhai's medicine couldn't bring him back. Our responsibility now is to get you three back to your families."

Bobby frowned. As much as he wanted to go home, he felt like he was just getting started with the Lamotelokhai. "We don't even know which way to go," he said.

At that moment Samuel entered the hut. "It is not the direction that is important, so much as the capacity to maintain your bearing," he said. "And what may prove fatal is your want for food and water."

Matiinuo followed Samuel in. Samuel sat on the floor, but the Papuan stood back.

"Samuel, please don't try to stop us," Mrs. Darnell said. "We don't belong here."

Samuel looked at her like he was afraid to say what was on his mind. "As you know, my inclination is to shelter the indigenes from the world, and at the same time shelter the world from the secret that they have guarded for so many ages. But once again I find that I have little influence on their ways of thinking, particularly with Matiinuo here."

"Meaning what?" Mr. Darnell said.

"My indigene hosts wish for you to go. They believe you have come here with the charge of assuming stewardship of the Lamotelokhai. They have supposed for many years that a man would inevitably come who could speak to the Lamotelokhai. As they put it, this event was to turn their world upside down." He frowned. "And indeed it has." Samuel then gestured toward Bobby. "This man they supposed would come is not a man after all, but a boy."

Bobby spoke up. "We can take the Lamotelokhai with us?"

"They will even assist you on your journey. My journey, as well, I suppose, as I will have no further purpose here."

Mr. Darnell cleared his throat. "You've changed your mind? You were convinced the Lamotelokhai should never be revealed. In fact you had just about convinced me."

"I still have doubts. But the villagers believe this to be the natural succession of things, and perhaps they are correct. Bobby's ability with the Lamotelokhai seems to support that. And if they were to prevent your departure, there would someday be others, and others after that. I can only hope that the sensibilities of mankind have progressed such that the Lamotelokhai will be used wisely, and for noble purposes." Samuel paused. "It is worth noting that the literal meaning of the word Lamotelokhai is, *the world will be destroyed.*"

Everyone was silent.

"We can't carry it on foot," Mr. Darnell said, finally. "If we make it to civilization, we'll tell others about it. They can send a helicopter."

Samuel frowned. "A helicopter."

"It's a flying machine."

"That is not satisfactory." Samuel's voice was almost angry. "My indigene hosts have lived as savages for thousands of years, and they resist alteration with passion such that you could scarcely imagine. And yet they insist that you remove the one thing that has determined their physiology and habits of culture for many centuries. So I am concerned for the fate of the surviving villagers. Do you truly wish to bring upon them the cruelties of—"

Mr. Darnell held up his hand. "No, I see your point. They deserve to be left alone."

"So what are we supposed to do?" Mrs. Darnell said.

Samuel waved toward Matiinuo. "The villagers and I will help to carry it. We brought it to this place, after all. When I first stumbled upon their village, it was far to the north, near the Sentani seacoast."

Bobby stared at Matiinuo. The Papuan returned his gaze. His skin was smooth and his clear eyes were like those of a young man. But Bobby thought he saw something more. From deep within the man's eyes shone the Papuan's wisdom—the wisdom of ten thousand years. Matiinuo smiled at Bobby. It was sad and tired, but still a smile.

———

AFTER SAMUEL and Matiinuo left the hut, the growing darkness seemed to fill the confined space with misery, so Bobby returned to the larger central hut. He stood staring at the Lamotelokhai. He could now talk to it. Better than anyone else, apparently. If they took it home with them, people would take it away. Bobby didn't want that to happen.

"It's really ugly, isn't it?"

Bobby started. He hadn't seen Ashley come in.

"I mean, if it's from an advanced alien race, why would they make it look like a big piece of crap?" She spoke without taking her eyes off the Lamotelokhai.

Bobby shrugged. "Maybe their crap doesn't look like this." After a few minutes of silence, Bobby said, "I'm sorry about Miranda."

Ashley looked at the floor. "Miranda was a good person. Better than the rest of us. I wanted to kill Addison." She looked up at Bobby. "You could have killed him, but you didn't. Everyone wanted to kill him, even Mr. Darnell. But you didn't." Her face was close to his and she eyed him without blinking.

Bobby felt his face flush, so he turned back to the Lamotelokhai. "I don't want to kill anyone."

"I think I was wrong about you, Bobby."

Bobby said nothing.

"Before, I thought you were just a nerd."

Bobby shuffled his feet. "Thanks."

"But I think maybe you're something else."

"What?"

"I don't know. Not really a hero. You don't look much like a hero."

"Thanks again."

She laughed. "How about this, then: When I'm afraid—when I want to be safe—I feel like I should be wherever you are."

Bobby felt his face flush again. "But I can't—"

"Let me finish. I don't think it's your job to protect us, or anything. But it seems like maybe you're important in this whole thing."

Bobby considered this. "I guess so." He put his hands on the Lamotelokhai. The hut was almost dark, but the symbols were clear. "What do you want me to ask it?"

Ashley put her hands next to his. She stared at the symbols that appeared before her eyes, invisible to Bobby. "I have no idea what all this shit is."

"It's Kembalimo. What do you want me to ask it?"

"Ask it if Addison is coming back."

Bobby shuffled the symbols. "What is the distance of Addison?"

"The distance of Addison is 9,016 feet."

Bobby turned to her. "He's still moving away from us. He's a long ways away."

"I hope so. Ask if we're going to die."

He did. The Lamotelokhai replied that it could not know this, and Bobby told her that.

"Figures," she said. "Ask if it minds if we take it with us tomorrow."

Bobby struggled with this one. "We want to take you away from here. Will you help us take you away from here?"

"Yes."

"I guess it doesn't mind," Bobby said.

"Then ask what it will do when we get it home. Is it going to take over the world?"

This was a good question, but Bobby had no idea how to phrase it. "That's too hard to say."

"Then ask if there's an easier way to talk to it."

Bobby should have thought of that before. He shoved the symbols around. "I want to ask you questions. I cannot ask you some questions. Are there other ways to talk to you?"

"Yes. Many ways."

Bobby remembered his idea from earlier. "Can the mbolop help me ask you questions?"

"Yes."

"Can the mbolop help me now?"

"Yes. Mbolop will come."

Ashley cleared her throat. "Do you two want to be alone?"

"Sorry." Bobby explained what they'd said.

Ashley laughed. "You're going to use a tree rat to talk to a big piece of crap?"

Just then Carlos came in from one of the tunnels. Bobby was a little disappointed. His conversations with Ashley were different when they were alone.

"The Lamotelokhai says the tree kangaroos can help us talk to it," Bobby said.

Carlos stepped between them. "You mean help *you* talk to it."

"Yeah, I guess so. But I'll ask it things for you, if you want."

Carlos put his hands on the stuff, and then frowned at the symbols that appeared. "Actually, that's what I was hoping for."

"What do you mean?" Bobby said.

Carlos hesitated. "You gave Addison some medicine that made him forget."

Bobby didn't like where this was going.

Carlos stared at the tree. "I want some of that. Mr. Darnell says we're leaving tomorrow," Carlos said. "But I don't care if we do."

"Don't you want to see your parents?" Ashley said.

"Why? So I can tell them why Roberto was killed instead of me?"

Ashley scoffed. For a moment Bobby thought she was going to laugh, but she didn't. She said, "Do you have any other brothers or sisters?"

"No."

"So if you stay here, they lose all of their kids. If you go home, they still have a son."

Carlos frowned at this, but he didn't argue. He adjusted the remains of his jeans wrapped around his waist. "I just think it would be easier if I didn't remember everything that's ever happened to me. The Lamotelokhai didn't even ask if that's what we wanted."

Bobby's thoughts returned to his first fight with Addison, when he was forced to remember what had happened on the airplane. Why was this nagging at him now? "Do you guys remember what happened on the plane before we crashed?"

He got blank stares from both of them.

He continued. "There was another airplane. It was really close."

Carlos said, "What do you mean, another plane?"

"Addison made me remember it. I thought maybe that's why we crashed. But I saw something out my window, in the other plane. Something really weird." He hesitated, but they were watching him now, waiting. "It was Addison. He was there, looking back at me through the window."

Ashley snorted. "Bobby, we've seen a lot of crazy shit, but that's *truly* crazy."

Bobby regretted bringing it up. "Never mind. It doesn't matter."

They waited for him to say more. When he didn't, Ashley said, "You were traumatized at the time, that's all." She walked around the tree, poking at the Lamotelokhai. "I don't see how we're going to carry this. How much do you suppose it weighs?"

"Matiinuo said they would help," Carlos said.

"They shouldn't do that," Ashley said. "They'll be discovered. Everyone will want to come study them."

Carlos said, "So?"

Ashley raised her voice. "We've pretty much wrecked their lives already. We crash here. Addison goes crazy and kills most of their tribe. Then we take away the thing they've worshipped for a gazillion years. Can we do anything more to screw them over? Oh yeah—let's show the whole world where they live. They can build an airport and a strip mall."

Ashley's eyes dared Carlos to argue. She was right. The Papuans didn't deserve that. Bobby wondered what would happen to the natives without the Lamotelokhai. Maybe they would start to grow old, like normal people. But at least they could live the rest of their lives in peace if they could stay here, hidden. He put one hand on the Lamotelokhai and moved the symbols. "You said you would help us take you away. How will you help us take you away?"

"I will help you in the way you ask me to help you."

Bobby thought hard. "Can you change your shape?"

"Yes."

Bobby suddenly stepped back. He stared, frowning, an idea forming in his mind.

Ashley said, "Bobby, your tree rat is here."

Bobby turned to see a shadow hop across the floor. Mbaiso stopped next to him and began moving his forelimbs. Bobby knelt closer so that he could see in the fading light. Some of the motions he knew from before, but others were new. A vision appeared, and Bobby immediately noticed that unlike the others this one had audio with it.

"The mbolop can help you talk to me."

It was Bobby's own voice, but these were not his words, or even his thoughts. Bobby looked at Carlos and Ashley. "Did you hear that?"

They answered together, "Hear what?"

THE NIGHT WAS long and cruel. Quentin needed solid sleep for the next day's efforts, but each time he closed his eyes the slightest noise or movement drew his attention. His mind raced with the past days' events and the logistics of tomorrow. And when he managed to push those thoughts aside, he could think only of his son wandering aimlessly through the pitch-black forest. What would become of Addison? How long would it be before he died of thirst and starvation? In the few seconds that Quentin had seen him after the substance stripped away his memories, Addison had shown that his strength and agility were intact. So perhaps he would be able to gather food and water to stay alive. Perhaps he would stay near the Papuan village where food was plentiful. Would the villagers kill him on sight? And what if the effects of the substance wore off, and he tried to kill them again?

Finally Quentin left Lindsey's side and felt his way in the darkness to the Lamotelokhai hut. As he neared the hut, he saw an orange glow. Inside the hut, several villagers tended a smokeless fire as they watched Bobby work with Mbaiso and the Lamotelokhai. Carlos and Ashley were sprawled on the floor, clearly exhausted.

Quentin watched Bobby. In the last day or so the boy had somehow become fluent in the kangaroo's sign language. His hands moved rapidly, but with precision. Each time Bobby completed a set of signs, Mbaiso followed with an equally elaborate set. And then Bobby would pause, as if listening or watching something.

"It looks like you have an audience." Quentin said. "How's it going?"

Bobby glanced at Quentin, his wide eyes accentuated by the flickering light of the fire. "Mr. Darnell. Sorry, it was talking to me."

Quentin raised his brows. "Talking?"

Bobby looked at Mbaiso and back at Quentin, apparently reluctant to interrupt what he was doing. "It speaks to me now. Mbaiso helps."

Quentin eyed him. Bobby seemed jittery. "Are you feeling okay, Bobby? Maybe you need to get some sleep."

"I'm okay." Bobby glanced at Mbaiso again. "I'm just kind of busy here."

Another mystery. It was too much. Quentin suddenly felt drained. He needed to sleep, to shut out all the violations of his perception of how the world should work. So he patted Bobby's shoulder. "Don't stay up too late." It was a ridiculous statement. It was what he would have said to Addison before going to bed on a Friday night, knowing his son would stay up as long as he wanted playing video games.

Bobby mumbled something and returned his attention to the tree kangaroo.

The villagers—there were five of them by the fire—seemed interested in what Bobby was doing, and Quentin decided they posed no threat. So he rousted Carlos and Ashley to their feet and herded them back to the sleeping hut, leaving Bobby to his task.

***

QUENTIN AWOKE with the sensation of being watched. Lindsey sat cross-legged beside him, staring at his face. The early morning light made her hair and skin look gray. The remains of two t-shirts, crudely tied together, were all that covered her breasts. She'd wrapped a half-disintegrated pair of khaki pants around her hips. Her skin was smudged with dirt and dried blood. Her hair was tangled and wild.

He reached out for her. Her shoulder felt cool and smooth. He ran his hand down her side, letting the backs of his fingers stroke the skin between the t-shirts and the khaki pants.

Lindsey nodded to her left, where Ashley and Carlos lay sleeping only a meter away.

Quentin sighed and withdrew his hand. And then the horrendous events of the previous day flooded his mind—from Miranda's dying words to the moment Addison fled from them for the last time. He tried to focus on Lindsey instead.

"You look beautiful," he whispered. It sounded awkward, forced.

Lindsey shook her head slightly.

"Well, you do." Quentin sat up. Bobby was still not back. "Damn. I told him not to stay up all night. He's going to need his strength."

"Are you still willing to leave, knowing Addison is alive?" Lindsey asked.

Quentin avoided her gaze. "We don't have a choice." He reached for the container of water Samuel had given them and took a long drink. "If you have a better idea, let's hear it." This came out with more edge than he intended. He put his hand on her knee. "We have to get the kids back to their families." He held the water out to her, but she made no move to accept it.

"I'm sorry for saying it, Quentin, but it would have been better if he had died. If we leave him out here, it will haunt us forever." Her eyes were welling up with tears.

Quentin felt a rush of sadness. Perhaps it would be better if they had all been killed in the plane crash. He pressed his palm against her cheek and wiped a tear away with his thumb. "We still have each other, Linds. And three of our students are alive. We have to accept that Addison isn't one of them."

"Three kids. That's less than half—"

"But they're alive. And don't forget, we're taking the Lamotelokhai with us. It has to be the most significant discovery in history."

Lindsey shook her head. "We don't even know what it is. It scares me. What if Samuel is right? What if this is a big mistake?"

This question had been nagging Quentin, too. "It saved our lives."

"But it killed more than it saved. What about all the dead villagers? And Miranda—I didn't see it saving Miranda's life, did you? And look what it did to Addison. What if that happens again, on a larger scale?"

Quentin pulled his hand away.

"I'm sorry, Quentin, but it scares me. I mean, how does it know how to play Kembalimo? How is that possible?"

Quentin had no answers, so he turned away. That was when he saw that Ashley and Carlos were awake. They both stared at him.

"We're just trying to figure out what to do next," Quentin said to them, realizing that it didn't sound very encouraging. He rose to his feet. "I'll get Bobby so we can get out of here."

But just then Bobby stumbled into the hut, breathing hard. "Mr. and Mrs. Darnell," he panted. "I have something to show you."

"Have you been awake all night?" Quentin asked as Bobby led them all through the hanging tunnel.

Bobby ignored the question. "I figured out a way so the Papuans don't have to go with us."

"How's that?" Quentin said.

Bobby hesitated. "I just have to show you."

As they approached the central hut, Quentin heard voices. They rounded the last curve in the tunnel, and the opening loomed ahead, growing larger with each step. The massive tree was framed in the opening. But somehow it looked different. The juncture of spreading branches seemed smaller. As they stepped through the opening, Quentin realized the Lamotelokhai was gone.

"Bobby, what's going on?" Then Quentin froze.

The Papuans stood in a cluster to one side, talking excitedly. And in the middle of them stood Addison.

It was Addison the boy, just as he had been before. He was naked, and Quentin took in the familiar spindly legs, the wispy promise of pubic hair, the dime-sized birthmark above one nipple. He looked feeble among the Papuans, but his demeanor was relaxed, even authoritative. And the villagers held no weapons. In fact, they chattered at Addison as if he were a long-lost companion.

Addison's eyes floated casually from Ashley to Carlos to Lindsey, and then to Quentin. The Papuans still talked, but Addison stepped away from them. He spoke. "You are Mr. Darnell and Mrs. Darnell, the father and mother of Addison." He turned to Ashley and Carlos. "You are Ashley. You are Carlos."

No one spoke.

"What's going on, Bobby?" Lindsey said.

"I wanted to find a way that the Papuans wouldn't have to leave," Bobby said. "Then I got this idea. The Lamotelokhai said it could change shape. So, well, I asked it to change to this shape." He pointed at Addison.

Quentin pulled his eyes away from Addison to face Bobby. "What?"

"I thought you'd like it, since Addison is—you know—gone."

Ashley whispered, "Jesus, Bobby."

Quentin steadied himself. One second he felt anger, then sadness, quickly replaced by compassion for Bobby. And then, of all things, a brief urge to laugh out loud. Finally, he stuttered, "This is the Lamotelokhai?"

Bobby nodded. "Now he can walk with us."

THE INITIAL SHOCK GRADUALLY RECEDED, giving way to numb acceptance of yet another unforgiving truth. For the briefest moment, Quentin's eyes had convinced him that Addison was back, returned to his former self by some miraculous feat of the Lamotelokhai's curative power. But it was not to be. What remained of Addison was still out there somewhere, perhaps already dead, having fallen from a tree or drowned in a river.

But this person in front of Quentin—this *thing*—was not Addison. It was merely a portrait of Addison. The clay-like substance had somehow been molded into Addison's shape, nothing more than a resourcefully-crafted sculpture. But Quentin could not take his eyes off it. And the more he stared, the harder it was to believe. The figure before him was Addison's body, down to the tiniest detail. The skin and hair were identical in every way. The voice was Addison's. It even moved like Addison.

Ashley approached and inspected the figure from top to bottom. Its nudity seemed to have no effect on her. Carlos followed, but kept his eyes on its face. The thing watched them, showing no expression.

"Another thing—it's easier to talk to now," Bobby said. "Just ask it something."

Ashley looked it in the eye. "Who are you?"

The thing returned her gaze, but remained silent.

"Sometimes you have to change the way you phrase things," Bobby said. "It doesn't understand."

Ashley tried again. "Are you really the Lamotelokhai?"

"Yes," it said without hesitation.

"Why do you look so much like Addison?" Ashley asked.

"I was asked to look so much like Addison."

Ashley wrinkled her nose. "No, I mean *how* do you look so much like Addison? How did you do that?"

"What I know of Addison is what helps me look so much like Addison."

Ashley turned to Bobby. "It talks funny."

"It's still learning how," Bobby said.

Carlos raised his hand like he was in school. "Where is the real Addison?"

"I cannot know where is the real Addison."

"But it knows how far away he is," Bobby said. "Lamotelokhai, what is the distance of Addison?"

"The distance of Addison is nine four three one foot."

"That means nine thousand, four hundred, and thirty-one feet," Bobby said.

This shook Quentin out of his daze. Addison was two miles away. He willed himself to speak to the thing for the first time. "Can you tell us where Addison is? What direction is he?"

The thing eyed Quentin, but still its face was blank. "I cannot know the direction."

"But you know his distance. How do you know his distance?"

"Information from Addison comes to me. I get the information from Addison. When Addison is near, the information from Addison is much. When Addison is not near, the information from Addison is little."

As peculiar as the thing's words were, the meaning was clear to Quentin. Addison was somewhere on the perimeter of a circle with a two-mile-radius, a circle with an area of something like fifteen square miles. It was hopeless.

"Does Addison remember us?" Quentin asked.

"Yes. Addison saw you before Addison went away."

"No, I mean does Addison remember us from before that?"

"No. I removed Addison's memories."

Quentin considered this. "If I asked you to put Addison's memories back, could you do that?"

Bobby interjected, "Mr. Darnell, I already tried. The Lamotelokhai said it couldn't make Addison the way he was before the plane crash, because it didn't *know* Addison then."

Quentin looked at the copy of Addison. "Is that true?"

"Yes."

Quentin sighed. He had to accept that Addison was simply gone, but now he found himself face-to-face with an identical copy of him.

Ashley circled the new Addison, looking it over as if not convinced it was real. "My friend Miranda is dead," she said. "Did you kill her?"

"Yes."

Ashley stopped. "Why?"

"Addison asked me to help kill Miranda."

"Miranda was my best friend," Ashley said, her voice becoming lower.

The thing did not respond. For a moment Quentin considered intervening, but the look in Ashley's eyes stopped him. Perhaps she needed answers. Maybe they all did. But then Ashley's next question took him by surprise.

"Before you helped kill Miranda, you got inside of her, didn't you?"

"Yes."

"So you know all about her?"

"Yes."

Quentin exchanged a concerned glance with Lindsey.

Ashley's brows furrowed. "Could you make a living person with all that you know about Miranda?"

The thing answered without hesitation. "Yes."

Quentin wasn't sure he'd heard this right. He said, "You can make a living organism, a human being?"

"Yes."

"How?"

"Pieces of the organism could be gathered. Some of the pieces are not here, but I could make them. The pieces could be put together to make a living human being that I know of."

"And you know of Miranda?" Ashley said.

"Yes. And I know of you."

That made Quentin uneasy. "Exactly how much do you know of us?"

"A unit of knowing is needed."

Quentin shook his head, not sure how to respond.

"So you could make Miranda come back to life?" Ashley asked.

The thing did not respond.

Ashley shook her hands, aggravated. "Could you make a living human that is Miranda?"

"Yes."

Ashley's eyes were now wide, her voice urgent. "Would she have Miranda's personality and her memories?"

"Yes."

Ashley turned to them. "Did you hear that?"

Quentin's mind reeled. Even if the Lamotelokhai could somehow create a living, breathing Miranda, and even if it could somehow give her all of Miranda's memories, would it really be Miranda? Miranda died. There was no changing that.

Ashley persisted. "Let's do this. We have to!"

Lindsey raised her hands. "Slow down, Ash. This is creepy beyond words. Even if he could do this, it wouldn't actually be Miranda."

Ashley wouldn't give up. "He just said it would! And what about Miranda's parents? Don't you think they would rather have Miranda come home?"

This was a legitimate question. Apparently this was not an option for Addison. But if it were, would Quentin do it? Probably. After a moment he said, "Shouldn't we let them decide?"

"It might be too late then," Ashley said. But then she fell silent.

Quentin felt besieged. What effect would the ability to reincarnate the dead have on the world? What other capabilities did this thing have? But for now the questions would have to wait. He said, "We all wish Miranda were alive. But we need to be careful about what we do until we get the Lamotelokhai to people who can comprehend it."

As if on cue, Samuel entered the hut bearing several woven bags loaded with food and supplies. He stopped short when he saw that the tree was bare. His eyes darted about the hut and then fell upon the replica of Addison. He dropped the bags to the floor. "God blind me!"

"It's the Lamotelokhai," Bobby said.

Samuel stared at the figure as if it were a ghost. "What manner of malice is this?"

Bobby explained as Samuel glanced back and forth from the bare tree to the transformed Lamotelokhai. He approached the figure and prodded it.

It responded by speaking to him. "You are Samuel."

Samuel stumbled back a step. He turned to the villagers, who chattered at him, obviously enthusiastic about the situation. "Extraordinary," Samuel muttered.

Bobby suggested he ask it a question.

Samuel cleared his throat and hesitated. Finally he spoke. "The prospect of speaking to the subject of so many years of study is quite beyond my command. It has long been my purpose to better communicate with you. And now that the opportunity is upon me, I fear I am without words." Samuel forced a smile, but it faded as the Lamotelokhai stared back without expression.

"Do you hear me?" Samuel asked.

"Yes."

"And all the years that I studied you, did you hear me then?"

"Yes."

"Could you not have transformed yourself in order to speak, as you now have?"

"I was not asked before to transform myself."

"I had only to ask?" Samuel seemed to say this to himself as much as to the figure.

"Yes."

Samuel sputtered a pitiful guffaw. It was the closest thing to laughter that Quentin had ever heard from him. "Confoundingly extraordinary," he said.

PREPARATIONS FOR LEAVING WERE BRIEF. They had no belongings other than their ragged bits of clothing and the bags of food. When they descended to the forest floor, several of the remaining Papuan men joined them. There was no sign of the women. The men hovered near the Lamotelokhai, still speaking and gesturing to it. Samuel was planning to leave the village with Quentin's group, and he stood to the side, patiently waiting.

As the Lamotelokhai talked to the Papuans, Quentin was still transfixed by the thing's resemblance to Addison, from the cracking adolescent voice to the navel shaped like a crescent moon above the woven loincloth Samuel had provided. Disquieted by the immediacy of their departure, Quentin spoke to it. "I would like to know the distance of Addison."

The figure turned to him. "I do not know the distance of Addison."

A lump swelled in Quentin's throat. "What does that mean? Is he dead?"

For the first time, the figure's face changed. Although barely discernable, it seemed to soften. *It's learning from watching us,* Quentin thought.

"Information comes to me when the distance of Addison is little. If Addison dies when information comes to me, the information tells me Addison dies. The information did not tell me this. The information stopped coming. The distance of Addison is great. Do you understand?"

"Yes," Quentin said. *Its conversation is getting better too.*

Quentin turned away, uncomfortable with the thing looking directly at him. He considered this news about Addison. He'd expected the last moments before leaving this place would produce second-guessing. But he'd been through it all a hundred times in the night, and had grown weary of useless analysis. Now Addison was too far away for the Lamotelokhai to sense him, and this made things easier.

Quentin turned to Lindsey. She had heard the Lamotelokhai's words and appeared to be barely suppressing tears. Quentin chose to say nothing about it. "We should go," he said.

Lindsey wiped one eye with her palm, and then she nodded slightly.

It was time.

WITH SINANIE GUIDING THEM, it took only a few hours to reach the same rusty-brown river where Quentin had washed the blood from his ankle days before. Brilliant sunlight filled the gap in the canopy where the river flowed. Quentin's eyes were long adjusted to shadow, and the river was like a tunnel of luminescence cut through the forest's gloom.

"*Méanmaél,*" Sinanie said, pointing to the river. Samuel explained that this meant 'the world sea,' which was a body of water leading to the end of the world.

They stopped at the path flanking the river. The plan was to follow the river downstream until they encountered another village. According to Samuel, this could take at least three days of walking, made difficult by treacherously muddy slopes.

But everyone seemed strong, even Bobby, who still had not slept. Among them there were no wounds, no disease, and no insect bites. The flies kept their distance, hanging in clouds above as if an invisible barrier held them at bay. In spite of the stifling heat, Quentin felt relatively cool. He began to let himself believe they could make it to civilization.

Sinanie told them, through Samuel, that he would leave them here at the river's edge. He then spoke one last time to the Lamotelokhai. "*Lamol mano-mano-po-dakhu-fekho.*"[46]

The Lamotelokhai gazed at him without responding. Quentin shot a glance at Samuel, but Samuel didn't offer to translate.

Despite the devastating blow that had been dealt to his tribe, Sinanie seemed to be at peace. After learning that the Lamotelokhai could reincarnate living people, Bobby had suggested that it bring back the villagers Addison had slaughtered. But the Papuans refused this, claiming that such an act would defy the obligatory fate of their companions.

Sinanie turned to Quentin and said, "*Nggulun, nun e khelép-té. Wolakholol be-lembu-té-n-da.*" He then spoke to Lindsey, Carlos, and Ashley—a different phrase for each of them. When he faced Bobby, he said, "*Khofé mano-pelu-m-é-o. Ge imo lalé. Lamol mano-mano-po-dakhu-fekho.*" As he spoke, Sinanie pointed to Bobby's eyes and then indicated the entire world with a sweep of his hand. Quentin sensed that Bobby was being told what he should do with his ability to see.[47]

And finally Sinanie spoke to Samuel, slowly and deliberately. "Samuel. Go now. Remember." Sinanie then put his hand on his own chest. "We remember Samuel."

Samuel straightened his shoulders. "Yes, I will remember. *Nggé, nu lenggile-lé-dakhu. Nu gelilfo.*"[48]

"*Gekhené ané kha-mén-é,*" Sinanie replied. And then he turned back toward his hanging village. They watched after him as he disappeared into the foliage and shadows.[49]

Samuel shook his head. "I fear the fate of the indigenes is uncertain." He eyed the Lamotelokhai. "We are taking that which has shaped their existence for centuries."

The thing stared blankly at Samuel.

"And now," Samuel said, "I wonder what will become of civilized men."

The Lamotelokhai spoke. "Samuel, you are afraid. Why?"

Before Samuel could answer, Lindsey said, "I'll tell you why he's afraid. Because we don't know what you are. We don't know your intentions."

The figure tried to smile, perhaps for the first time. "I have no intentions. I am a gift."

"A gift from who?" Lindsey asked.

"From those who created me."

"Who are they?" Lindsey said. "What do they want?"

"It is likely they are dead. They do not want."

After a moment of silence, Quentin asked, "A gift of what?"

The figure smiled again. This time it was a confident, warm smile. "A gift of what they knew."

"Do you have any intentions of hurting us?" Lindsey asked.

"I have no intentions," it repeated.

"My fear," Quentin said, "is that you might be used badly, perhaps to do harm. And you could change our civilization. Some people won't like that."

Suddenly Bobby spoke up. "Diffusion. You taught us about that, Mr. Darnell. You're afraid of cultural diffusion."

Quentin frowned. He hadn't thought of it quite that way.

Bobby addressed the Lamotelokhai. "Diffusion is what happens when different types of people meet and change each other. The Papuans changed when other people came here. It just happens."

"Yes," the Addison replica said. "I was created to share what my creators knew. It is likely this will change you."

Quentin considered this. Bobby had come to his conclusion about diffusion because he had accepted from the start that this thing was an alien intelligence—something bigger than the human species. Nearly all his life, Quentin's views had been forged by the tragedy following his parents' careless actions. And that was a mistake made on such a very small scale.

A shadowy dread that had been lurking in the back of Quentin's mind began to expand.

Samuel adjusted the bag of food that hung from his shoulder. "Since there is little will among us to prevent this diffusion, may I suggest we continue our journey?"

The seven figures made their way along the river. Eventually conversations stopped, and the only distraction was occasional rustling above them as three tree kangaroos moved through the canopy, keeping pace.

First, I must say that I have the deepest respect for the unique cultures of the Papuan peoples. Obviously I have taken liberties with developing the characteristics of Sinanie's tribe, but I intended no disrespect by doing so.

I adapted this language from the amazing work of Gerrit J. van Enk and Lourens de Vries in their studies of the language and culture of the Korowai, a Papuan community of treehouse dwellers of southern Irian Jaya (now called Papua). Astoundingly, the Korowai had never come into contact with outsiders until the early 1980s. Each word or phrase is referenced by number in the text of the novel.

1. *Méanmaél* (the world-sea, a body of water leading to the end of the world)
2. *Kembalimo* (This is the name of the online problem-solving language game that Bobby and Addison play. It also means *to return* in the language of Sinanie's tribe.)
3. *Gu mbakha-to-fosu le-bo? Mba-mbam?* (Where have

you come from? Children?) *Walukh, khomilo?*
(Sick, dead?)

4. *Yu le khomilo-mbo. Khomilo.* (He begins to die. Dead.)
5. *Gu mbakha-to-fosu le-bo?* (Where have you come from?)
6. *Nu pesau im-le. Pesua.* (I saw the plane. Plane.) *Friend, gu spirit lai-ati-bo-dakhu. Lele-mbol-e-kho-lo? Laleo? Spirit.* (Friend, are you coming as a spirit? How are you coming?)
7. *Mbakha lekhen, Jesus? Laleo khop.* (What reason—why Jesus? Bad spirit there.)
8. *Gu laleo-lu de-te-dakhu, Jesus.* (You are a spirit for sure, Jesus.)
9. *Gu mbakha-lekhe wa-mol-mo, dodepa-le Lindsey? Lindsey gekhene mbakha mo-mba-te?* (Why do you do that, call Lindsey? Lindsey what are you doing?)
10. *Yu Khentelo! Yu beben!* (He angry! He strong!)
11. *Yu khentelo tekhen. Khedi belen. Khedi belen.* (He angry for a reason. Do not kill. Do not kill.)
12. *Ané kha-fen.* (Let us go.) *Ané lai-m!* (You must come!)
13. *I mbakha? Yu le khomilo-mbo. Ané lai-m.* (What is this? He begins to die. You must come.)
14. *Laléo-khén! Laléo!* (Angry spirit! Spirit!)
15. *Fano! Mbolop manop.* (No! The tree kangaroo is good.)
16. *I mbakha?* (What is this?)
17. *Soyabu* (local word for the dorcopsis wallaby used for food)
18. *Kembakhi live in the lepun melun.* (Aggressive ants live in the leaf stem gall bladder.)
19. *Anggufa diabo?* (Why – to know? Or: How can you know this?)
20. *Nu khomile-lé-dakhu khosü kha-lé. But I'm better now.*

Khi-telo. (I died and went there – to the place of the dead. But I'm better now. Healthy-be.)

21. *Khosükhop, khaim.* (There, tree house.)

22. *Yebun* (rope ladder)

23. *Hey n-até-o.* (Greetings, my father – a term of respect from a young Papuan to an unrelated man)

24. *Gu laléo-lu.* (You bad spirit)

25. *Senggile-lé.* (Be frightened) *Yanop khomile-lé-dakhu* (People will die. Or: I will kill them)

26. *Gekhené pesua im-le* (You saw the plane.)

27. *Nu lefaf! Yu be-khomilo-n-din-da. Ya nokhu wola-maman-é. Nokhu solditai imoné khomilo.* (I am finished! He cannot die. Yes, as for us, the end of the world is there. We begin to die now.)

28. *Noadi, gu mbakha-lekhé wa-mol-mo?* (Noadi, why do you do this?)

29. *Nu if-e-kha misafi gup-tekhé fédo-p. Nokhu-yanop-tu* (I want to give these things to you. It is our people.)

30. *Nokhu-yanop-tu. Wolakholol lembu-té-n-da* (It is our people. The world will get out of order.) *Yu nggulun. Yu manop. Gu di mbolombolop* (He is a teacher. He is good. You tell our ancestors.)

31. *Maf lebil lefu-manda* (Picture tooth no more. Or: This is the last picture tooth.)

32. *Ané kha-fén! Nokhu ima-fon khüp Lamotelokhai!* (Let us go! We wish to see the Lamotelokhai!)

33. *Nu khén-telo! Gekhené pesua im-le!* (I am becoming angry! You saw the plane!)

34. *Mbakha-leké mbolop?* (Why are you with the mbolop? Or: What reason the mbolop?)

35. *Yu nggulun!* (He is a teacher! Or: He is a communicator!)

36. *Khofé mbakha mo-mba-té?* (Youngster, what are you doing?)

37. *Walukh, Joamba.* (Sick, Joamba.)

38. *Nu be-khomilo-n-din-da. Nu khén-telo!* (It is impossible for me to die. I am becoming angry!)

39. *Gekhené khup lefu. Gekhené wola-maman-é.* (Your time has ended. Your universe is now out of order. Or: Your world is ended.)

40. *It has your keliokhmo.* (It has gathered together knowledge of you.) You did not like the *khofémanop*, Addison. (You did not like the boy (son), Addison.)

41. *Ya nokhu wola-maman-é. Nokhu solditai imoné khomilo.* (Yes, as for us, the end of the world is there. We begin to die now.)

42. *Yu khokhukh-telo-dakhu dialun.* (He is strong and clever.)

43. *I le-ba-lé ye-mén!* (Come here, to this side!)

44. *Gu nu u-ngga-lekhén-ma-té.* (You want to kill me.)

45. *Manda-é. Yu lé khomilo-mbo iMoné.* (No. He is going to die now.)

46. *Lamol mano-mano-po-dakhu-fekho.* (Set the world right. Or: Make the world good.)

47. *Nggulun, nun e khelép-té. Wolakholol be-lembu-té-n-da.* (Teacher, it is clear to me. The world will not get out of order.) *Khofé mano-pelu-m-é-o. Ge imo lalé. Lamol mano-mano-po-dakhu-fekho.* (Boy, grow well. You see greatest. Make the world good.)

48. *Nggé, nu lenggile-lé-dakhu. Nu gelilfo.* (Friend, I am frightened. I am going away.)

49. *Gekhené ané kha-mén-é.* (You can now go home.)

50. *Nggé, gu mbakha-to-fosü le-bo?* (Friend, Where have you come from?)

ACKNOWLEDGMENTS

I am not capable of creating a book such as this on my own. I have the following people, among others, to thank for their assistance.

When it comes to editing, my son Micheal Smith is extremely talented, and his tireless and meticulous suggestions are invaluable. If you find a sentence or detail in the book that doesn't seem right, it is likely because I failed to implement one of his suggestions.

My wife Trish is always the first to read my work, and therefore she has the burden of seeing my stories in their roughest form. Thankfully, she kindly points out where things are a mess. Her suggestions are what get the editing process started. She also helps with various promotional efforts. And finally, she not only tolerates my obsession with writing, she actually encourages it.

I also owe thanks to my former colleague, Monique Agueros. She provided expert editing suggestions in spite of being an amazingly busy person. Thanks, Monique!

Finally, I am thankful to all the independent freelance designers out there who provide quality work for independent authors such as myself. Jake Caleb Clark (www.jcalebdesign.com) created the awesome cover for *DIFFUSION*.

ABOUT THE AUTHOR

Stan Smith has lived most of his life in the Midwest United States and currently resides in Warrensburg, Missouri. He writes adventure novels and short stories that have a generous sprinkling of science fiction. His novels and stories are about regular people who find themselves caught up in highly unusual situations. They are designed to stimulate your sense of wonder, get your heart pounding, and keep you reading late into the night, with minimal risk of exposure to spelling and punctuation errors. His books are for anyone who loves adventure, discovery, and mind-bending surprises.

Stan's Author Website
http://www.stancsmith.com

Feel free to email Stan at: stan@stancsmith.com
He loves hearing from readers and will answer every email.

I am thankful for the hard work of those who have painstakingly researched the cultures, wildlife, and ecosystems of Papua. The following are recommended books (and one video).

Flannery, Tim. *Mammals of New Guinea*. Chatswood, New South Wales: Reed Books Australia, 1995. Print.

Flannery, Tim. *Throwim Way Leg: Tree Kangaroos, Possums, and Penis Gourds – On the Track of Unknown Mammals in Wildest New Guinea*. New York: Atlantic Monthly Press, 1998. Print.

Marriott, Edward. *The Lost Tribe – A Harrowing Passage into New Guinea's Heart of Darkness*. New York: Henry Holt and Company, 1996. Print.

Merrifield, William, Gregerson, Marilyn, and Ajamiseba, Daniel, Ed. *Gods, Heroes, Kinsmen: Ethnographic Studies from Irian Jaya, Indonesia*. Jayapura, Irian Jaya: Cenderawasih University, 1983. Print.

Muller, Kal. *New Guinea: Journey Into the Stone Age*. Lincolnwood, Illinois: Passport Books, 1997. Print.

Souter, Gavin. *New Guinea: The Last Unknown*. New York: Taplinger Publishing, 1966. Print.

Van Enk, Gerrit J. and de Vries, Lourens. *The Korowai of Irian Jaya*

– *Their Language in its Cultural Context*. New York: Oxford University Press, 1997. Print.

Sky Above Mud Below. Dir. and Perf. Pierre-Dominique Gaisseau (organizer and leader) and Gerard Delloye (assistant leader). Lorimar Home Video, 1962. VHS.

This is an amazing video filmed as it happened in 1959, when a group of explorers set out on a seven-month attempt to cross the jungles of Papua (then called Dutch New Guinea). Winner of the 1961 Academy Award for Best Documentary Feature.

Quentin, Samuel, and Gregory were confined to their room well into the afternoon. Quentin requested to see Lindsey and the students but was told to wait. Gregory asked endless questions about the Lamotelokhai and its capabilities and origins. But finally he seemed to reach cerebral overload, and he lapsed into silence. He was taking it pretty well, Quentin thought, considering all he'd been forced to absorb in a single day.

Samuel passed the time by asking his own questions, mostly regarding the various devices he had encountered since leaving the forest: radios, smartphones, and the hospital intercoms that interrupted them every few minutes with announcements in Indonesian. He never passed up a chance to physically touch anything unfamiliar to him, including the glass window and its plastic frame in the door of their hospital room.

It was late afternoon when Santoso led two men into the room. One stepped forward and extended his hand. He wore a gray suit and was tall and thin, perhaps sixty, with almost-white hair impeccably combed straight back.

"Gentlemen, Sterling Hess, Regional Security Officer, U.S.

Embassy Jakarta. This is Dr. Paul Saskia." The other man appeared Indonesian, though he was dressed in an American-cut suit almost identical to Hess's. They shook hands all around and gave their names.

Hess sat in a folding chair. The man had a relaxed but commanding way about him, and he seemed to consciously ignore Santoso, as if he had already decided he was tired of dealing with him. He pulled a digital tablet from his black bag. "There is some confusion over your situation," he said. "The first order of business is to clear that up." He tapped his way through some screens. He stared directly at Quentin for a moment and then looked at something on his screen, frowning. "Where are the others?" Hess asked Santoso. "Mrs. Darnell and the other passengers of the flight?"

Santoso answered, "We have put them in other rooms in order to facilitate their medical examination."

Hess addressed Quentin. "Do you wish to be separated from your wife and the others at this time, Mr. Darnell?"

"No, I don't."

Almost before Quentin finished speaking, Hess boomed, "Then this is bullshit. You are isolating these guests of your country against their will. Please bring the others here. Now."

Santoso's face reddened, but he nodded to someone outside the door. Within seconds Lindsey entered the room, followed by the students, including Addison. They all sported the same white t-shirts and pants that had been given to Quentin and Samuel. Quentin introduced all of them. He presented Addison as his son, which was easier to do than he expected.

Hess looked back and forth from his tablet screen to each of them. "Roberto Herrera, Miranda Henry, Russ Wade," he said. "Do you know the whereabouts of these people?"

After a few uncomfortable glances, Lindsey said, "They were killed when our plane crashed. Along with the pilot and two Indonesian passengers."

Hess hesitated a moment. "I'm very sorry to hear that." He then stood up. "If you will forgive me, there is something I must clear up right away. Dr. Saskia here is an American doctor. After what you have endured, you must surely have some use for his services."

Hess stepped into the hall but did not close the door. Dr. Saskia smiled at them and approached Ashley first. Santoso motioned for one of the Indonesian doctors to stay close and observe Dr. Saskia's activities. Quentin tuned them out and listened instead to Hess.

"Cameron, Sterling Hess here. There's been a major gaffe. I'm here with the people now and have confirmed their identities." A pause. "Cameron, they were standing right in front of me." Another pause. "Well, they're quite obviously wrong." A longer pause. "I don't know that yet. Yes, I'll find out. I'll get back to you. Oh, and Cameron, they say three Americans were killed. Students, in their teens. Along with three Indonesians. Yes, indeed it is."

Hess re-entered the room. "Who was it that called the United States earlier today?" He glanced at his tablet screen. "The call was made to a Dr. Phil Bollinger."

Gregory raised his hand.

Hess motioned to the door. "I would like to speak to you alone."

Santoso looked as if he might interfere with this, but then he let them leave the room.

"You're wasting your time," Ashley said to Dr. Saskia. "You won't find anything wrong with me or any of the rest of us."

The doctor appeared to be flustered. Clearly this was not what he had expected.

"These people claim to have discovered a remarkable curative agent," Santoso said, without hiding his skepticism. He pointed at Addison. "Perhaps that boy is the one you should examine first. The boy somehow fooled us, making it appear that he was injured."

Dr. Saskia approached Addison with a warm smile and urged him to move to one of the patient beds. Addison was soon lying on his back with his shirt off. The Indonesian doctor hovered near as

Dr. Saskia asked Addison questions and palpated his abdomen. Quentin held his breath, hoping neither of the doctors would notice him tensing up.

Hess entered the room, frowning. Apparently Gregory's words had done little more than irritate him. Gregory followed behind him. His eyes met Quentin's, and he shook his head.

Hess spoke, obviously trying to keep his voice calm. "I must say, I can scarcely imagine what motives you people have."

"I assure you," Quentin said, "we have something that must be taken to the United States right away. You simply need to trust us."

Hess glared, a darkness gathering in his eyes. The man truly had an imposing presence. But before he could speak, Dr. Saskia's voice filled the room.

"What in God's name?" The doctor's hands were on Addison's knee and thigh. Even from where Quentin stood, he could see that the leg was moving, as if the bones were shifting beneath the flesh. The doctor gaped at the leg. "How did you do that?" he said.

Addison did not answer. Instead he looked at Hess and smiled.

Hess said, "Paul?"

The doctor's face had gone white. "I don't know. I have no way to explain what just happened."

Hess eyed Addison for a moment, as if trying to make a decision. Then his features hardened, and all signs of hesitation were gone. "Mr. Santoso, we are no longer willing to share this investigation with your doctors. It is clear that these American citizens have medical conditions that can only be addressed in a fully-equipped American facility, staffed by American doctors." He approached Addison. "Son, can you walk?"

"Yes."

Hess turned to Santoso. "We will immediately transport these people to the airport, and they will be flown to the U.S."

Santoso appeared frozen in place. Dark veins pulsed in his forehead. Suddenly he spoke to the two guards standing in the doorway. One of the men yelled down the hall, presumably to other policemen, and the two men entered the room with their hands on their side arms. Within seconds several more armed men blocked the door.

Santoso turned back to Hess. "It seems we are at odds, Mr. Hess. Perhaps you wish to rethink your decision."

Hess pulled his smartphone from his belt and punched in a sequence of numbers. The guards looked to Santoso for instructions, but he shook his head, allowing Hess to make the call.

Hess spoke loudly. "Cameron, Sterling Hess. We have just been forcibly contained at the hospital. I don't have details at this time, but there may be something to the UMBRA security report we discussed. We need these people in American custody pronto." He paused, and his brows shot up as he listened. "You're kidding me. Why are they interested? It's just a mistake at Qantas." He listened. "Good God. I hope it's worth it. Make sure they know we're on the first floor, north wing. It doesn't look like we're going anywhere." He returned the phone to his belt. "Calvary's almost here already. They were sent before I even called."

"Why?" Quentin asked, but Hess had already shifted his attention to their captors.

"Mr. Santoso, you are minutes away from having an international relations incident on your hands. You and I are diplomats. Let's talk this out before things escalate."

Heavy footsteps clattered in the hall, and more Indonesian police appeared outside the door. Quentin heard others in the building, shouting curt commands to each other. It sounded like they were positioning themselves for an attack. The whole situation seemed surreal.

Santoso now sweated profusely, his face still red. "Yes, Mr. Hess. We will begin with you explaining exactly what it is that you are so eager to take from our country."

"We wish only to take our citizens back to their home where

they can receive proper medical treatment. Please have your men stand down and let us pass. You have no legal course for holding us. I have been informed that a United States Special Operations Forces unit will be on site very shortly. A hospital is no place for a confrontation."

Santoso's expression was venomous. "We have no intention of using force. We merely wish to know the truth. If force is used, it will be a result of your people's eagerness for violence. Perhaps you should use your phone again and put an end to this nonsense."

A cacophony of sounds suddenly poured in from outside the hospital: vehicle tires screeching, men shouting and running, an unintelligible bullhorn voice. Santoso's eyes grew wide. He started to speak but then thought better of it and left the room. Indonesian policemen now formed a semicircle outside the door, their pistols drawn and held pointed upward against their chests.

Hess stepped toward the door but was repelled by the guards. He wheeled around. "What exactly in the hell are we risking so much to protect? It damned well better be important."

Quentin said, "What we have with us is more important than you can imagine, but this is a mistake. We can work together—."

Suddenly there was a gunshot from outside the hospital, and then another.

Hess shouted, "Jesus Christ!"

Quentin and Lindsey forced the students into the corner of the room and onto the floor. Angry yelling from outside the hospital was now constant. But then suddenly, as if it were orchestrated, things quieted down. Only the garbled bullhorn could be heard, but shortly even that stopped. Quentin looked at the nearest police-man, and their eyes met. The man forced a nervous smile. He was visibly shaking. A single gunshot rang out from the street, and the man's smile faded. For a moment following the shot there was total silence, and the man's eyes seemed to plead with Quentin. Then the silence was torn apart by a scream of anger from outside. Before the cry ended, gunshots filled the afternoon air. It sounded like someone had lit a whole strand of firecrackers in the street, and for a moment Quentin could almost convince himself that this was all it was.

Santoso stormed into the room. "Do you have any idea what you have done?" he managed to scream in a mix of Indonesian and English. Two policemen followed him into the room, their pistols drawn and eyes wild. "And for what?" Santoso cried. "A boy and his tricks?" Spit flew from the man's mouth as he spoke, and Quentin realized they were in immediate danger. Santoso had been driven over the edge.

From the corner of his eye, Quentin saw Bobby lean over and whisper to Addison. This was not the time for another wild idea. Quentin started to warn Bobby, but Santoso yelled at them, "Maybe you are not worth it, no?" He motioned for the policemen to point their weapons at Addison. They glanced at each other, but then complied.

"If you are so valuable," Santoso cried, "then perhaps we should put an end to this!"

Addison rose to his feet. He moved toward the men. This had an almost calming effect on Santoso. He stopped talking and watched Addison approach, as if mesmerized by this unexpected behavior. Both policemen's guns were pointed at Addison. Addison took another step, until the nearest gun pressed against his neck. The man holding the gun muttered what could have been either a curse or a prayer. Addison stepped directly in front of Santoso, pushing the policeman and his gun back a step. The room was quiet, although sporadic gunfire could still be heard outside.

Barely above a whisper, Lindsey pleaded, "Don't shoot. Please don't shoot."

Addison deliberately lifted a hand and grasped the policeman's wrist. With his other hand he reached for Santoso's hand. He held them, smiling gently. The policeman seemed to relax, and his gun moved away from Addison's neck. Quentin's eyes were drawn to their hands. Where Addison's skin touched the men, it appeared to flow into them like liquid.

"Do not be afraid," Addison said.

Santoso and the policeman looked down at their hands. Both men tried pulling free, but Addison held tight. The policeman's gun fell and clattered on the floor. Santoso's eyes grew wide as he watched his own arm change shape, becoming shorter. He babbled something unintelligible and tried desperately to free himself. The policeman simply stared at his arm, silent but horrified. The other men looked on helplessly. Santoso's arm was no longer even recognizable, and his babbling had turned into pleading screams.

Abruptly the nearest policeman stepped forward, raised his pistol, and shot point blank at Addison's face.